The Ranchers

A Modern Family's Inspiring Odyssey

Art Martin

To my wife, Jan, around whom my earthly world revolves.

Acknowledgments

I received incredible editorial help from Matthew Arkin of My Two Cents Editing, the wonderful creation of Meghan Pinson. Their brilliant advice was so helpful in my writing.

Also, I received wonderful support and advice from Mary Ann Mackin whose Foreword sets just the right tone for this book.

Cover credit: V. Hawley Smith, Jr. – "Big Dog."

Foreword

Growing Up a Rancher

Art's wonderful book tells the story of a modern family, their trials and their road to reconciliation and redemption. The story is set in the West, where Art now lives, and where he learned to appreciate the ranching life even though he was not born into a ranching family.

I grew up in a ranching family as the sidekick of a father who was both a cattleman and my first true friend.

Those early formative years during which I helped my dad on the ranch and traveled around with him as he worked in the cattle business became the basis for my understanding of the world.

We had a ranch in the Pacific Northwest with a view of Mt. Rainier. The hub for activity on our ranch was a big red barn, and it was in the barn and in the ranching life where I discovered my definition of what character is and the roles things like love and fear and God play in our lives.

This may explain why, during difficult times, I have often dreamed at night that I was back in the barn with my father—no doubt my subconscious way of drawing on the simple lessons I received there in order to try to find solutions to current problems.

My father was about 5 ft. 11 inches tall, lean and agile and strong. He had hazel eyes and a face that was always the tanned color of a man who had spent his life in the outdoors. Balding since his twenties, he always wore a gray Stetson hat as well as dark green work pants and some kind of shirt and Wellington cowboy boots

I remember watching him in the barn taking on a horse that was out of control or working around a bull 15 times his weight. This is where I first learned what physical courage is.

Physical courage was also called for when we doctored and tended to cattle in the barn.

With a cow securely restrained in the shoot, we could dehorn, vaccinate or brand it. Of course, a cow often went crazy, once it felt the sting of a needle dispensing a penicillin shot or the burn of the branding iron pressing against its flesh.

I remember that the cows' gyrations scared me half to death sometimes but my father was always unruffled.

When we were shipping cattle to California and there was the vet and the hired man and a lot of commotion in the barn I was always placed out of harm's way, posted on a set of steps that led to the hay loft where I sat and documented all the records and medical history on each animal being prepared for sale.

What I didn't know then was how much business stress there was for him in trying to get four kids through college and higher degrees— as a cattle dealer in a world where being that was almost an anachronism.

My father bought from the farmer by the head and sold at market by the pound. He couldn't be a few dollars off on the market and survive.

He also had to have a sixth sense for conditions like hoof rot and Bangs disease—a condition that would cause a cow to abort its calf—and a million other ills that threatened our stock.

My father, Elmer James .Mackin, had been raised during the depression on a wheat ranch in the eastern part of Washington State in a town called Walla Walla.

That life and hard farm work had left its imprint on him.

It had given him an outlook I've seen in ranchers and others who lived their lives close to nature experiencing on the one hand, its life-sustaining bounty and on the other, its sobering indifference.

The indifference of a scorching sun beating down on the back of a young boy (my father) as he helped harvest his family's wheat alongside a twenty horse combine on days so hot that horses had been known to drop dead in their tracks.

Or the indifference of a hail storm that could pummel that same wheat field so hard that it could make a whole year's crop worthless in a matter of minutes.

My father had come to terms with the trials and tradeoffs of living close to the soil. He had seen the same unforgiving sun that killed horses and men rise in stultifying beauty, morning after morning over the wheat fields of his youth, and he had decided that the certain occurrence of that never ordinary event sort of evened things out.

This blend of optimism and resignation was one of the things that made him and some other ranchers and farmers I knew rock solid.

His family had lost their wheat ranch during the depression but he seldom talked about the difficulties of his childhood, only the positives.

However, on a trip with my sister and I back to Walla Walla, he had admitted that in his senior year of high school he had been the only kid in the class disadvantaged enough to still have to ride a horse for an hour every morning to get to school.

On that same trip we met the family that had ended up in possession of the ranch that was to have been passed onto my father and his siblings.

My sister and I sat rapt as our father told the current owner of the land who was an old school chum of his that he harbored no hard feelings about the fact that the other man owned what was to have been our father's land.

Then, he expressed his admiration for the success and prosperity this man had created with the land.

My father was a man of faith.

Before he asked my mom to marry him he made a nine-day novena. A novena is a Catholic thing where you attend the same service nine days in a row to pray for a specific thing. In this case, my father was praying that my mother would say "yes."

Even when they were in their eighties if you ever walked by my parents' bedroom door near bedtime, you would see them kneeling on either side of the bed they shared, old and broken rosaries in hand, saying their prayers.

His theology was fairly simple and might be considered secular and a little too progressive when set against the stone hard structure of the Catholic Church.

It called for a lot of personal responsibility.

He believed as he put it that "the good Lord gave you a head to use" and he believed that charity begins at home where one has enormous power to help or hurt the ones to whom he or she is closest.

That value somehow made ordinary moments sacred.

I think the other reason I like what the Catholic church calls ordinary time--which is time where there isn't lent or Christmas or something else special going on-- is that some of the best days of my life were ordinary days riding along with my dad in the truck in which we transported cattle. I was an eight or nine year old alternately writing poetry and talking away to him.

My father was a man who listened to his children. He could exult in the details of a nine-year old's days and respond in the way other men night respond to listening to the singer James Brown sing "I feel good" or to watching the last 10 minutes of the NBA playoffs.

I was a 4Her and my father was a 4H leader helping children band together to learn the things they needed to know to pursue life in the farm and ranching world, each one with a project to manage and tend to like a horse or a cow or even a crop if their parents were farmers.

The 4-H creed was "I pledge my head to clearer thinking, my heart to greater loyalty, my hands to larger service and my health to better living for my club, my community and my country.

Art thinks the 4-H creed is the youth version of the cowboy code.

I have witnessed the fact that ranching is a hard life., I was blessed to encounter in it many people who were good and wholesome to the marrow. Some I knew I would call righteous.

My dad was the epitome of a righteous man to me.

Mary Ann Mackin

THE RANCHERS

Mary Ann Mackin has provided speechwriting services to CEO's of foundations and corporations in a number of industries. She is co-author of the book *Showing Up for Life*.

Chapter 1

"Wait 'til you guys hear what the newbie clerk at the Co-Op said to me yesterday," Jerry said.

It was Sunday, the 6th of July, 2014 and, being Sunday, Jerry was in "church" with his breakfast buddies. Of course, for him, that meant the Two Rivers Café in Livingston, Montana, his cathedral of breakfast which happened to be his favorite meal. He always got the same thing, two fried eggs over medium, very crisp bacon, country potatoes and whole wheat toast, which made him wonder why they brought him a menu. Even more puzzling to him, anyone could name whatever combination of stuff they might like, whether it appeared in that form on the menu or not, and they would make it for you. It made him wonder why they bothered with menus at all—why not just ask folks what they want?

"Okay, I'll bite," said Barry Rickety, a lawyer, "what did the newbie say?"

"Well, I was checking out at the register and the kid doesn't know me. So, I say, 'This is for the Johnston Ranch' and the kid looks it up and says, 'Your name, Sir?' and I say, 'Jeremiah Johnston' and he says, 'Really? Like the movie, "Jeremiah Johnson"? I mean, that's almost like being Robert Redford!'"

That brought guffaws all around because the breakfast bunch knew Jerry's opinion of Hollywood, at least the Hollywood of modern times. Of course, it was also preposterous that anyone would think Jerry was almost like Robert Redford because, for starters, Redford was notoriously liberal. Jerry was conservative, maybe even libertarian.

"I mean, how dumb is that? I swear, young people these days aren't any smarter than a box of rocks. You know the other night I saw some guy on TV doing a street interview in L.A. and he was

1

asking people if they could name the three branches of the federal government. I swear to God, one kid said. 'Um, the military, the Post Office and the IRS?' It makes me think you should have to take a test to be able to vote."

"Good luck with that idea," said Tom. Tom Daniels was a banker. "Why don't we poll the customers in Two Rivers on that idea?"

Two Rivers had been the height of funk at one point in time in the past. It had about half a dozen each of tables and booths in the main eating area plus another five or so on the bar side. The booths had needed some repair work and most of the table and chairs looked like they had been obtained one at a time from here and there as opposed to matching sets. In the men's bathroom was a picture of a stagecoach being hauled by a team of apparently terrified horses who were looking back at the driver who was whipping them furiously. All of the horses had their eyes bulging out in fear. Over the picture that hung over the urinal, one comic had penciled in "Hey, put that thing away. You're scaring the horses!"

But as Livingston became a little more upscale, the owners had renovated. It still was funky but now only half as much. But they had managed to retain the relaxed nature of the place which made it very appealing to the locals, whether ranch types or business types. Most importantly, if you liked the basics, they made about the best breakfast you could want and it came out of the kitchen in nothin' flat. It was the place everyone went to whether they were cutting a deal or just looking for good grub and a friendly environment.

Cattle ranching was pretty much a 24/7 occupation but this was one luxury that Jerry just had to have. He always had one of his hands take charge at the ranch telling everyone, "I'm goin' to church." Of course, he wasn't fooling them or anyone else. Everyone in town knew that every Sunday, he and five good friends would gather and eat and talk. Men love to talk just as much as women, they just didn't admit it. They generally would talk about sports, politics and women, and not necessarily in that order. Ranchers, and farmers, would also talk a lot about the weather and the markets for their products.

Jerry's group of six was split between three ranchers and three non-ranchers, the latter being two bankers and a lawyer.

Originally from Canada, Loren Wilson was a rancher like Jerry. In fact, their ranches partly adjoined and they helped each other quite a bit with various tasks like gathering, branding and other activities where help was needed.

The other rancher was Gordon O'Laughlin. He had a somewhat smaller ranch than Jerry but had a big family who all worked on his ranch and so his labor costs were effectively zero. Gordon was even more conservative politically than Jerry. He was short but wiry.

Then there was Barry Rickety, a new lawyer in town who had taken over the practice of a man who had done legal work for most of the guys at the table including Jerry. Considering that many people in town didn't have much respect for lawyers, he had gained their trust rather quickly. Barry had played college football at UCLA. He was tall and well-built and looked like an athlete.

Finally, there were the brothers, Tom and Tim Daniels. Tom was several years older than Tim but they looked a lot alike. They owned the First State Bank of Livingston which was where Jerry did his banking as his father had before him. The bank had been owned by the Daniels family for nearly as long as the Johnston Ranch had been owned by the Johnston family. They were both large men, tall with a bit of heft.

As for Jerry, he was about six feet two inches tall, blue eyes and his brown hair had long since turned a silvery gray. He had a constant battle with his waistline but was only ten pounds over what the charts said he should be. With a Scottish heritage, his skin was fair with freckles. Women generally considered him handsome with rugged good looks.

Jerry was a cattleman's cattleman. He was third generation-born into it. His family had been in Montana for over 100 years and had one of the biggest and most profitable ranches in Montana. His grandfather and father had developed the ranch and guided Jerry to the rancher's way of life. Jerry considered that way of life to be true and good and almost holy, though a cowboy like him might never put it that way out loud, except maybe to his best friends.

"Yeah," said Loren, "sometimes it's frustrating that today's Hollywood crowd can use their notoriety and their money to try and influence things when they often really don't know what they're talking about. I'm not sayin' they're bad people, just uninformed or misinformed. Seems to me that's how some liberals are. They have feelings about things and are well intentioned but are divorced from reality. They just ought to stick with acting; at least that's something they know somethin' about."

"Here we go," warned Tim Daniels, the lone liberal in the group. "Let the cannon fire begin." That brought more laughter because they knew Jerry would have to speak out.

"Well, for Pete's sake," said Jerry, "how can anyone be happy with the way things are? I mean, the economy sucks, there's international strife everywhere, the new healthcare plan is a mess and going to get worse and we're borrowing money like a drunken sailor about to go on leave!"

They all pretty much agreed with Jerry but in varying degrees. They found it amusing when he got all worked up and started making speeches because, normally, he was no more talkative than the typical cowboy and the typical cowboy was practically a sphinx compared to the average person. But get Jerry going on the Feds and he'd be a Montana version of Fidel Castro.

"I just think we're turning into some kind of social democracy," said Jerry with his finger pointing in the air, ironically, almost like a politician.

"What do you know about social democracies?" asked Tim.

"Don't you know?" asked Loren, laughing. "Jerry isn't just some dumb, hick cowboy; he's a well-read, dumb, hick cowboy."

That was true. Jerry had read a fairly large number of books and had secretly taken some correspondence courses on philosophy when he was younger since he hadn't had the chance to go to college. Now in the age of the Internet, he also found more courses and all kinds of sources to learn about all kinds of things that one wouldn't normally associate with the image of a cowboy.

Probably the primary source of Jerry's day-to-day news came from the Wall Street Journal which he had to get online since you couldn't get a real paper delivered anymore to rural areas. He had tried a number of papers but over time he believed that the editorial bents of those papers began to creep into their news coverage. Some of the other sections were really good but he was often steaming when he read the main section. He felt they can be whatever they want on the editorial pages, but in the main news section, be objective. And they weren't except for the Wall Street Journal which he came to believe was the best, most well written newspaper in America.

But far more than any other source, Jerry had inherited much of his philosophy of life from his father. It wasn't like Joe had ever sat Jerry down and said. "Okay, here's how life works." It was more the way he, Joe, had lived his life; that and the occasional vague admonition like "Be a man" and "Have faith in the Almighty" and others. And by those thoughts, Joe didn't mean for Jerry to be macho, he meant believe in God (which Joe took as a given), work hard, take responsibility, love your family and serve your country, and so on.

"Hell, I ain't no cowboy, at least the way I think about them. I may be a little nostalgic but I like to think about the kind of guys you saw on the old Western movies and TV shows. Guys like Joel McCrea and Randolph Scott are what I think of when I think of cowboys. They stood up against bad guys; they went on long cattle drives; they were nomads and lived pretty much day-to-day. Yes, I am on a horse a fair amount and deal with cows, but those are just my choices. In truth, I'm a business man in the ranching business. And the age of long cattle drives is long over. Nowadays, you have don't have to drive cattle a long way to market like they did when cattle were driven up from Texas to the rail lines in Kansas and elsewhere. As y'all know, today they come to you and pick them up in big rigs. I'm not a cowboy like they were, but sometimes I wish I were. It is true, however, that I try to read fair amount and keep up with what's going on in the world. Gotta say, though, it's pretty depressing."

But now having been provoked, Jerry went on for several more minutes, criticizing Washington politicians, tax and spend policies, income redistribution, over-regulation, the numerous scandals and so on. The boys' amusement slowly turned to boredom because they had heard it all before.

"What the heck has you so riled up today?" asked Tim. "Emily chew you out again for being such a pig?" Emily had been the nanny to Jerry's kids and was still his full time housekeeper.

"No," answered Jerry. Then, hesitating more than a little bit, he continued, "Ryan came home for a visit a few days ago. He left this morning and, well, it didn't go very well. We had a fairly big argument last night." Everyone fell silent because they all knew that Jerry's relationship with his three kids was mediocre at best.

Jerry sat quietly for a few seconds, looking at all of them looking at him. He knew how they felt about it and if it weren't for the fact that these were his best friends whom he had known for a long time, except for Barry, he would have just told them it was none of their business. Actually, he had said that in the past but they didn't let that stop them because they felt they were good enough friends that they could raise the topic and because they felt they were doing him a favor by trying to get him to mend fences with his kids.

"I know what you're thinking, but how many times do I have to tell you guys? They left me, I didn't leave them. I gave them a chance to be a part of the family ranch that can provide a very good living for anyone willing to work hard. I'm the third generation and I was hoping that there would be a fourth generation; but right now, it's looking like there might not be." Jerry paused to see if, after the umpteenth time he had unsuccessfully made his case to them about him and his kids, that maybe this time would be different. Not seeing any sign of success, he tried to explain the previous night's argument with Ryan.

"Well, anyway, Ryan doesn't seem to be particularly happy but he wouldn't admit that his place is back here on our ranch.

So, I told him he was being a stupid and stubborn so and so and he said the same about me. I just don't get why he wants to be off in Chicago."

Barry said, "I know you're disappointed but it's natural for kids these days to want to see something of the world beyond Montana. It's great for us but we're all old and settled. Julie's got a great job and doing well and you've got to be proud as hell of Colin. Just give it some time; they will get tired of the city life and before you know it they'll probably be begging you for a chance to come back."

"Ha!" snorted Jerry. "Don't count on it. Look, I love'em and all but, I'm sorry, I think all of them leaving demonstrates a lack of gratitude. What I was offering them is priceless. How many poor people do you see in the cities on TV? How many really happy people do you know that live in a big city? OK, so I love the country and the cattle-ranching life but I thought they did, too. Instead, they all told me that they had to get away. Well, so be it!"

"Jerry, didn't you ever want to get away when you were their age?" asked Barry?

"Not really," Jerry replied somewhat defiantly. Then, he clearly recognized that what he had just said wasn't accurate. "Well, that's not totally true. I did try something else once but my dad expected me to work on the ranch and take it over one day and that was that."

"But Jerry, that was a different time," stated Tim. "I mean kids today have been exposed to so much more. They're not going to stay put just because that's what *you* want. They think they will find happiness and fulfillment in the city," he said making quotation marks with his fingers of each hand. They may be right or they may be wrong, but don't you think it's OK for them to find their own way?"

"You guys just don't get it," Jerry answered. "There's an obligation here to me and to my dad and to my granddad. And I don't deny that I find it disrespectful to me and to them that not one of my kids seems to understand that. What my dad and granddad built is darn difficult to replace. Hell, you guys know

7

that most cattle ranchers make peanuts on their operations. It's the appreciation in the land value that brings any degree of wealth. But because of the hard work and sacrifices of my dad and granddad, those kids could make a real good living on our ranch that most cattlemen would die for. But it's more than that. I think this way of life is special. There's no bright lights and no fancy restaurants, but there's a feeling that comes with this life that's downright spiritual, almost divine." At this, Loren and Tom were nodding like they knew what Jerry was saying was true. "By God, I must be a failure in not being able to make one of them see that."

"Jerry, you were so hard on those kids growing up how could they see this wonderful life you're talking about when all you did was come down hard on'em every time they did the kinds of things that all kids do?" said Tim. "I knew your dad some and he was a strict man raised by another strict man and there's nothing wrong with that. In fact, you turned out OK, maybe," he said with a bit of a smile. "But as has been said, if you would reach out to your kids and show them a little love, I bet you'd see a big change."

"Look," said Jerry, "I'm not mean to them. I don't shun them. I don't yell at them or criticize them when then they do occasionally call. But I'll be damned if I am going to beg them to accept the gift of being a rancher. Bein' a rancher is the epitome of bein' an American. And I am not talking about cowboy shit. I am talking about having values that made this country great: hard work, self-reliance, helping your neighbor and so on, all because it's the right thing to do. It's by living your own life in accordance with Western values with no one telling you what to do or say that makes you moral, a good person. Now, there may be other ways to make a living that offer the same chance as ranching to have that kind of life but, frankly, I am not familiar with them. But my kids are all over and not here. When they show a little gratitude for what they grew up with and the opportunity I offered each of them, well, then I'll show a little love."

Everyone just sat there trying to digest that speech—there were a lot of pieces and trying to figure out a reasonable response wasn't easy. Certainly, some of what Jerry said was true but somehow for the rest of them, the end result shouldn't be this estrangement between Jerry and his children. But it was difficult to sort out.

"Gordon, you've got a big family and most of them did stay on. What do you think?" asked Tim.

"I think I have to use the restroom," said Gordon, not eager to jump into the fray.

"Seriously, though," said Tim, "what do you think?"

"Well," he replied, "I can understand where Jerry's coming from. I was lucky that my kids largely wanted to stay on. But my family didn't have to put up with the shit that Jerry's did."

They all knew what Gordon was referring to. Jerry's wife, Jackie, had died giving birth to their third child, Colin. Jackie was a wonderful lady, a true rancher's wife. Jerry had been devastated when it happened and was a changed man thereafter. It was correct that Jerry's father and grandfather had been strict, old-fashioned men, but compared to them, Jerry had been as light hearted and as happy-go-lucky as was possible under the circumstances. But when Jackie died, his world came to an end. He just didn't handle it very well and, among other things, became stricter and harsher with his kids. It had been nearly twenty-nine years since she had died and as far as they knew, Jerry had not so much as looked at another woman, much less looked for a relationship.

Turning to Jerry, Gordon said, "Jerry, we all know it's been tough on you, especially me and Loren since we know what you go through on the ranch. But every one of us here just wants the best for you and we think that includes having a good family situation. You know, sometimes on the ranch you have to do stuff that you really don't want to do whether it's a chore of some kind or puttin' down an animal. But, you know, we do it because that's just what has to happen. Well, it's the same thing with your kids. Maybe they should be more grateful for the way you brought them up and the things you allowed them to experience.

Maybe they should have been more willing to stay on. Maybe they should be the ones to communicate with you instead of the other way around. But what has to happen for your family life to have a speck of a chance to get normal is for you to suck it up and reach out to them."

"Thanks, fellas, I really appreciate your concern," said Jerry, "but that ain't going to happen."

As that sunk in for a moment, there was silence. Then Tom said "You know, Jerry, if you look up the word stubborn in the dictionary I think there's a picture of you."

"Well," said Jerry, "it may seem that way to you boys, but I think I am just holding the line." The phrases "holding the line" and "crossing the line" were two of Jerry's favorites but none of his five friends knew why he referred to "the line" so often.

Barry, the new lawyer in town, thought the topic had been thoroughly discussed and saw an opportunity to change the subject. "So, Boys, how are things on your ranches?"

"Pretty good," answered Loren. "It's been kind of slow since the calving season but that was pretty good for us this year. Thank God, because that's a hard time and a lot of work. We only lost a couple calves and one cow. That's pretty good. Of course, it may be slower now than during calving season but there's still a lot of work. I really shouldn't be here but if the hardest working rancher in Montana," he said gesturing to Jerry, "can take a morning off, I guess by God I can, too."

"Well, what's so hard about calving?" asked Barry. "I mean, don't you just let the cows out and let them drop the calves? What's so complicated about that?"

Jerry and Loren looked at one another and laughed. The others who had been around ranching much longer than Barry simply wore the soft smile of knowledge.

"Well," said Loren, "most of the time it isn't all that complicated and it works pretty much the way you say. But there's still a fair amount of work to make everything ready. And then there's the last one or two percent that causes all the fun."

"Like what?" asked Barry.

Jerry looked at Loren, gave him a wink, and said, "Go ahead. Give this city slicker a taste of ranching."

"Well, OK. For example, when a cow actually goes into labor, when the cervix is dilated enough for the front feet to start through, the cow is stimulated to begin straining or pushing, just like a pregnant woman does. If the calf is positioned in the normal way the whole thing doesn't take too long. Heifers, however, sometimes take longer because they're not as developed for the birthing process. Sometimes you have to help the cow or heifer by putting chains around the feet and pulling. You can also use mechanical calf pullers. If only one foot is showing or no feet or you don't see the head, you have to reach into the birth canal and try and figure out what's going on."

Barry was starting to look like he was getting a little nauseous. Jerry noticed and, with a mischievous grin, said to Loren, "Tell him what happens when the calf isn't situated just right."

Loren knew what Jerry was doing so he went along with it. "It gets really tricky when the calf isn't positioned correctly. You have to manually check things out. Now, I won't go into all the detail, but you have to stick your arm right up there." As he said that, Loren pretended he was pushing his hand and arm up into a cow in labor. "You can use an obstetrical glove but some people think you can tell more when you just use your bare arm and hand." Barry winced at the thought and the picture he had in his mind. "You may only have to reach in a short distance or you may have to reach all the way up to the uterus with your arm in all the way to the shoulder. Then there's all different kinds of bad positions the calves can come—backward, breech, head turned back, legs turned back; and each of them requires a little different treatment. Now, in a normal birth, the cow licks the calf and that stimulates the newborn to breathe. But sometimes, especially in a problem birth, the calf won't start to breathe and you have to administer artificial respiration."

"Mouth to mouth?" Barry exclaimed in horror.

The other five erupted in laughter.

11

"No," laughed Loren, "you can use a suction bulb but if that doesn't work you may have to hold the mouth shut and pinch off one nostril and blow into the other."

"Oh my God!" said Barry, pushing away the rest of his unfinished breakfast.

Loren sat back, amused at the look on Barry's face and said, "Well, those are just the highlights. I could go on for a lot longer but I assume you get the point that there's more to it than just letting the cows out and watching the calves drop."

"Welcome to the West, Newbie. Maybe you should join up with that kid at the CoOp," laughed Gordon.

"Well, I know I have a lot to learn," he said making a face. Then, recovering after a few seconds he said, "Still, I'm glad I asked. It's interesting. You think being a lawyer is all that interesting?"

"Obviously not," said Loren. "Your wife's been tellin' everybody how boring you are."

That attempt at a joke provoked only minimal laughter followed by quiet. Tim thought he'd try once more with Jerry about his family. "So, Jerry, have you heard from Julie lately?"

"A few phone calls, a few voice messages, otherwise haven't heard much from her," Jerry snorted.

"Well, have you tried calling her?" asked Barry.

"Look, they all know where I am," answered Jerry. "I figure it's up to them to get in touch with me—not the other way around."

"Jerry," said Tim, "don't you think you could ease up a bit on'em? Cripes, you at least ought to give Colin a break. I mean, he was in a damn war zone up until six or seven months ago."

Jerry shot back, "Well, he ain't now!"

Loren stood up and said, "Well, Guys, tryin' to convince Jerry to change his mind about anything is a full time job and one that's likely to end in failure. And I've got a ranch to tend to so I am going to hit the road. Stay good until next week."

A great scraping sound was heard as everyone else got up and pushed their chairs back. They divided the bill six ways equally including a very generous tip for the waitress, Laurie, said their goodbyes and headed for the door.

When they got to the door, Tim said, "Jerry, we all want what's best for you, you know that. Just think about what we said."

Chapter 2

When Jerry walked out the door of Two Rivers he saw that it was a beautiful, sunny day but he didn't even notice. He couldn't appreciate it one bit because his mind was racing—playing hide and seek with itself. The mention of the "shit" he had gone through started this tug of war where his brain inexplicably wanted to both pull up these mostly buried memories of the death of his wife while at the same time trying to think of anything else and keep the memories suppressed.

It was all Jerry could do to keep from getting teary-eyed when the topic came up. And now, he was trying every little trick he knew to keep from thinking about Jackie. He hoped to distract himself by stopping in the market and picking up a few things that Emily had asked him to get.

He was making sure he bought the precise stuff as specified by Emily and by focusing on those little details he tricked his mind into pushing those haunting memories back in their place. The fact that Emily would be sure and comment if he didn't shop carefully gave him extra motivation. Heaven forbid he should get crunchy peanut butter when she wanted creamy. When he left the store, he decided that on the drive home, he would turn his mind to his kids, calculating that he sure wouldn't get maudlin if he was thinking about them. Of course, Jerry loved his kids as much as any parent but that didn't mean that he would be all soft and cuddly about them.

Everything he said at breakfast he felt deep in his bones. He did think they were ungrateful. He did think they should have stayed on the ranch out of respect for him, his dad and his granddad. He could have accepted it if they had said they were just going to go out to the real world and look around but that

14

they would come back in a couple of years but none of them had said any such thing.

In his mind, he acknowledged that having their mama die was a tough thing for them, but he felt it was infinitely tougher on him and that that fact should have made them feel sorry for him and therefore eager to please him. What he never really understood was that it was not only her dying that affected them, it was the effect her dying had on *him* and how that changed the way he interacted with them. He wouldn't have admitted it, hell, he didn't even know it, but her death made him a little nuts. He buried himself in his work and put up an emotional barrier between himself and any other human being. With his kids, he largely abandoned his role as a loving, warm-hearted dad and became the strict father, even while turning much of the child-rearing to Emily which she had readily accepted.

Now, after some twenty-nine years being with but not married to Jerry, she no longer lectured him at length about his kids. They still had brief exchanges on the matter but they had more or less adapted to the other's viewpoint. In that way, and not in any romantic way, they were now like an old married couple. They would bicker and banter and shake their head at something the other would do or say but they had been doing and saying those things to each other for so long that the emotional heat was mostly gone.

Jerry opened the door to his Ford F-150 pickup and put the groceries inside. The F150 was the "car" for the family. It was a crew cab so there had been room for five and it was a comfortable ride but still able to do light-to-medium duty. He had a couple of other pickups but they were heavy duty and fairly beat up. He started the truck up and as he shifted from "park" to "drive," he executed his plan and allowed his brain to shift from peanut butter labels to his kids. As his close friends knew, his kids were an emotional subject for him, almost as much as the death of his wife. The big difference was that there was an element of anger mixed with the love and guilt that was not in the equation relative to Jackie.

Jerry was aware that he wasn't the "world's greatest dad" like the tee shirts read because he hadn't been able to show the love that a dad should. He felt bad about that but after Jackie died, his capacity for love went dormant. It was there, somewhere, but any recognition of love for them at the conscious level would necessarily bleed into his feelings for Jackie and guilt over her death and his subconscious just wouldn't let him do that because it might have killed him. In his mind, he had done the best he could, including getting Emily who had done a fantastic job with the kids.

In Ryan, he had had the son every father wants. Jerry had relished the time he spent with Ryan and felt so good when Jackie would look at them together and smile approvingly. And when Julie came along he felt truly blessed. He had the son every father wants and the daughter every father treasures. Even though only two, she would climb all over Jerry as he would be playing with Ryan and all of them watching Jackie make dinner. If a picture had been taken, it might have made the cover of the old Saturday Evening Post. Everything changed when Colin was born and Jackie died.

Jerry had assumed that when Ryan got older, he would come back and help Jerry run the ranch. Oh, if Ryan wanted to go to college, sure, that would be fine, especially if he went to Montana State which was nearby. He had recognized the value of those correspondence courses on philosophy he had taken and they had nothing to do with ranching. Hopefully, if Ryan did want to go to college, he might study agribusiness or something similar. Ryan had been expected and, indeed, had helped out with all the ranch operations and chores and he knew quite a bit about cattle ranching, horses, irrigation and the myriad of things it takes to run a working ranch. Jerry never really sat down at length with Ryan and talked about Ryan's role or future on the ranch; he made vague suggestions and just assumed that Ryan would be thinking the same way as he. Instead, one day in Ryan's senior year of high school, he told his dad that he had been accepted to DePaul University in Chicago to study broadcast journalism. He wanted to be a TV news reporter. They had quite an argument over it and Jerry told Ryan how disappointed he was but Ryan was adamant.

With Julie on the other hand, Jerry never anticipated that she would stay on at the family ranch, never really cultivated her or tried to teach her about ranch operations. Oh, she did her fair share of chores like gathering and branding and helping with difficult births and feeding and you name it. And, truly, she was just as comfortable in jeans as in a dress. But since Jerry had mentally put all his chips on Ryan taking over, he had just never thought about Julie. A wee bit old fashioned in this regard, he had assumed she would just marry another rancher and be a rancher's wife. He hadn't known that she would have killed for him to ask her to come back to the ranch but she sure wasn't going to let him know that.

When she went off to college, he was OK with that but he was more than a little surprised when she decided on a double major in political science and communications. At least she had chosen MSU so that she was close by, not that he or she took advantage of the proximity. But "poly sci" as she called it apparently had a lot to do with politics and government which seemed to Jerry like twin heads of a mega criminal enterprise. And now she was working at some PR firm or whatever they did in Washington D.C. and clearly did not have the ranch in her plans.

As for Colin, well, the truth was that every time Jerry looked at him or even thought about him, he would be reminded, way in the back of his mind, that Jackie's death and Colin's birth were intertwined. Colin literally never knew his mom and, emotionally, he only knew his dad at a relatively superficial level. Their relationship always had her death between them, choking it of relationship oxygen. When Colin followed Julie to MSU, Jerry was actually happy that he was going to study agribusiness. But then, after once heeding Jerry's admonition to not enlist in the Army in 2004, two years later he defied Jerry and went ahead and enlisted. Jerry was angry that Colin had enlisted against his wishes but secretly proud of his service. But then, after eight years of service including deployment to Iraq, when he got out, an Army buddy talked him into joining him to ride motorcycles in Southern California, doing what Jerry had no idea. Jerry couldn't figure that one out. Whatever, he wasn't back on the ranch.

"Hard to imagine," Jerry told himself, "three kids and not one willing to help out the old man. No gratitude for all the opportunity I provided. Well, so be it. But then don't be expecting me to pick up the phone and chit chat. You know where I am."

As Jerry was driving along, this little mind game that Jerry was playing with himself was working well enough. Indeed, he was practically mouthing the words of his speech of indignation as he stopped for the last stoplight on the way out of town. Suddenly, everything changed. As luck would have it, crossing the street right in front of him was a young woman probably in her mid-twenties that was the spitting image of Jackie at the same age. She even carried her handbag the same way Jackie did with the shoulder strap over her head and diagonally across her chest. Jerry had no idea who this woman was but for him, it was a painful reminder of the woman he had loved and lost.

The light changed and Jerry hit the gas and headed out of town. He tried to get back to thinking about his kids and all the faux rage that had kept his mind off of Jackie but it just wasn't going to happen. Jackie had been the love of his life and he had had her for such a short time.

Chapter 3

Jerry's reached the main ranch gate and turned onto the one mile drive up to the main ranch house. The road was not paved but consisted of crushed rock and dirt. Because it wasn't as smooth as a paved road, one had to drive relatively slowly and so it took a while to get to the house. Unfortunately, that gave Jerry plenty of time to think about his first and only wife.

Jackie Kay Houston was born in Livingston, Montana in 1950; a year after Jerry was born. They both attended the same high school but a year apart and while they knew one another they tended to run in somewhat different circles—somewhat different because the circle overlapped in such a way that they were often in the same large group but just not together. Mentally and, at times, literally, they would see each other across the room and be attracted but neither would ever act on it.

Jackie was attractive so she had a number of suitors. The same was true for Jerry; he never had a problem getting a date. So the two of them went through high school dating other people, never confronting the apparent attraction.

Jerry graduated a year before Jackie and, of course, plunged totally into the ranch and all the work that it entailed. He had a girlfriend, Lucy, and they dated for five long years and it was a nice relationship, comfortable and convenient, but it wasn't going anywhere. Neither of them minded and neither of them was in a rush to change. Jerry's life was mostly about the ranch and working with his dad and taking care of his granddad and when he needed a date for the occasional dance or whatever, Lucy was a good companion. As for Lucy, she was working at a dead-end job at a retail store. Not the brightest person, she was basically incapable of putting together a plan of how to do something with more potential. So, she plodded along, year after year, wondering how she might change things. Finally her cousin in Phoenix asked her to join her in a woman's clothing business that her cousin had started. She didn't know that much about women's clothing but it was a chance to escape Livingston and it was a warm weather destination to boot. So, she said goodbye to Jerry and was gone.

It surprised Jerry that he didn't miss her a bit. Oh, he missed the convenience, he missed knowing that he always had a date if he needed one and he missed driving her car—a real car and not a pickup. But by that time he didn't care that much about dating and, though he was a little conflicted about promiscuity, he was able to satisfy his needs by taking short trips and seeking women who were cooperative. He was sure his father would not approve had he known.

A few years after Lucy had left, one of Jerry's friends was getting married and Jerry was invited and the invitation specified "and guest." But Jerry had let his dating life slip so far that for one of the few times in his life, he could not find a date. So, he went by himself. He was sitting in the church, looking toward the front where his friend, the groom, was waiting for the music to signal the actual start of the wedding. When it did, he swung around in order to see the bride and his eyes immediately fixed on Jackie. She looked terrific. She was looking at him and he felt a "zing" that he couldn't really describe but it was a wonderful yet puzzling feeling; puzzling because it wasn't a feeling one experienced more than once or twice in a lifetime. All during the wedding ceremony, his mind was racing, wondering what was going on. He looked back a few times, as discreetly as he could, to have another look at her. She was always looking straight ahead.

At the reception, he sought her out and discovered much to his dismay, that she *did* have a date. But Jerry and Jackie and her date were at the same table and so he was able to catch up with her life since high school. She had studied bookkeeping in high school and had taken a job with a local accounting firm after graduation. She said she enjoyed the work and liked the people she worked with but she didn't sound very passionate about it. When her date excused himself to go to the restroom, he asked for her telephone number and said he's like to go out with her. He figured if she and her date were tight then she would say no. She didn't say no.

He called her the next day and asked her out for the following Saturday and Jackie accepted. It turned out that her date was the same type as when Jerry had dated Lucy—comfortable and convenient but nothing more. Each confessed to the attraction that had felt in high school but had never acted on and laughed as to how silly that seemed. They dated regularly for a couple of months and then exclusively. Marriage was only a matter of when. Nevertheless, they took their time and enjoyed the courtship. When they did marry, Jerry was as happy as a man could be and Jackie was equally ecstatic. In fact, she suggested holding off on having kids for a time so that they would really have the chance to settle in together. She also admitted to herself that she was a little nervous about the prospect of being a mother and about the birth process itself. They lived at the Johnston ranch and Jackie gave up her job to be a full time wife and homemaker.

Eventually, their first child, Ryan was born in 1979. It turned out that Jackie's concerns about motherhood were groundless. She took to being a mother with zest and very naturally. She was a very loving mother though not particularly strict. She left discipline issues up to Jerry who had been brought up in a "Yes, Sir," "No, Sir," environment.

It was nearly five years before Julie came along and the birth process left Jackie somewhat sick and exhausted. It had been a hard pregnancy and then labor had to be induced and it took a very long time and it was just everything that Jackie had once feared. Jackie loved having another female in the house and absolutely cherished both her children. At the same time, she was grateful that they had had a boy and a girl because now they had the full experience, children of each sex, and both were healthy and normal. There would be no wondering as there would have been had they produced two boys or two girls. As far as she was concerned, she was done. She even talked about having her tubes tied.

Jerry, however, felt differently. He wanted more kids; as far as he was concerned, a bunch more would be fine. He had always wished that he had a brother, even a sister would have been better than being an only child. Some of the other families he knew growing up had five or six or even seven kids. So, by his way of thinking, two kids was just getting started. So, he began a campaign with Jackie to have more kids. Back and forth they went for months. She didn't like disappointing Jerry but she felt pretty strongly that she didn't want to go through the whole ordeal again. But Jerry wouldn't take "No" for an answer. He bitched and moaned and pleaded and cajoled and eventually wore Jackie down. He was ecstatic when in the spring of 1985 she announced she was pregnant. When they later had all the tests done and knew it was a boy and Jerry was thrilled.

Four months later she went into labor and they headed to the hospital. At the hospital, Jerry stayed in the waiting room for fathers-to-be. Jerry was old fashioned about this, he didn't want to be there for the blood and screaming and whatever else went on. He was fine with having the nurse bring him his baby when it was all done. There were a couple of first time fathers there and Jerry felt like an old, calm hand compared to these frantic souls.

But then word came that there was a problem—the baby was fine but Jackie was having problems. "What kind of problems," Jerry asked nervously. He was told they were not sure but they were doing everything they could. Jerry's head was spinning; he felt he had suddenly entered a bad twilight zone where everything seemed to be unreal. "What could be happening?" he wondered. "Why aren't they telling me anything?"

Then he prayed. "Please God, let everything work out okay and I'll do anything you want."

He wanted to believe that everything was going to be fine but he had a bad feeling. Minutes seemed like hours and still there was no word. Finally, a weary-looking doctor came into the waiting room and took Jerry over to the side. "I have bad news," he said. "I don't know how else to say it, but we lost your wife. The baby is fine."

Jerry's mind totally stopped; he thought he had heard the doctor say something, something awful, but now he could only gape at the doctor. Finally, he managed to say, "She's gone?"

And the doctor answered. "Yes."

"How is it possible? What happened?"

"We think she had an amniotic fluid embolism. Sometimes, amniotic fluid can enter the bloodstream triggering cardio respiratory arrest. I'm very sorry, Mr. Johnston."

Jerry knew Jackie was dead but his mind just wouldn't allow itself to think about that. It was pure defense mechanism for a man who was all tough and strict on the outside but very emotional at his core. Instead, his sole thought was that it was his fault. He had pushed her and pressured her to have another child when he knew she didn't want another. But he had been persistent, persistence which caused her to die. Had he acceded to her wishes, this would not have happened. At that moment, he wanted to die himself. He could barely breathe. His whole world had crashed around him and everything was a blur. He felt a pain like he had never known; a pain that felt like it would never go away.

Somehow, Jerry had the hospital call Gordon O'Laughlin to come and take Jerry home. The baby would stay at the hospital. When Jerry got home, he told Gordon's wife who was babysitting Ryan and Julie. Then, he told his father what had happened. Joe Johnston tried his best to comfort his son but Jerry was inconsolable. He went to his bedroom and wept and wept and wept.

Presently, Jerry had driven ten miles from town toward his ranch but had no awareness that he had. All the thoughts about Jackie and her death in giving birth to Colin swept over Jerry and he lost it. He began to cry as if it had all happened yesterday. He was so overcome with grief that he had to pull the car over to the side of the road. He only hoped that no one would stop to see what was wrong, because that's what people did in these parts and he really didn't want to explain to some kind person, but still a stranger, why he had pulled over. After a time, the memories and feelings passed sufficiently so that he could resume his trip home. The pain wasn't quite like it was the night she died, but, surprisingly, after twenty-nine years, the pain was still intense. "Will I never get past this?" he thought to himself.

When he got home mid-morning, Emily was doing her usual household chores. Emily had been a very good looking woman in her prime and was still good looking considering she had just turned seventy-one. When she was young, she had definitely wanted to marry and for her, marriage had always seemed just around the corner. Two times she had been engaged and then something happened each time that made her question if marriage was her destiny.

Normally, she might be starting to fix something for lunch but not on Sunday. Jerry would have eaten a big breakfast at Two Rivers and he would not have been out working so he wouldn't be hungry for a big lunch. He tried to say a quick hello and blow past her before she could see his face because he did not want her to know that he had been crying but it was no use. He couldn't get anything past that woman, no matter how he tried. And while he might have liked a little sympathy, he knew he was unlikely to get it from her.

Emily said, "You've been crying, haven't you? OK, what triggered it this time?"

Though he knew it was useless, he tried to pretend he didn't know what she was talking about. "What makes you say that?" he asked.

"Oh, Lord, Jerry, don't play games with me. I know you have been crying, now answer my question!"

Although he knew the real reasons why she had never been married, he pretended he didn't and thought, "No wonder she's never been married!" Out loud he said, somewhat sheepishly, "Oh, somebody kind of brought Jackie up at breakfast and then on the way out of town, I saw a young woman who looked a lot like Jackie and it just got me thinking."

"And I know what you were thinking about; you were thinking that her dying was your fault. How many times do I have to tell you that you're an idiot to think that way? You didn't force her at gunpoint to have another baby. She made her own choice. God just had a different plan for her than the two of you did."

"Why? Why would God, if He even exists, why would He want or need to take her away from me? Why would a loving God do such a thing?"

"Oh, so it's all about you? If God had a reason to take her before *you* were ready, that makes Him a bad God? Or maybe you think He's supposed to communicate His reasons to you? Get over yourself! The universe revolves around Him, not you. You should just thank Him for the years he gave you with her instead of blaming Him, and yourself and your kids."

"Well, that's easy for you to say—you've never been married. And I should thank Him for my kids?" He knew what he said about her never being married was a little cruel but he hoped to throw her off a little. The woman had a sharp tongue and he was no match for her in that regard.

"Oh, and now it's the kids turn. Let's kick them in the butt, just like you always used to, because you felt life had dealt you and bad deal. They're not ungrateful, Jerry. You just never gave them a reason to want to come back. What did you expect when you were always telling them they had "crossed the line" when they had done some little thing wrong. They were some of the best behaved kids I've known and you always acted like they had just committed a felony."

Crossing the line was one of Jerry's favorite pronouncements to his kids when he felt they had misbehaved. Good behavior, he felt, was clear cut. The phrase came from one of his favorite books, "Lonesome Dove." The book was about two former Texas Rangers in the old West who were on a cattle drive but were diverted to chase down some very bad men who had stolen horses and viciously killed innocent people. A friend and former fellow Ranger had fallen in with the bad men and had tried to get away before the killing started; indeed, he wasn't a killer himself, but the gang had threatened him if he tried to leave. So, when the Rangers caught up with the whole bunch and were going to hang them, the friend included, the friend proclaimed he was no killer, that he shouldn't have to hang. But the Ranger said, "Ride with an outlaw, die with him. I'm sorry you crossed the line." Jerry had always interpreted that to mean morality is black and white, there is no gray area. You're right or you're not, there is no middle ground. And that's pretty much the way he was raised and the way he thought his kids should be raised. Jackie hadn't belonged to the black and white school of child-raising, but after she died, that's how Jerry operated. He had used that line so often on his kids that when they got older, they just rolled their eyes when he said it.

"Well, someone had to teach them right from wrong," he said.

"Of course," Emily replied, "and you did it and I did it. But these weren't little machines; they were little people, who make mistakes, same as you. You wouldn't expect perfection from a young colt, would you? You never really showed them the love to go along with the discipline. They all loved you, they told me so, but they never felt your love in return. And the fact is, underneath it all, they still love you. But they're not going to take the first step; they have waited too long for you to return their love. So, you have to be the adult in the room and take that step toward them."

Having been lectured for the second time in one day on this topic, Jerry was a little thin skinned. "Well, it's not going to happen, and that's that!"

"Like I said, you have to be the adult in the room and that's not happening, either," lashed Emily. "Now go on; get out of the house. I have work to do."

Generally, when they would have a disagreement, it usually ended with her issuing an order and him slinking out of her presence. He would wonder to himself who owned the place, anyway. But leave he did; he went to his bedroom to change clothes so he could saddle up and go out and find his crew to see what was happening. His last thought as he headed to the barn was, "I guess it's better to be scolded like a two year old by your housekeeper than to be sad and crying; but not by much."

Chapter 4

The rest of Jerry's day went considerably better, even though it involved a lot of work. On a working cattle ranch, there is always more work than there is time or money. Today, Jerry let most of his crew handle the herd; he took one young cowboy and worked on some fences. Cattle, and horses, too, for that matter, have an uncanny ability to find a weakness in any fence. Thus, the old line about being "out mendin' fences" was a constant reality. There were always fences to erect, repair, or re-build. For the most part, Montana is an "open range" state, meaning a landowner has to fence out the livestock of a neighbor rather than fence his own in. Nevertheless, fence maintenance is something that needs to be done all the time.

The young cowboy, who happened to be originally from Mexico, called Jerry, "Patron" or "boss". Among other things, this meant the young man didn't think he should speak unless spoken to and on this particular afternoon, this suited Jerry just fine. With just a few tools that have been developed over many years of fence work, two people can take care of a lot of fence. The afternoon passed quickly and when it got to be around six o'clock, Jerry sent the young man back to his crew chief and he headed for home.

He and Emily did not eat together every night but tonight they did. Mercifully, she didn't make any mention of their discussion earlier in the day. They talked about politics because politics was one subject where they were in agreement. They both had little regard for politicians even though they had to admit that there were some good ones on both sides. But the bad ones were such liars and hypocrites that they tended to obscure the good ones.

When supper was done, Jerry let Emily clear the table and load the dishwasher. Back when Jackie was alive, they didn't have a dishwasher; Jackie would wash and he would dry and they would talk about anything and everything. It was a favorite part of Jerry's day. Sometimes, he thought, technology doesn't make life better.

It was Jerry's custom on most days at the end of the day to pour himself a generous glass of red wine and get something to read. In fact, he often had a second glass and, occasionally, even a third. He told himself that it was simply that it tasted so good, that he wasn't reacting to the numbing effect of the alcohol even though down deep he knew better. In summer, he would go out on the porch, but most of the year it was a little too cool, if not downright freezing, and he would go into the study/library. In terms of speed, he had never been a very good reader, tending to silently say each word instead of just reading it. He was getting up in age, "65 years young" he would say to himself; but as a result, he found that when he read at the end of the day and had a glass of wine, he would get drowsy quite quickly. Reading a book seven or eight pages at a time meant you didn't read too many books in a year. He wasn't sure how someone smarter would classify or group his favorite books, but they included "Lonesome Dove," "The Caine Mutiny," "Angle of Repose," and The Bible. He found the Bible confusing—all the killing and mayhem in the Old Testament and the peace and love of Jesus Christ in the New Testament.

Tonight, he picked The Bible to read, but somehow the sheer heft of it deterred him. As he plopped in the easy chair in the study, he put the book on the table next to him and just savored his wine. His mind drifted to the conversations of the day and the exhortations of Tim and Barry and, especially, Emily to reach out to the kids and ease up on them. A part of him wished he could but something held him back from doing so. He wondered what his dad and granddad would have thought. What would they have said to him? Well, he knew a little of what his dad, Joe would have said because he was still around when Jackie had died. He first had tried to console Jerry but then, as Jerry put up an emotional barrier between himself and everyone else, Joe had tried to get Jerry to take it down. Jerry hadn't been able to. He also thought that Joe would have understood about succeeding generations staying on the ranch because that had been important to Joe and to his father Paul. "What would granddad say?" said Jerry out loud to himself.

Paul Alexander Johnston was born in Voss, Norway in 1889, the same year Montana achieved statehood. Though born in Norway he was of Scottish descent, his parents moving to Norway a few years earlier for work. Paul had always reminded his son Joe and his grandson Jerry that he, Paul, had been born less than a year after and in the same town as Knute Rockne, the famous football coach who played and coached at the University of Notre Dame. As a result, the members of the Johnston household were staunch Notre Dame fans.

When Paul was nineteen, both his parents contracted influenza—the flu, and they died within a few months of one another. Paul was nineteen with no parents, only a high school education and no real prospects. He scraped together just enough money for the lowest class on a ship and made it to New York City.

Like so many immigrants before him, he found New York to be rough and loud and getting work was not easy. So, he worked his way west to Chicago, then St, Louis, then Kansas City. He had a variety of jobs but many of them had some connection to the stockyards of each town. Working in slaughterhouses he sometimes would meet people who were ranchers, the people who raised the cattle he was helping to slaughter. Several of them suggested he should come out to their ranches; one was in Colorado, another in Texas and yet another in Montana. Paul thought he would like the weather better in Montana. Originally being from Norway, he liked cold; he didn't like hot.

So, Paul came out to work on the ranch of a man named Jennings. It was a fairly small ranch of about 150 acres a little ways west of Bozeman. For fifteen years, Paul worked extremely hard for Jennings, learning everything he could about cattle ranching. The Jennings ran Black Angus which Paul liked because the breed had Scottish origins like Paul. He also liked their smaller size as compared to some breeds and, of course, the quality of the beef. Some years were good and some not so good. In the not so good years, Jennings would sometimes pay Paul in heifers. In the good years, he paid Paul in dollars and he was a fair and generous man so Paul was accumulating a fair amount of both capital and heifers.

In his fifteenth year of working for Jennings, Paul met and married a woman by the name of Sally Cummings and their son, Joe, was born a year later in 1925. Sally was by no means from a wealthy family but she had a little money saved and her dad gave her a modest but meaningful sum as a wedding gift. Together, Paul and she had enough to buy a 500 acre ranch south of Livingston in 1929 when Paul turned thirty.

Of course, 1929 saw the advent of the Great Depression and the '30s brought drought and the Great Dustbowl. Montana wasn't hit as hard as some other states but, nevertheless, many ranchers in Montana were hit hard enough that they were not able to hold on to their ranches. Paul had good land and superior water rights and he knew that out West, water was more valuable than gold. Also, the fact that he had a herd of heifers from his past paydays, meant he was basically in a great financial position relative to other ranchers.

In prolonged bad economic times, ranching can be a heavy burden. Many of his fellow ranchers who were less fortunate had to sell and Paul bought just about everything he could get his hands on. He'd go to the owners, sometimes people he knew, and tried to see if he could help. Very often, the owners didn't want a loan or help, they wanted out. So, Paul would ask what they thought was fair and then give them twice the amount asked. His reputation for fair dealing and integrity grew tremendously over the next decade. By the time the U.S. got yanked into World War II he had accumulated nearly 25,000 acres of prime Montana ranchland, both north and south of Livingston and most of it connected.

Paul built a large ranch house, at least large by the standard of when he built it. He anticipated and hoped for a large family so he built seven bedrooms along with study/library, the "radio" room where the family could gather and listen to the radio broadcasts about the war, storage and utility rooms, a den and, of course, a large kitchen. It wasn't particularly fancy but it was roomy. And no animal head or antler chandeliers; he thought those were stupid.

Paul planted lawns and a number of trees and little flower gardens and rock walls and other features all intended to communicate the idea that this was a home; the ranch was "out there." Although he had built seven bedrooms, he also built a number of guest cabins that were charming in their own right.

The war ended in 1945 and it didn't take long for things to begin to boom. Those fortunate enough to be well positioned in 1945 stood to make a fortune and Paul Johnston was certainly well positioned. He owned a lot of prime ranchland, he had money in the bank, he had a large herd of cattle, he had a wife who was a great partner in everything he did, and he had a twenty-year old son eager to join him in running the ranch. "What a blessing," Jerry thought, "to have a son eager to stay and work on the ranch."

Joseph Martin Johnston was the only child of Paul and Sally Johnston. They certainly had planned to have more children but complications from the birth of Joe made that very unlikely. Jerry remembered his granddaddy Paul lamenting that they had only been able to have one child when he had hoped for a bunch. In Jerry's young mind, then, a bunch of kids was better than one.

From before the time he could walk he was put on a horse and walked around in a corral. He was brought up to be a hard worker, to be honest and humble, and to believe in God. In particular, he was raised to be respectful of his elders; and for Paul, respect meant keeping your mouth shut and doing your job, whatever that may be, like a man. That, in turn, meant no whining or complaining, no shirking and not needing to rely on other people. In addition, Paul had always expected that Joe would follow him on the ranch and Joe wanted it as much as Paul expected it.

The Johnston family formula, then, was based on old-fashioned ideas of men being the strong, silent type and the women silent. The men were clearly in charge, the women were equal but silent partners. There wasn't a lot of happy talk or constant saying "I love you" or any of that. It was the land and the weather and the life that influenced them, that molded them to be as tough as one had to be to survive. The land was a beautiful but brutal mistress that demanded those who wanted to live off of it be as tough as the middle of a Montana winter. In that kind of environment, you gritted your teeth and went about your business. There was no patience for weakness because weakness and the ranching life could not co-exist. If you wanted one, the other could not be allowed.

Nevertheless, Joe did have a weakness for his son, Jerry. He didn't coddle him or anything like that; but when Jerry was a newborn, Joe had loved to hold him and look at his blue eyes and little smile and he couldn't help but say, "I love you, Jeremiah Johnston." After all, Jerry had been born a couple of months premature on April 7, 1949 and in those days, dealing with premature babies mainly involved putting the newborn into the equivalent of a toaster oven and hoping for the best. Joe couldn't believe how tiny and fragile his new son was and that resulted in a soft spot in Joe for Jerry.

Joe hadn't known what to make of how small Jerry had been at birth; in fact, he didn't know much about babies at all. But he believed Jerry to be a fighter as every day Jerry got a little stronger and after a few weeks the doctors said they were confident he would make it. Of course, when Jerry got older, the relationship generally reverted to the Johnston family formula. But just every now and then, Joe would break the formula and tell his son that he was proud of him and that he loved him. Joe wouldn't know until years later how much of an impact those few occasions had on Jerry.

As Jerry continued thinking about his family history and how the ranch came to be, he chuckled quietly and took another sip of wine. His dad hadn't known, and Jerry never told him, but even old grandpa Paul had broken the formula once. Paul had died in

1962 when Jerry was just thirteen. He didn't have any particular disease, he just wore out. Near the end, Joe was out working on the ranch and Jerry was in the house and Paul called him into his room where Paul was lying in bed. Jerry assumed that Paul needed something or was hungry or needed help with something.

Instead, Paul said," I want to tell you something that's just between you and me, OK?"

Jerry nodded his head.

Paul said, "I've been on this earth for near seventy five years and they've been mostly good ones. There've been some bad moments, like when your grandma died, but the good Lord has been good to me; I've got no complaints. The good times included when I met and married your grandma, when your dad was born and when you were born. Like your daddy, I have loved you since the moment you were born and I am proud of the man you are becoming. Here's my advice to you: Be proud to be a rancher and be proud to be an American because one begets the other. Someday soon, you'll have a family of your own. I won't be there to see it so I have to tell you this now: be tough, be fair but be sure and let them know you love them."

Jerry didn't say a word; he was stunned. He had never heard his grandpa talk this way and he didn't know how to respond.

Paul smiled weakly and said, "Go on now, go on with your chores." Jerry left the room and headed for the barn and tried to process what he had just been told. Paul died two days later. His grandpa's death put a focus on the words Paul had spoken to him.

Taking another sip of wine, Jerry thought about that scene of which he had never told anyone including his dad. He remembered his initial confusion and then remembered how he had cried that night, thinking of his grandpa, how he loved him and how he wanted to be like him, and, especially, to be a rancher. Being a rancher and being an American *was* kind of the same thing. "Why aren't my kids like that?" he thought.

And so a rancher he had become. What would he have done if he hadn't become a rancher? Hard to say but it probably would have been physically easier, financially more lucrative and, yet, less rewarding to his soul. Had he liquidated the ranch when he took over and put the money in the stock market and real estate and technology and stuff like that he'd probably have his own jet and be mingling with the rich and powerful. He could have had women, all the toys a man could want and a life of pleasure. When he'd jokingly mention those thoughts to his dad, Joe would quote Jesus Christ and say, "For what does it profit a man to gain the whole world and forfeit his soul?"

He'd reply, "I was just kiddin', Dad"

Joe would mutter, "Nothin' to kid about."

Jerry thought about his dad now, down in an assisted living facility in Scottsdale, Arizona. The doctors said the warmer temperatures and lower elevation would be good for him but it was tough on Jerry. He didn't get to see his dad but a few times a year when he would travel down and stay a few days with him. Joe was getting more frail with each visit but his mind was still clear.

Jerry was getting a little drowsy but his mind shifted from the ranch to the business of ranching. Most people tended to think that ranching had to be easy; after all, what could be hard about it. You get some cows, get'em pregnant, wait for nine months until the calves pop out, put'em on some grass to fatten'em up and then sell'em and make a bundle. Simple. Of course, there was hard work involved but the basic business model was pretty simple. You didn't have to figure anything new out, just do the same thing you did last year.

Jerry was fortunate in a number of ways. First, he had inherited incredibly valuable land. His father had continued the practice of buying other ranches and land when the price made sense so now the Johnston Ranch was about 34,000 acres. On a couple of occasions, he had sold land he didn't really need to provide capital. Second, their herd of cows was plenty big enough that it replenished itself given the number of calves they needed to produce to generate a very good income. He didn't need or want to be the biggest. His crew chiefs or foremen had lived on ranch property in homes they had been given long ago and they were paid decent wages. The basic labor was paid well enough that there was no trouble getting good cowboys. Years before, Paul had made a handshake agreement with a large food company to buy all his calves, at least the ones that weren't rejected by common agreement, at the market price at a date agreed upon every year. In short, inheriting all the capital and infrastructure and relationships gave the Johnston ranch a built-in advantage. Of course, advantages are not a guarantee of success. The ranch continued to prosper through Jerry's own efforts and those of his crews.

As much work as it took, there were aspects of the life that he felt, no he knew, were priceless; like the feeling when a job was well done by a crew working together. Working in such a glorious physical setting was a privilege that city slickers regularly paid for. It was you and your crew dealing with nature with no intermediary; thus it was pure. And, most especially, when you were sitting on your favorite horse, working as a team, looking at mountains and valleys that made your jaw drop with their beauty, you had to believe in a divine being. Of course, Jerry had been struggling with that ever since Jackie had died but when he was up on his favorite horse, Rocket, that's what he felt.

Rocket was a Palomino quarter horse that Jerry had bred himself. Gelded at about the age of one, he was now six and was a beautiful horse. When Jerry was riding Rocket they were a team. He really enjoyed when they were out without other ranch hands; somehow in that isolation, Jerry's connection with Rocket was heightened. Usually, they would be accompanied by Puck, Jerry's black lab and mutt mix of a dog that was about the same age as Rocket. Puck's tail never stopped wagging when they were out. Dogs are quite obvious in their emotions. Horses are much more subtle. Jerry loved them both.

He finished the last of his wine and his eyelids were starting to droop. He went into the kitchen and put his glass into the sink and then headed for his bedroom. Emily had already gone to bed apparently and Jerry was ready. He washed his face and brushed his teeth thinking about Ryan and Julie and Colin and wishing things were different.

He got into bed and as his head hit the pillow, he thought, "This life is priceless. Why the hell can't my kids see that?" He fell asleep immediately.

Chapter 5

The following Tuesday was a windy but clear July day and Jerry had been up early as usual. It was light but the sun wasn't quite up yet in their valley. Emily had gone away for a few days to tend to a sick friend and so Jerry was on his own for meals which usually meant something fast and unhealthy.

Looking out his bedroom window, Jerry saw a passenger balloon down the valley which was pretty common in the summertime. Tourists liked the view of beautiful Montana that they could get from the basket of a balloon. Obviously one got a much better view than from an airplane and it was much quieter than a helicopter. He noticed the balloon moving up valley, toward his house at a fairly rapid pace but didn't think much of it. These balloons always drifted a little bit and today was pretty breezy. Still, this one seemed to be on a different track than most.

Jerry dressed hurriedly and went outside where he could see the balloon, now only a few hundred yards away and still coming. He could feel a strong wind that was pushing the balloon down in spite of the attempts of the pilot to keep the balloon higher. He could see that there were four or five passengers in the basket who looked afraid, not sure how this ride might end. It appeared that the pilot had been trying to get the balloon high enough to go well over Jerry's house but for whatever reason had failed to maintain enough altitude. So now he was doing the opposite, trying to get the balloon down before it slammed into Jerry's house.

There was a small white picket fence about fifty yards from the front porch of Jerry's house. The balloon was coming along at a rapid pace and looked like it might either hit the house or the basket might plow into the fence. Instead, probably through sheer luck, the basket cleared the fence by inches and then touched the ground. However, it was moving too quickly and caught an edge and toppled over onto its side, spilling the passengers part way out of the basket. The pilot, holding onto the controls, was able to stay totally in the basket. The balloon lay toward Jerry's house and was still catching some of the hard blowing wind, thereby dragging the basket little. Eventually, however, the balloon began to collapse and, finally, everything was stable.

Jerry rushed over to help and saw that there were, indeed, five passengers. They were trying to crawl out of the basket which was lying on its side. The first ones he caught sight of and looked to help were a man and his wife and two children, the children being around ten years of age or so he thought. They were able to get out with his assistance and the father and mother immediately began to profess their gratitude. One of the smaller children was crying but from shock as opposed to any injury.

Jerry only heard about half of what they were saying because he went to help the last passenger, a woman that seemed around his age; and as he was helping her get up and got a full look at her, he felt something he really hadn't in years—attraction. Not just the kind of surface level, shallow physical attraction that all men feel throughout their lives, but a deeper, more powerful feeling that comes as a big mystery to men when it does happen because they can't explain why, they can only acknowledge its presence. This kind of attraction had one characteristic that didn't happen with the other kind of attraction and that was the possibility of something beyond casual.

When some men are in this kind of situation they trip all over themselves; the mere possibility of something serious begins to interfere with their normal abilities in the areas of logic and behavior. Jerry normally was not flustered by much, but it had been so long since he felt real attraction that he was somewhat flummoxed. He was simultaneously staring at this woman while another corner of his brain was screaming at him to see if the other passengers were okay and, oh yeah, the pilot still had to be assisted. Finally, Jerry broke out of his semi-trance and helped the pilot and then asked, "Is everyone okay?"

"We're okay'" said the father of the family of four. "But what the heck happened there?"

The pilot said, "I really don't know for sure. There was a real strong downdraft and, for some reason, the balloon didn't respond as it usually does."

Jerry turned to the lady that had created the stir inside of him and asked, "How about you, Ma'am? Are you okay?"

In a clear and strong voice she said, "I'm just fine; bumped my head a little but nothing at all serious. I know someone might have been hurt, but no one was and I have to say that was rather thrilling."

Still looking at her, Jerry said, "My name is Jerry Johnston. Why don't you all come into my house and you can wash up a little, use the facilities and relax until they come to pick you up. Come on, folks." And with that, he turned and headed toward the front door. They all followed except the pilot who was inspecting the basket and the balloon and attending to the tanks and other controls.

Once inside, he turned to the father of the family of four and pointed to a door and said, "Why don't you take your family and use that bedroom. It's got a large bathroom that you all can use. When you are done, come on out here and I'll get you all something to drink."

As they headed to the bedroom door, Jerry turned to the lady in question and took just a moment to look her over. She was not tall and not big; she had a very nice figure and a pretty face and short brownish hair. There was just something about her demeanor that set her apart although Jerry wasn't sure exactly what it was.

He said, "Well, Ma'am, what can I do for you? Would you like the use of a bathroom or would you like something to drink or what?"

"Well, for starters," she said with a bit of a chuckle, "you can stop calling me Ma'am; it makes me feel old. My name is Jan, Jan Martino. And it would be nice if you had a bathroom I could use and then I think the only other thing I need is a drink of water." There was no whining or concerns about the accident; no timidity about what she wanted or how she wanted to be addressed. At first blush, she seemed about as self-confident a woman that Jerry could ever remember.

He escorted her to another bedroom and pointed to the bathroom. "There you go," he said. For just a moment, he watched her from behind as she took the few steps to the bathroom. He was experiencing thoughts and emotions far faster than he could process them. He felt the attraction but wasn't sure what, if anything, to do about it. He had brief thought about Jackie since he really hadn't had this type of feeling about a woman, however raw this feeling might be, since Jackie. There was also a little fear, fear of exposing himself to the possibility of romantic disappointment. After all, his life in that regard was very safe and stable—no romance meant no chance of being hurt and he was content with that. Jerry was thinking all these thoughts but then knowing that she would be back in just a moment, he forced himself to think about it all later. He settled down and recovered from his earlier discomfiture.

When she did come back, she said, "How about that glass of water?"

He reached for a glass from the cupboard and said, "I think I can handle that. So, Jan Martino, are you from somewhere around here or are you just visiting? It's probably the latter because I know just about all the good looking women who live around here and we haven't met."

She gave him a look and a little laugh that he interpreted as saying not unkindly, "That's a little lame but on short notice so, C+ ."

In reality she said, "Well, actually, neither. I'm from back in the Midwest but I am in the process of moving here. I'm a school teacher and I've accepted a job here starting in the fall and I was here on an apartment hunting trip and saw the ad for the balloon ride and thought I'd give it a try. I guess I got a little more adventure than I had originally thought."

Jerry noted that there was no mention of a husband or partner or family. "What do you teach?" asked Jerry.

"Grade school. Anything from first through eighth grades."

"So, you don't have a home, yet? Where are you staying?"

"At the Livingston Hotel."

Jerry heard some stirring in the bedroom where the family had gone and something inside told him if he wanted to pursue this, whatever "this" was, he had better do it quickly. So, he blurted out, "Well how about having dinner with me tonight? I'll tell you all the secrets you need to know about Livingston and get you the best steak in town."

"Well, I don't know. I mean, I don't want to put you to any trouble and you've already been very nice to all of us."

"Well, that's the way most folks around these parts are. And as for dinner, it's no trouble. I'd really like to get acquainted since you're moving here. How about it? I'll meet you in the lobby of the hotel at 6:30."

Jan blushed just a little at Jerry's pronouncement about wanting to get acquainted. She said, "I can't tonight but would tomorrow night work for you?"

"Tomorrow night it is," he said. "I'll see you at 6:30 tomorrow night at the hotel."

Just then the family, whose name Jerry did not know came out from the bedroom and at the same moment that the pilot came into the house and said, "Okay, everybody, our van is here to take you back to town."

They all went out the front door and, now by himself, Jerry tried to figure out what had happened. He was happy that he had made the connection and happy he would be able to pursue the attraction the next night. He did have a little hesitation, though; this was the first time he had even been interested in another woman, other than in a purely sexual way, since Jackie had died and he didn't quite understand it. Sure, she was attractive but there were plenty of attractive women around. Why her? Why now?

The rest of that day and much of the rest were a bit of a blur for Jerry. He joined up with one of his crews that was both tending to a herd of weanlings and fixing some fence. He alternated as to whether to think about the date or not. Sometimes, he would let himself think about Jan and how their date might go and what he might say and what he might tell her about himself and what he might say about Livingston and on and on. Other times he didn't want to think about it at all, instead just trying to focus on whatever he was doing as if there were no date. Nevertheless, everyone noticed that he seemed distracted; he would reach for the wrong tool or not hear a question. His mind was clearly elsewhere but no one said anything because, after all, he was the boss.

As it got around to five o'clock on the date night, Jerry made an excuse to the boys about having to take care of something and went home to get cleaned up. He found himself taking extra time in bathing and washing his hair and cleaning his nails. He shaved with extra care both to look good and so that he didn't nick himself. He trimmed his eyebrows, applied body powder, brushed his teeth, used mouthwash and applied cologne. He didn't really want to admit it, but he was a little nervous and he didn't like that although it did tell him this was somehow more than just a casual date, at least to him. He wore a pressed, clean pair of jeans with what city folks would call a cowboy shirt with white pearl buttons and a brown, suede Western jacket that had fringe on the upper chest. He combed his hair over and over trying to get it to lay just right.

A little after six o'clock, he headed into town and arrived at the Livingston Hotel at around 6:25. Jan was not yet in the lobby and Jerry had a momentary panic as to whether she might not show. But, he took a seat in the lobby and looked around at the décor since he hadn't been in the hotel for several years. He noticed that they had upgraded everything since the last time he had been there and thought it looked nice but, maybe, not as Western as before.

At exactly 6:30. Jerry heard one of the elevator doors open and he looked over and there she was and, by golly, he thought his heart skipped a beat or, at least, he felt a little blip in his emotions. She looked even better than the day before. She was wearing a simple skirt and blouse with a jacket that somehow managed to show off her figure. She looked around and spotted

Jerry and smiled a big smile and headed over without hesitation to where he was now getting up.

As she approached him, Jerry managed a smile himself and put out his hand and said, "Well, howdy, Ma'am; I mean, Jan." A millisecond after he said it, he closed his eyes, wishing that he hadn't made the mistake of saying Ma'am and shook his head the way people do as if they could somehow erase the last few seconds and get it right the first time.

Jan laughed, appreciating his discomfiture and appreciating that he must be sufficiently attracted to her to make him nervous enough to trip up. Just about all women like it when a man is a little nervous, especially over them; it makes them feel good, not in a malicious way, and it gives them more control than when a man can take them or leave them.

"Well, howdy to you, Jerry,' she said. "I'm glad you didn't forget."

"Why no, Ma'am; I mean no, I wouldn't forget," said Jerry, swearing at himself silently. For God's sake, you're sixty-four years old and run a big ranch; can you please stop making a fool of yourself? Out loud he said, "Well, shall we go? The restaurant's just down the street."

The Cattlemen's Club was, indeed, just down the street from the hotel which was good because Jerry needed a little time to recover from his flubs in the hotel lobby and he was able to just make small talk in the short walk to the restaurant. The Cattlemen's Club was a club because the owner ran it as a private club, charging a mere one dollar to join and a dollar a year to be a member which was always subject to his approval. The club rules allowed him to expel any member with or without cause at which time he would return the one dollar initiation fee. This method allowed him to control who could eat there and how they behaved. You would not be rowdy in the Cattlemen's Club more than once. And, since it was the consensus that it had the best food in town which no one wanted to miss out on, it was as genteel an establishment as you could find in Montana.

As they were about to go through the door, the door opened toward them and what Jerry feared might happen, did. He was spotted by someone he knew; worse, it was Tim Daniels and his wife. They had been laughing and not looking forward and literally bumped into Jerry and Jan. When Tim saw Jerry with a woman, he did a double take and then exclaimed, "Holy Cow! Jerry is that you?"

He had to look twice to be sure it was Jerry. Then he turned his attention to Jan and gave her a big smile although it was as much as for what he had stumbled onto as it was in being friendly. Tipping his hat to Jan, he said, "Ma'am, you must be something special to get ol' Jerry here to go out." Tim was clearly enjoying having "caught" Jerry doing something that few of his friends could remember him doing—going on a date.

Jan replied with a smile, "Well, I'll have to let others decide about that. But I had the impression that Jerry went out a lot; that he knew all the attractive women in town."

Glancing back and forth between Jerry and Jan, Tim said, "My name is Tim Daniels and this is my wife, Lucy." Jerry introduced Jan to Tim and his wife. Tim, turning back to Jerry said, "Jerry, you old son of a gun!"

Jerry had feared he might bump into someone he knew but had it just been a casual friend or business acquaintance; it would have been no big deal to him. What he had hoped to avoid was running into a close friend. That would mean lots of questions that he simply wasn't prepared to answer. And, of course, a heap of razzing. Jerry was feeling sufficiently strange about the whole dating thing himself that he didn't want the extra complications. The Cattlemen's Club was the best steak place in town so he had gambled that he wouldn't be spotted.

After a long pause with Tim grinning from ear to ear, he finally said to both Jerry and Jan, "We'd hate to be so abrupt but we are headed to the theater and have to get going. Nice to meet you, Ma'am."

Jan looked up at Jerry and said, "I take it this is somewhat unusual for you?"

Jerry laughed like it was nothing and said, "Oh, never mind him. Let's go in." And as they did, however he was thinking about the grilling he was going to get the next time the gang had breakfast at the cathedral.

They were seated and began looking over the menu and Jan commented, "Well, with the name of this place I was sure there was going to be nothing but beef on the menu but I see that there is a very broad selection; how nice."

Jerry said, "Well, I am a cattleman and so I am a beef guy but I'm glad that there's a good selection for you. I'll probably have the eight ounce filet, my usual. Have you found something that looks good to you?"

"I think I'll have a salad and the grilled salmon," replied Jan.

"Great," said Jerry, as he motioned to their waiter who came over and took their orders.

"So, you said that you were in the process of moving here to teach, right?"

"Yes, I am going to be teaching at Livingston Elementary starting in the fall. I had come here to look for a house but instead, I have decided to rent an apartment to make sure that I like it and everything works out okay."

"Well, how did your moving here to teach come about?" asked Jerry.

"I'm from the Midwest, I teach there, or, at least I did. Of course, now it's summer and we're off for a while. So a lady friend of mine wanted to take a trip "out West," Jan making quotation marks with both her hands held up and showing first and middle fingers, "and so we wound up coming here and a few other places like Bozeman and Cody, Wyoming. I really liked it here and saw a story in the paper about how they needed teachers in the school district. So, I went and spoke with the superintendent who gave me an application. Then, when I got home, I sent in a resume and the completed application and, lo and behold, he offered me a job, I said 'Yes' and here I am."

"Are you from the Midwest originally?"

"I am," she answered. I was born in Granite City, Illinois, down near St Louis but on the Illinois side of the Mississippi. I grew up in Alton, Illinois."

"Am I right in assuming that since you are a teacher you must have gone to college?" Jerry asked.

"Yes," Jan replied. "I went to college at Southern Illinois University. After college, I moved to Chicago and taught in the public school system which was a challenge for a girl from southern Illinois. I taught there for eight years but eventually just got a little burned out and when I got a job offer to teach in Dunlap, Illinois I took it because while it wasn't as rewarding as the Chicago job, it was easier. So, I taught there for many years until this little trip to the West occurred and appears to be changing my life."

Jerry was quiet for a few moments. He was impatient to get into the nitty-gritty of her life but was afraid of moving too fast. Then he decided there wasn't much point to waiting and, anyway, he was just too curious.

"Were you ever married? Do you have any kids?" asked Jerry.

Very briefly, a pained look crossed Jan's face and a shadow passed behind her eyes. "No kids, but I was married for a brief time," she answered, looking down.

Again, Jerry wasn't sure whether to pursue the topic but before he could decide the waiter came with their drinks. He took a few moments to set them down and tell them he'd bring their salads shortly. While he was doing this, Jerry was looking intently at Jan, trying to discern anything. He couldn't; but the realization hit him that the strange sensation that he had felt the day he met her was still there. It hadn't been a momentary thing. Jan had his attention, and more. He knew he should be more circumspect than his natural predilection to be direct but found it hard not to ask about her history, especially her marital history.

"What happened, if I may ask?"

Jan took a deep breath and exhaled. "I had met a man named Bruce Wilder in Dunlap and we got married and a little more than six months after the wedding he was killed in a car crash. The other driver was drunk and his license was suspended but he was driving anyway." Jan paused, swallowed and took a sip of water. "I never had a chance to say goodbye," she said softly.

Jerry was moved. He barely knew her but he wanted to comfort her, give her a hug. Instead, he settled for simply saying, "I'm very sorry."

"Well," she said, shaking her head as if shaking the memory away, "that was a long time ago. But I just never wanted to get married again."

"And too short a time for kids, I guess."

"Naturally, we thought we had all the time in the world and had planned on having lots of kids but waiting for a little time before we started."

There was a little pause and then, "How about you? I've naturally assumed you are single, unless Livingston is a different place than I think, but do you have kids?"

"I am, indeed, single; widowed some twenty-nine years ago when my wife died having our third child. I have three kids, all basically okay and off doing their own thing."

Jan said, "How nice. What are they doing?"

"Well, my oldest, Ryan, is a newscaster in Chicago. My middle child, Julie, works for a political consulting firm in Washington D.C. And my youngest, Colin, just got out of the Army after about seven years including several tours in Iraq."

"Oh," Jan exclaimed, "you must be very proud of them."

"Well, I guess I am, up to a point. I wish at least one of them would have stayed around to help me run our ranch. They're going to get it one day and I think they should be helpin' me now. To my way of thinking, they're a little ungrateful."

Jan frowned. "Oh, I'm sorry to hear that. How are they ungrateful?"

"Instead of sticking around to help on the family ranch, or at least go to school with the intention of returning to help me, they are all off doin' their own thing and no thought about coming back. In my book, given everything I've given them and offered them for the future, that's ungrateful."

"How old are your children?"

"Ryan is thirty-five, Julie is thirty and Colin is almost twenty-eight."

"Well, it sounds like Ryan and Julie are honorably employed and Colin served his country. That doesn't sound too bad to me. Besides, they are still pretty young. Don't you think it's fairly normal for young people to want to find their own way?"

Jerry hadn't really want to get into this but now that it had come up, he had hoped that Jan would take his side and see things his way but he had a sinking feeling that she was like everyone else and thought he was wrong.

"I didn't go out to 'find my own way,'" Jerry said with a hint of anger and sarcasm, especially when he parroted the words Jan had used. "I stayed and helped my dad because that's what was expected. I offered them a way of life that has been in our family for a long time and no one's going to convince me that what they've done is okay. It ain't!" he ended with a loud and emphatic level to his voice.

Jan was taken aback. First, she was surprised how Jerry felt about his children. Maybe there was more to that part of the story, but she hadn't heard anything that she would consider indicated a lack of gratitude. What really troubled her, however, was how Jerry's demeanor changed. Up until that point, he had been all charm albeit a little bit corny. But this topic revealed a vein of bitterness and she wondered how deep it ran. She also wondered how many such veins there might be. Just when the silence was getting a little awkward, the waiter showed up with their salads and they began to eat. Jan and Jerry concentrated on eating their dinners for a few moments which gave them time to let things settle a little. The rest of the evening was filled with small talk and with Jerry talking about some of the history of Livingston.

Finally, Jan said, "Have any of your kids indicated that they might come back? Have you talked to them about it?"

Jerry responded, "Not sure there's much to talk over. They know how I feel and until they bring it up to me, I'm not going to go crawling to them."

"Well, Jerry, it seems to me that someone has to take the first step and since you're the oldest and presumably most mature, why don't you try talking with them and, in particular, asking them to consider coming home? Don't you think that might break the ice?"

"Nope," answered Jerry. It wasn't clear if he meant it wouldn't break the ice or that he wouldn't talk to them. Either way, Jan didn't care for this mean, stubborn streak. Jerry continued, "Look, I believe in family and country, hard work and integrity, gratitude for what we've been given and responsibility. I don't mind that my kids went off to try different things; I just want them to be grateful for the opportunity I gave them and to show that gratitude by coming back here to help me. But, so far, it doesn't seem like it's going to happen."

When dinner was over, Jerry walked her back to her hotel and along the way said, "I enjoyed the evening. I'd like to see you again. When might that be?"

"I'm leaving tomorrow to go back to Illinois to take care of a few things. I am going to go to church in the morning. If you'd like to join me, we could have breakfast afterward."

Jerry shook his head and laughed just a little the way one does when a request has been made that has no chance of happening. "I'll have to pass on church," he said, "I haven't had any use for God since my wife died. But I'll join you for breakfast afterward," he said with a bit of a question in his tone.

Jan looked at him for a few seconds. Then, she said, "Maybe it would be better if we just wait until I come back from Illinois.

Although he hadn't been, Jerry felt like he had just been slapped. "Well, okay. Will you call me when you come back?"

Again, there was a pause while she seemingly considered that simple request. Finally, she said, "Yes, I will. Good night." And with that, she shook his hand, turned and headed toward the elevator.

As she made her way to her room, Jan was up in her hotel room trying to assess her feelings. Jerry was an intriguing man, something she didn't often say or think. She had dated many, many men over the years and had enjoyed many of them and enjoyed being with many of them; but, always, she didn't think much more about them other than that they were worth dating and was never really troubled when the dating ended. She thought him sufficiently good looking but, at this stage of her life, it wasn't looks that resulted in attraction. Oh, there were some minimal requirements that most women wanted and many men didn't pay attention to—grooming, reasonable weight and so on. Jerry was pretty good in those areas. But she thought she might be attracted to his deeply held values on family and integrity and so on. At the same time, she was troubled by his apparent poor relationships with his kids and that he seemed to not want to try very hard to improve them. And, of course, the fact that he was apparently not religious, or worse, was a problem. But those things could always change. She had to admit there was attraction and that felt good. Jan went to bed simultaneously happy, troubled and confused.

If Jerry had felt a little discombobulated before dinner, he was definitely disoriented now. Never in his life had he encountered such a woman. Of course, he hadn't dated in years so he hadn't exactly been in around a lot of women but, still, he didn't think that any woman he had been around over the past thirty or forty years had been like Jan. It wasn't so much anything that she said, although she was blunt bordering on sassy to Jerry's ears, it was more how she was in control. Jerry wasn't used to that with men for heaven's sake, much less with women. It felt just a little uncomfortable and certainly unfamiliar but it also felt quite good. Jerry went to bed simultaneously happy, troubled and confused.

Chapter 6

The next day was Sunday which meant breakfast at Two Rivers. Jerry was prepared for a lot of kidding and a lot of questions and his friends didn't disappoint.

"Hey, Jerry," said Tim Daniels, "what did the clerk at the Co-Op call you this weekend, Romeo?"

"Or maybe Clueless," chimed in Barry.

"Or Dopey."

"How about Casanova?"

"How many bases did you make?"

"Are you kidding? Jerry's forgotten where the batter's box is."

"He doesn't even know where his "bat" is."

"Word is it's no Louisville Slugger anyway!"

"Okay, okay," Jerry said, holding up his hand, hoping to quiet the building laughter. "Enough." Jerry knew they were only kidding in the way only close friends can do.

"Maybe, at least for now. What's her name, Jer'?" asked Gordon.

Tim said, "I told you, Jan Merton, or something like that."

"Her name is Jan Martino," said Jerry in a somewhat exasperated tone, "and she's a teacher, moving here from Illinois."

"How'd you meet her?"

Jerry told them the story of the balloon accident and how they met.

"Well, that settles it," said Tom. "Must be the hand of God. You'll be married in a month."

Jerry could only smile and shake his head.

"Seriously, Jerry," said Tim, "what's the deal? Why her after all these years?"

Tim didn't know it but he had asked the question that had been in front of Jerry for a couple of days but which Jerry hadn't had the guts to tackle. Indeed, why her? He really wasn't sure of the answer. It wasn't completely "love at first sight" although it kind of seemed that way. Somehow, in some way he didn't understand, she had interrupted his cosmos. Of course, he wouldn't have put it that way; he would have said something like "She got under my skin." But he didn't understand it to even make that small a declaration. So he said simply, "I don't know. It just seemed like a good idea at the time."

"Are you going to see her again?" asked Barry.

Jerry replied, "She's going back to Illinois to take care of business there and when she returns here, I expect to."

"Well good," said Tom, "you can bring her to breakfast so we can all meet her."

"Fat chance of that," replied Jerry.

"No, seriously," said Tom, "we'd really like to meet her some time.

"Well, if I can trust you guys to be respectful and not try and make a jerk out of me, maybe I'll arrange something."

"We'll at least be respectful," chuckled Barry. "Heck, it's fifty-fifty that you'll make a dang fool of yourself without our help anyway."

Jerry's turned the conversation to politics and he made one of his usual little speeches. In so doing, he had temporarily removed Jan from his mind because he was so passionate about what he felt was the wrong direction of the country. It didn't take long for that to prompt everyone to get up to leave.

Tom said, "I think meeting this gal, Jan, is going to be good for you, "Jerry."

Jerry could only say, "I hope so."

At the mention of her name, she was back in his mind and would stay there throughout the day, sometimes in front, sometimes in back, sometimes hidden, but always there.

Chapter 7

The kids that Jerry thought were blind to what the ranch offered were Ryan Michael, born in 1979; Julie Ann, born in 1984 and Colin Lucas, born in 1986. Even Jerry would admit that all three were good children. In their early years, they did what they were told, kept reasonably quiet, except among themselves, and weren't any serious trouble.

Ryan would fuss some as he got a little older; it was hard to figure what would trigger some little emotional outburst but they came and went and, if they didn't, Ryan and Jerry would have a little "time out". Ryan adored his dad and he himself didn't like the fact that these little tantrums occurred. He would just shrug his shoulders and say, "That's just me."

What Ryan really liked was when Jerry would spend time with him at night. Ryan didn't know it, but it was a big alteration of the Johnston family formula. They would talk about the ranch and cattle and baseball and football and all kind of things. Ryan didn't really care about the topic; he just wanted to be with his dad. He wanted to be like his dad.

"When I grow up," he'd say, "I want to be just like you, Dad." And he meant it. His mom was there sometimes, too, but often she would tell Jerry, "I've been with him all day and you've been working. I'll do the dishes; you spend some time with him."

Once, when Ryan was three going on four, Jerry and Jackie took him all the way to Chicago to see a baseball game; at least that's what they told him. Jerry had been invited by the big food firm the family had been doing business with for years to come to Chicago for a gathering of customers, industry related meetings and other such stuff. The mini-convention lasted three days and every night there was a dinner which Jerry skipped so that he could be with Ryan and Jackie.

Jackie had a chance to experience a big city for the first time, shopping on Michigan Avenue and enjoying the art galleries in the River North district. Of course, she had to bring Ryan along and she wondered how he would deal with time in an art gallery. But Ryan was so amazed by everything, he never had time to get bored or wish they were doing something else. The buildings were so big, especially when Jackie took him to Sears Tower and they went to the top. He was pretty sure that he could see their ranch in Montana and Jackie agreed with him.

But the highlight of the trip for everyone was going to a game at Comiskey Park, home of the Chicago White Sox. Because Jerry couldn't attend the dinners, the food company had arranged excellent box seats. In addition, someone knew someone who knew someone and they arranged for Ryan to meet two of the stars of the team—Carlton Fisk and Harold Baines before the game. Jackie and Jerry couldn't help but laugh, looking at Ryan's wide eyes and gaping mouth. When they went to their seats and saw the expanse of the field and the big scoreboard and all the other wonders of a major league ball park, they *all* were agape and had their eyes wide open. The perfect evening ended perfectly when the White Sox won on a walk-off home run in the bottom of the ninth inning. As they were filing out of the park, Ryan turned to Jerry and said, "Thanks, Dad. This was the most perfectest night ever!"

A little after Ryan turned five, Julie Ann was born and, unlike some young boys, Ryan was thrilled. He loved the idea of a little sister that he could protect and care for and now he would have a playmate. When Jackie came home from the hospital with little baby Julie, Ryan was as proud as if he were the father. He had decided that he would be Prince Valliant and be the protector of his little sister. And now in the evenings there were the four of them. Jerry and Jackie would both do the dishes and then Jackie would hold and bounce and coo at Julie and Ryan and Jerry would watch them as well as talk to each other. Ryan was now an avid White Sox fan and he followed them on radio every night. Sometimes they would all listen to part of a game but rarely made it to the end because they were all tired and would go to bed before the game was over.

Julie was a precocious toddler. Jackie would often put her to bed listening to classical music because Jackie had read in some magazine that it was a good thing to do. Jackie enjoyed classical music but wished she knew a little more about it. They had a little tape player and set of headphones they would put on Julie and she would go to sleep listening to the tapes. The tapes were just music with an announcer indicating the piece that was about to be played. It did seem to work; Julie would listen for five or ten minutes but then drift to sleep and Jackie would gently remove the headphones.

When Julie was just about to celebrate her 2nd birthday, Jackie was doing some work at her desk and Julie was playing on the floor nearby. Julie had been talking for a few months but, of course, her vocabulary was somewhat limited. Jackie had the radio on and tuned to the station in Livingston that played classical pops for at least part of the day. One piece ended and, without introduction, the next piece began whereupon Julie announced, "Oh, that's Chopin." Jackie almost fell over. When Jerry came in from the day's work, Jackie told him what had happened. He went over to Julie and picked her up with his large hands around her tiny waist and lifted her high in the air and exclaimed, "What a smart girl you are! Maybe you'll be the one to run the ranch one day!" It was another example of the new Johnston family formula. Julie was so happy and could feel how happy her father was. Of course, with his single-minded focus on the ranch, it never occurred to Jerry that Julie might one day use those smarts to do something not involving the ranch.

Jackie was pregnant with their third child. A few months later, when she went into labor in the early-afternoon, Jerry got Gordon's wife, Fran, to stay with Ryan and Julie and took Jackie to the hospital. The kids were excited; they were going to have a younger brother and another playmate. Julie didn't fully comprehend everything but knew there was going to be a baby and that everyone was excited. In their little world, to the extent they could understand, it was a wonderful time.

When Jerry came home that night, as young as they were, Ryan and Julie sensed something was wrong. They saw their dad and Fran O'Laughlin have a whispered conversation in the kitchen. She hugged him and asked if there was anything that she could do. He was weeping and shook his head no. He looked over at Ryan and Julie and wanted to tell them but he just couldn't find the words much less the will. He turned and trudged off to tell his father what had happened. Joe consoled Jerry as best he could but Jerry was in another world. Jerry went off to his bedroom and closed the door. He knew he should say something to Ryan and Julie but he just didn't have it in him. He left that task to Gordon's wife and she did the best she could do under the circumstances.

For Ryan and Julie, they went from being in a comfortable little world, warm and cozy, almost like being in utero, to one that was cold and uncertain and frightening. Their little minds had envisioned a continuation of the joy they had experienced earlier. Now, Mrs. O'Laughlin had said something about mommy not coming home and they couldn't really grasp it.

"Why not?" they said. "When will she come home?"

Fran O'Laughlin was struggling. "Your momma has gone away to another place and won't ever be back."

Ryan and Julie went off to bed in various stages of confusion. Mostly, they wondered if things would return to normal. They wouldn't.

The next few days were awful. Their dad didn't speak to much to them and when he did it was so different than before. He seemed to be upset and given the way they perceived how he was interacting with them, it seemed to them like he was upset with them. And they did not understand why. Ryan now understood that his mom had died and Julie was also aware but couldn't fully comprehend what that meant.

A few days later there was a funeral that they went to and hated; everyone was somber and dressed in black and said things to them to which they didn't know how to respond. Their dad only spoke to them in clipped phrases, mostly just telling them to come or go or sit or whatever. They were deeply affected by his behavior toward them and hoped that he would soon revert to the loving daddy they had known just a week before.

Jerry stayed home to take care of Ryan and Julie except for a few hours a day when Fran would come over and give him a break. Her help was especially important when Colin came home from the hospital; Jerry wasn't adept with infants and needed Fran to show him what to do which he learned quickly. Julie and Ryan watched their father with Colin and were puzzled. Again, they weren't sure of anything but it just seemed like there was no joy in him. They had been used to watching him enjoy interacting with them, but now it was like he was doing a chore; like he was handling a young calf for which he had no particular affection.

Then one day a woman named Emily came to the house and Jerry told Ryan and Julie that she would now be taking care of them. He didn't say much more, didn't elaborate—he just said she would now be their nanny. They knew or sensed that she was "the replacement." Some kids in that position would have rejected such an idea but they didn't dare. Daddy was no longer someone to mess around with, to frolic with on the floor; he was someone to fear because he was perpetually quiet and occasionally angry. One time when Jerry was on his hand and knees trying to clean a spot on the carpet, Ryan took advantage and jumped on Jerry's back like the old days, hoping his dad would play the part of the horse. But Jerry brushed Ryan off his back with a big sweep of his hand and said, "Not now, Son." He saw Ryan's keen disappointment but said nothing more. He generally didn't have big bursts of anger but just short little rockets; otherwise he was emotionless.

Over time, the kids actually grew to like and then love Emily. For Julie and, especially, Ryan, she wasn't like Jackie. Where Jackie was all warmth and tenderness all the time, Emily was more businesslike and practical. But, when tenderness was particularly needed, Emily was there; in fact, she was always there, sick or well, whatever, Emily was always there when the kids needed her. This showed in a variety of ways. One example was when the kids would bring home their report card, Emily would go over each grade with them and generally give encouragement with a small lecture about working harder. Jerry was almost the mirror image. He didn't want to hear excuses; he just wanted to see better grades. There grew a definite gulf between Jerry and the kids of which he was aware but didn't do anything about.

For Colin, the relationship with Jerry was especially troubling. He had been told that his real mom had died when he was born but not much more was said. It was Ryan who turned that information into a weapon when he and Colin were having an argument one day. At one point, after several minutes of childish bickering, Colin said, "You're a jerk of an older brother!"

In response Ryan said, "Oh yeah? Well, you're the reason mommy died!" That stopped Colin in his tracks. He went to see Jerry.

"Daddy, Ryan says that I'm the reason mommy died. Is that true?" Colin wore the expression of someone wrongly accused and wanted his daddy to say so.

Indeed, Jerry knew that he should strongly refute that falsehood; he knew it to be wrong, not only because it was untrue on the face of it but because Jerry blamed himself for Jackie's death. His persistence in having a third child was the cause of her death. Colin's birth may have been the cause of her death but, in more than just the physical sense, Jerry was primarily responsible for Colin's birth.

Jerry was so unnerved by the question and so quickly suffocated in his own guilt, he said, "you get Ryan and both of you come see me."

When the boys returned, Colin was still waiting for words of comfort; Ryan seemed unafraid as if he had spoken the truth.

Jerry said, "Ryan, don't you ever say such a thing to your brother again. You don't know what happened or why and you just keep your mouth shut about that, you hear?"

Ryan looked down and said, reluctantly, "Yes, Sir."

Jerry turned to Colin and said, "Colin, what Ryan said is not true." But he didn't say anything more to Colin. Colin was left trying to figure out why such a thing would have been said in the first place and what exactly he had done wrong; but he was left with the sense that his dad, too, at least partly blamed him for his mom's death.

Over the ensuing years, Ryan, Julie and Colin spent as much or more time with Emily than with Jerry. Of course, they knew their dad was working hard to provide the clothes they wore and the food they ate. After all, Emily told them that almost every day. And there were a few occasions where a little of the old Jerry would reappear, like when one of them would get an award in school or would do well in an athletic contest. For just a moment or two or three, he might hug them or give them a smile that reminded Ryan and, to a lesser extent because of her age at the earlier time, Julie, of the old days and showed Colin a side to Jerry that he wasn't familiar with. Every time that happened, there was great hope that things might be different going forward but it never lasted. And yet, at the same time, it was enough that all three sensed that there was love there, somewhere and enough so that they, quietly, almost secretly, loved their dad very much. Emily was his advocate in that regard; always telling them how much he loved them, even if they couldn't always see it.

So, when those moments came, she would say, "Did you see that? Do you see how your dad loves you?"

All the while Jerry was hating himself; hating himself for being the cause of Jackie's death and hating himself because he had lost the ability to love his kids the way he should. He knew it was wrong and knew he should change his behavior. He was like an alcoholic who knows what he is doing is wrong but hasn't found the strength to change. It takes more than wanting to change; it takes the will to change. For Jerry, the will, for now, was lacking.

Chapter 8

July was about the easiest time of year on a cattle ranch in Montana. Though he never stopped in busier times of the year, it was easier for Jerry to justify taking Sunday mornings off to go to "church" in July.

On the Monday after the Sunday Jerry had been razzed about his date, he met up with Cooper Landry, one of his three crew chiefs, and his crew. Cooper was an interesting guy, particularly to Jerry. Cooper understood what ranching was all about. In fact, his father had been an M.D., a radiologist, and wanted Cooper to follow in his footsteps. But Cooper had fallen in love with the ranching life as a young boy and, while he didn't have enough money to have his own ranch, he had the next best thing as a top hand on the Johnston Ranch. To Jerry, to have someone pass on being a doctor to be a rancher was vindication for his feeling that the ranching life was a high calling.

Everyone was on horseback, a bit of an anachronism in an age where many ranchers were turning to ATVs and even dirt bikes. The Johnston Ranch did use mechanical means when necessary but Jerry liked tradition and, in particular, loved riding horses. They were mostly quarter horses, some of which had been trained as cutting horses. As the name implies, a cutting horse is used to "cut" or separate a cow calf pair or a single arrival from the herd.

The calving was long over and, all in all, it had gone very well. They had only lost a handful out of a thousand calves. Each calf and its mother are a "pair" and stay close together for the first few days but then start to get a little mixed up with the others. The cowboys have to keep'em together to avoid orphans. Some ranchers put ear tags on the pairs but it's hard to do on a place as big as the Johnston Ranch. This crew was working a sizable group of pairs.

Jerry trotted over to Cooper and said, in his best cowboy patois, "All our little doggies been eatin' OK?" He wanted to know that all the cows had been suckled and that all the calves had had their milk.

"You bet, boss," answered Cooper. I think we're ready to move them out to pasture 14."

"OK," answered Jerry, "let's do it."

The ranch was set up with multiple pastures, ones at lower elevations used in the winter and the higher elevations used in the summer. Each pasture would lead "home" to a small gathering area which in turn would lead to pens for sorting, separating and other activities. Some pastures were best suited for growing hay and were never grazed.

Managing the land that comprised the ranch was a critical job and Jerry handled that personally. There were a number of variables to consider. For starters, the animals were generally sorted by gender, age, size, etc., so that each pasture area all had similar cattle. Jerry was lucky enough to have an excess of land so that he could not only change the use for a particular pasture, he could let it lie idle for a year. Some areas were better for haying. Some pastures, might have cows for a year or two, then nothing, then horses, then yearlings, and so on. Each type grazed a little differently and so this kept the land from being overgrazed.

Cooper and his crew spent all day and the next sorting out pairs that were ready to leave the pasture close to the calving area. Jerry helped a little with the cutting but was content to mostly watch. Cooper was his best foreman; a wisp of a man with character as rock solid as basalt, who had been working cattle almost as long as Jerry. The two other crew chiefs were Matt McFlynn and Elmer Perkins. Elmer's family had once owned a ranch that was now part of the Johnston ranch. The Perkins had had some bad luck with droughts and beef markets and had been deep in debt. Joe Johnston had tried to help but the Perkins just seemed to be jinxed. They sold out to the Johnstons at a much higher price than they could have received from anyone else. Joe also persuaded the Perkins to stay on and work on the ranch they had once owned. It was charity, plain and simple. Everyone knew it but it just wasn't an issue among men of this stripe.

There was a young man in his early twenties working on Elmer's crew by the name of Austin Harris. Austin was like an adopted son to Jerry, not in the formal sense but in the way they considered one another. Austin was born into a ranching family although it was not wealthy like the Johnstons. Perhaps more typical, Austin's family eked out a living on a small amount of acreage that always looked messy and disorganized. There just wasn't enough time and labor and money to do much more than the basics. But they did alright.

Austin's father had, over time, succumbed to the trials of ranching. He had worked hard but somehow could only stay even, at best, running in place. To him, the joys of ranching seemed to dwindle over time and the daily challenge ground him down like a giant millstone. He had begun drinking just to 'ease my aches and pains' he would say, when Austin was in grade school. By the time Austin left home, some would say his father was a drunk. It soured the relationship between Austin and his father and although Jerry, aware of his own shortcomings as a father, urged Austin to overlook the drinking, to Austin it was an unforgivable sign of weakness.

Austin was your typical "cow-boy," tall, lean and strong. Women and girls were drawn to him and while he enjoyed the attention up to a point, he didn't always know how to deal with it. One thing Jerry noticed, though, he didn't take advantage. Lots of men might have exploited that situation but Austin didn't and Jerry valued him for that and other qualities. When Jerry would be working with Elmer and his crew, Jerry always seemed to find time to find a small job where he and Austin could talk about life and ranching and other such things.

Every night, Jerry worked well past dinner. The days were still long, though getting shorter, which allowed for ample time with the herd. After that, he had to take care of his horse and tack and a hundred other little chores. Of course, Jerry knew that "being a cowboy" wasn't the romantic lifestyle that most people thought it was. Most people thought of cowboy movies and cattle drives which, when they did occur, were very short and boring. But he loved this time of year when the late afternoons and early evenings were getting cooler and there was a little extra time to get work done. This was the routine, after all—working long and hard and late but going home with the kind of daily satisfaction that most people just didn't experience.

In the cycle of the rancher's year, after the calving and when warmer spring weather came, the cattle would be turned out to pasture. You'd have to bring some in for doctoring and so on but, pretty much, they could take care of themselves. As the weather got warmer, there was the constant battle with weeds, some of which were noxious to cattle and horses. You'd have to spray from tanks mounted on tractors or ATVs or, in some places, from backpacks.

Then, in the fall, you bring the cows and calves back in to the home corrals and you'd start the weaning process which could be handled in a variety of ways. The cows go through a chute for a variety of treatments. As mentioned, the calves are weaned from their mothers and are readied for shipping.

Shipping day is a big day for any ranch because that is when they make their money and either have a profit or loss. Calves are sold by weight times an agreed upon price per pound. So, you want the calves to be as heavy as possible. Any time they are in corrals not eating nutritional grass they're probably going to lose weight which means losing money. So, you want the weighing and shipping process to be as quick as possible. The trucks are limited to 50,000 pounds to avoid overcrowding of the calves in the trucks. Once that's done, and hopefully you made money, it's time to take care of the cows. In the fall, the cows are put out on fall grass and they're pretty much OK until winter when they have to be fed. In the meantime, there are a million other repair and maintenance jobs—fencing, equipment, corrals, irrigation, etc.

Winter feeding of cows, especially on a big operation like the Johnston Ranch, was a big job. A crew would spend all morning dropping bales of hay for the herd and then spend all afternoon loading up bales for the next day.

The reality was that cattle ranching was a tough, hard business. So, what was the appeal? Why did Jerry think the life was appealing? Well, first and foremost, it was the independence. You were your own boss and outcomes were based largely on your own efforts. You couldn't control the weather or the market prices for beef on the hoof or a number of other things but at least you didn't have to march to the beat of someone else's drum. You were challenged almost every day and when you met that challenge, it just left a good feeling. Then, there was working on the land and with animals, the connections to which just somehow resonated with the nature of man. He couldn't imagine that someone who sold widgets by the gross could feel the same way.

Jerry didn't actually think about it in these terms, he just felt contentment with his life's work and that such a feeling was priceless.

Chapter 9

A couple of weeks later Jerry came in from a long day's work and saw the light on the telephone blinking, indicating that there was a voice message. He hit a line button, popped in the command for messages and his code and heard Jan's voice which thrilled him, much more than he had been prepared for, literally sending a shiver up his neck. Thank God it was a message and he didn't have to talk live.

The message was from earlier in the day and went "Hi, Jerry, this is Jan. I'm back in Livingston and calling like you asked me to. I hope all is well. You can reach me at ..." and gave her phone number. Jerry started to dial the number right away and then stopped, realizing he had no plan of what to say or whether he should ask for a date or what? Maybe he should wait until tomorrow and not seem so anxious. Maybe even wait another day. No, that would be too long wouldn't it? She might get annoyed, thinking I wasn't responding in a timely fashion. Okay, it's probably okay to call her tonight; she might be pleased that he was a little anxious. But then should he try to set up a date or suggest she get settled first or what? My God it's been a long time since I had to think about this stuff. I have no clue about what to do. Then he remembered what Emily said, "Be yourself." Well, what I want to do and I guess then what I *should* do is call her now and ask her out. That's the point, isn't it?

Jerry dialed her number and hoped inspiration would be his guide.

"Hello."

"Hi, Jan, this is Jerry, Jerry Johnston." He heard her giggle.

"How many Jerrys do you think I know in Livingston," she said in a pleasant tone. "I know it's you. How are you?"

"I'm great. Glad you're back. Maybe we could get together this Friday?"

Again the little laugh, not a tone of ridicule just a total lack of nervousness, unlike Jerry.

"Well, you don't waste any time, do you? I guess I should have remembered that from the day we met. Oh, by the way, I'm fine, too."

"Oh, I'm sorry. You're doing well? That's great, great. Um, so, does Friday work for you?"

She seemed to be in a constant chuckle now. "Yes, that would be fine. Why don't you pick me up around six thirty," and she gave Jerry her address.

"Okay, said Jerry, "I'll see you then" and then he hung up. He sat back in his chair and sighed, feeling two conflicting reactions. He was happy he had a date with Jan and that she had readily accepted but he felt like he had made a fool of himself. Then he realized he had sweat rings under each armpit. "How is that possible?" he thought, "I only was on the phone with her for a minute." He felt like the guy in the movie "Broadcast News"—instant flop sweat. But, importantly, the deed was done.

On Friday, Emily did double duty as a "pre-fight" coach and a wardrobe counselor. Jerry was going to wear jeans and a short-sleeved shirt because it was warm out to which Emily exclaimed, "Lordy, men around here are such slobs. Why don't you just wear shorts and a bowling shirt?"

While Jerry was considering that possibility, she took away the jeans and shirt and brought out a good pair of beige, gabardine slacks and a blue, button down collar shirt. She said, "Blue's your color; it goes with your eyes. You can wear your brown cowboy boots if you want, but the dress ones, not the ones you work in," she said, thinking if she didn't define it precisely he just might wear the more broken in, more comfortable work boots.

"Oh, I wouldn't wear work boots," Jerry said. "How uncouth do you think I am? Don't answer that."

"Now, here's what you have to concentrate on with her. It doesn't sound like you have to make her comfortable; she's apparently the confident type. *You* have to be confident yourself without being cocky. Women love a confident man. And get her to talk about herself, find out what's important to her. And be funny. Women also love a man with a great sense of humor."

"Oh great," Jerry thought to himself. 'Be funny.' You might as well say 'Be tall.' I mean, you were or you weren't; it's not like you can pick and choose—"Tonight, I will be funny, tomorrow I won't be."

For all the "pre-fight" jitters, Jerry was surprisingly calm and confident during the date. They went to dinner at a Chinese place that was Jerry's favorite. He didn't know it before but found out that Jan liked Chinese food as much as he, and Livingston, of all places, had a couple very good ones.

As they were eating their meals and each enjoying an ice cold Tsing Tao beer, Jan said, "So anything new with your kids?"

"You mean with them or with my relationships with them?"

"Both"

"No, nothing new. But now that you brought it up, I wonder if I gave you the wrong impression on our first date. I mean, I love my kids and I'm proud of them. I'm just disappointed that they turned away from the opportunities I put before them."

"Well, to be honest, Jerry, I got the impression that you didn't so much as put any opportunity before them but that you just expected them to follow in your footsteps. I mean, did you really lay out a role for them where they could use their knowledge and talents?"

Jerry thought about that for a few moments. "Well, I'd guess I'd say that I didn't do it quite like that but I assumed they knew my feelings."

"I think feelings have to be expressed, they can't be assumed. People are so afraid to express their feelings, men in particular. That whole thing that men joke about when they say that thing about 'I love you, man' is funny but also sad. People should be able to say 'I love you' without feeling funny about it."

Jerry took a sip of beer and considered her statement. He had read that type of advice in some magazines and knew it was fairly common among younger people. But he hadn't been raised in an overly verbal environment himself. His dad and granddad weren't much for that kind of thing and Jerry had tried to be somewhat different but had a hard time escaping from what he knew growing up.

"Well, how often do you say 'I love you,'" Jerry said with a bit of a grin, hoping to turn the tables a bit.

"I say it to my close friends all the time, Jan replied, "but, of course, they know it's friendship."

"How about to men, romantically?"

"For me, that's a whole different ball game. I don't use the "L" word with men unless I am way past just "being" in love. When I tell a man that I love him that means we're going to get married. So, in my case, I have said it to one man, my deceased husband."

"Oh, I'm sorry, I didn't mean to…"

"Nothing to be sorry about. I loved Bruce but the Lord taketh away. I haven't loved a man since."

Jerry thought it a good time for a break in the action and so he concentrated on his Moo Shu Pork. He loved the plum sauce and how it mixed with the pork and vegetables. He ordered another beer.

How's your Kung Pao Chicken," Jerry asked.

"Very good, " Jan answered. "It's got a little kick to it."

"Just like you," Jerry thought.

"What kind of music do you like?" he asked.

"I like all kinds but I guess I am pretty partial to classical music and opera."

Inwardly, Jerry groaned. He liked modern Country and Western. But, it was always good to know stuff like this.

He followed with, "I'm afraid I don't know much about it. What's your favorite?"

"I like a lot of it," she answered, "but I guess my favorite would be Beethoven's Sixth."

"Beethoven's Sixth what?" Jerry thought to himself but he kept quiet, not wanting to appear ignorant.

After a little more silence, Jerry said, "Another thing we touched on last time was God and religion. I gather you are a religious woman?"

"Yes, I am, it's very important to me. I was raised Catholic but I admit I have some problems with the earthly institution and I don't go to Mass every week. But I believe in the basics; I believe in God and Jesus Christ and I try to live my life according to Christian principles. Are you a believer?"

"I don't really know what I am. I, too, was raised Catholic and we used to go to Mass every Sunday. But when my wife died, I kind of gave it up."

"Why?"

"It was hard to believe in a God that would let such a good woman die before her time."

Now it was Jan's turn to go silent and consider what Jerry had just said. He interrupted her thoughts.

"What makes your faith so strong? Was it always that way?"

"The answer to the second question is no, it wasn't always strong. I was like you, brought up Catholic but kind of fallen away. I think there are a lot of us," she said with a smile, "we should start a club or something. As for how strong it is, well, I sometimes wish it was stronger; I still have some doubts. But a couple of things got me back from being somewhat agnostic to where I am today. Now you can make fun of this if you want, but the first thing was what happened to the husband of a very close friend of mine a number of years ago back in Illinois. He was in the hospital for some tests when he had a heart attack and even though he was right there, he died on the table, his heart was stopped. But they kept working on him and after a few minutes they got his heart working again but they were afraid of brain damage. He had gone several minutes with no blood going to his brain and they were certain there would be brain damage. But not only was there no brain damage, he swears that he died, came out of his body and saw a bright light and a glimpse of heaven. Then he was told by a voice that it wasn't his time yet so he would return to his body and have more time on earth. It's the same kind of story that has been reported I don't know how many times but this is someone I know well. Is it real? Who knows for sure but when you hear it directly and convincingly from a good friend, it makes you think."

Jerry had heard these stories before but he didn't put much stock in them and just shrugged them off. Seeing how intent Jan was, he kept quiet.

"So I wasn't sure whether to believe that story or not but it got me thinking. So I began to buy some books and do some research about God and Jesus and so on. There's a great book by a minister in New York called Timothy Keller called "The Reason for God" that explains a lot. I also joined a Bible study group and began to get more insights about the Bible and, particularly, the connections between some of the Old Testament and the New Testament." After a little pause she continued. "My faith is definitely a work in progress. You have to make a leap of faith yourself to get over at least some of your doubts but that doesn't mean they all go away. I have to work on it every day."

Jerry considered whether to follow up but decided enough serious talk for one night. Uncomfortable talking about religious faith, Jerry steered the conversation back to safer territory. He took the opportunity to play the welcome wagon and filled Jan in on her new town. On this safer ground, dessert and coffee went smoothly.

On the way back to her apartment, they chatted about inconsequential things. As they neared their destination, Jerry mentioned that he would be out of town visiting his dad the next weekend but suggested they do something in two weeks. Jan said, "Oh, I don't make plans two weeks out. Why don't you call me next week when you get back?"

Jerry was just a little floored. Won't make plans two weeks out? Most women would be happy to be booked but not her. Does she have some other plan? Any chance there's some other guy? Whatever, it's a woman's game and I just have to go along. "Oh, okay, I'll call when I get back."

Chapter 10

Ryan grew up working on the ranch—after school, on weekends and over holidays. Even though he didn't work full time, he became quite knowledgeable about the ranch and the ranch operations, about cattle and about horses. He loved to ride and spend time around horses. He enjoyed working on the ranch but he wished that he would always be with his father when he did. Oh, he and Jerry sometimes worked together but very often, when Ryan would come home from school, there would be a note for Ryan telling him to meet up with Cooper or Matt or Elmer and help them with something. The foremen all felt a little funny that Jerry didn't have Ryan work with him but instead with them but it wasn't their place to question. And Ryan took their directions without hesitation; he didn't act like the boss's son.

Ryan went to Livingston High where he got decent grades, was second string guard on the basketball team and was popular with the girls. His best friend was Dan Rothman who played on the football team and, like Ryan, came from a ranching family. When they were both a month or so into their senior year, Dan and Ryan were talking about what they were going to do after high school.

"So, what are you going to do?" Ryan asked Dan.

"Well, I haven't thought too much about it," answered Dan, "I guess I'll just follow in my dad's footsteps and one day run the ranch. What about you?"

"Well, I don't know anything 100% for sure but I think there is a good chance that I'll do something different."

"Like what?" queried Dan.

"Well, you remember that day a few weeks ago when that guy came by from some university and was talking about communications and broadcast journalism? That looks kind of interesting to me and maybe I'll look into doing something in that area."

"Man!" exclaimed Dan, "what do you think your dad will say about that?"

"Well," chortled Ryan somewhat sarcastically, "It's pretty certain that he won't like it. But you know, he hasn't really talked to me about my future or whether he wants me to stay on the ranch. Of course, I know he does, but it's just like him to assume something without talking about it. Besides, I'm not sure I want to spend the rest of my life under his thumb and with his attitudes."

"What attitudes?"

"You know, we've talked about it before. Ever since my mom died my dad's been a different guy, and not in a good way. I know it was tough on him but it was tough on all of us. Then add the fact that he's so tough and demanding; I don't know, maybe that's his way of coping but it doesn't work for me."

"Man, that's a hard one to figure out," answered Dan. "I heard my mom and dad talking about it one night—now, don't ever repeat this—but they said that your dad changed after your mom died and that even though he loves all you kids, he has a hard time showing it. But, do you think leaving is going to make it better?"

"Probably not," answered Ryan, "but I just think I have to get out on my own for a while. I'm not saying it will be forever but it's just something I think that I need to do."

"So, you think you're going to go to college and study broadcast journalism? Where are you going to do that?"

"Not sure," answered Ryan. But probably somewhere pretty far from here so I am really away."

That night, after Ryan had finished his homework, he thought about his conversation with Dan. He totally surprised himself. Prior to the conversation, he had formed no such resolve to leave and study broadcast journalism; it had just leapt from his lips on the spur of the moment. As he considered that, he realized that it must have been forming for a while but that he hadn't wanted to admit it, even to himself.

Over the next month, he began researching schools that offered broadcast journalism as a major. There were quite a few, some pretty famous. But the one that caught his eye was not because of where it did or did not rank but because of where it was—DePaul University in Chicago. Ryan had fond memories of Chicago from his trip there as a boy and it was also in a big city which would scratch that itch for him. In January of his senior year, surreptitiously, he applied to DePaul and was accepted. Now, all he had to do was tell his father.

It was winter, so the main chore was feeding all the pregnant cows. Ryan chose a night when he and Jerry had been working together, thinking he might develop a little rapport with his dad before be broke the news. He managed to persuade Jerry to go in early for dinner saying there was something that he wanted to talk about.

After dinner, while Emily was doing the dishes, Jerry asked what Ryan wanted to talk about.

"Well," said Ryan, "I guess about my future. You know I only have a few months left in high school and I have to make some plans."

"Well, that's simple enough," replied Jerry, "either you stay on the ranch or if you want to go off to college, MSU has a good agribusiness school. It would be a good thing for the ranch to have that knowledge base in the management. I know a lot but I don't have the schooling that you have or, especially if you went to MSU for agribusiness, that you would have. Now, how specialized do they get in those majors? I mean, for instance, do they have a sub specialty in cattle ranching or something that would particularly fit for our operation? I mean if you took one of those things that could really help us out. I try to stay up on the new things coming out but it's hard when you're working long hours and maybe not as good with computers as you youngsters are. But I think—"

"Dad! Dad," Ryan interrupted, "I'm not going to stay on the ranch or go to MSU. I am going to go to DePaul University in Chicago and study broadcast journalism."

Ryan waited for the explosion but there wasn't one. Instead, Jerry just stared at Ryan and then slowly sat back in his chair with an expression on his face like Ryan had just spoken to him in Chinese. They stayed that way for a long time, Jerry dumbfounded and Ryan actually relieved to have finally gotten this off his chest.

"When the hell did you come up with this idea? I always thought that you would stay with me on the ranch?"

"Dad," Ryan said as softly and as gently as he could muster, "you never talked to me about that. In fact, you hardly ever talk to me at all. How would you ever know what I wanted to do or what I thought about what you wanted me to do? This is just something I feel like I need to do."

"Don't you think you at least owed me the courtesy of telling me about this before? I had such plans for you."

"When did you think you were going to tell me about those plans, the day before they started? Look, Dad, I am sure you find this disappointing but that's not my intention. I just think it will be better all the way around if I go off on my own. I'm not saying it's forever; things may change. But, for now, this is the way it has to be."

With that, Jerry just got up and headed to his room. Ryan wasn't happy about it but was glad to have the conversation over. He quickly decided he'd go to Chicago early in the summer rather than wait until the fall term started. He knew the time between now and then was not likely to be pleasant.

When June rolled around, Ryan packed his bags and moved to Chicago. Jerry was there to say goodbye and they did hug but there was a bit of tension in the air. Jerry wasn't happy with Ryan's decision and still hadn't accepted it several months after first having been told. For Ryan, the move was bittersweet to be sure. He was going to miss the ranch and his horse and Emily and, he had to admit, even his dad. But he was excited to be embarking on something new and in a big city like Chicago.

He had found an apartment in the Lincoln Park neighborhood in an area often referred to as the DePaul neighborhood because the main university was located in that near North micro neighborhood. Chicago was definitely a city of neighborhoods; there was an official map of what the boundaries were. Ironically, the broadcast journalism school was located downtown in the "Loop". The Loop was formed by the roughly square elevated tracks of the city's elevated train, commonly referred to as the "el". So, every day, Ryan would walk a couple of blocks to the Brown line station at Armitage and Sheffield and take the "el" downtown for classes. To Chicagoans, the Loop and downtown were synonymous.

Ryan really enjoyed his time in Chicago. His schoolwork kept him pretty busy but he found time to enjoy all that a big city could offer. He had never been a classical music fan but he was told that the Chicago Symphony was among the finest in the world and maybe even the finest. So, he was able to go and get tickets that had been turned in by someone who could not go and, as a student, he got a discount. He went to Sox games and, every now and then, would go to a Cubs game even though they were the enemy. A true Chicagoan, he was told, could not be fans of both teams. Of course, he was not a true Chicagoan but he was trying to be. But even Ryan, a die-hard Sox fan had to admit that Wrigley Field was a great place to watch a game and it was closer to home. He was able to go to a couple of Bear games but only when someone would get him a ticket. They were expensive and hard to get. And, finally, he went to the occasional Bulls games and got to see the last of the Bulls' NBA championships with Michael Jordan.

Ryan did well in school, getting mostly "A's" and "B's" and graduating near the top of the class. He had specialized in general assignment news reporting and along the way had taken a few undergraduate business classes. He did pretty well with the technical side of things but was superior in his on-air presence and the construction of his stories. He had been able to get a summer internship with one of the major Chicago TV stations and learned a great deal; some good and some not so good. For example, he learned that while he always had ample time to set up a story and do it right, reporters are often under deadline pressure and sometimes balance and accuracy would suffer.

Upon graduation, many of his fellow students had immediately begun sending out DVDs of their capabilities and experience to TV and radio stations and newspapers but Ryan decided to stay at DePaul and get an MBA. He figured that having a good understanding of business would be useful in any reporting he might do. It took a little over a year to complete the MBA and now he was ready for the world.

Through help with people he had met during the internship, he landed a job at a TV station in downstate Illinois in Champaign. In this farm area, he found much of the news coverage to be on agribusiness which he was used to with his ranching background. Of course, there was general, local news and a wee bit of national coverage but the emphasis was local and a good deal of that around farming. Even though the markets were different, Ryan's ranching background coupled with his MBA and understanding of business quickly made him popular. He became somewhat well-known and was respected at the TV station and in the community. It didn't take more than a couple of years when a bigger station, located in Milwaukee, Wisconsin came calling with a higher salary and more input over what to report and more business and political stories.

After a few more years there, during which time he had a number of offers that he turned down for one reason or another, he was contacted by a station in Hartford, Connecticut. While the offer wasn't as good as some he had turned down, he was intrigued because he had never been east of Chicago and he wondered what it would be like to live and report there. In addition, it was a network station and so he would occasionally get to work with the network boys more so than elsewhere perhaps because of the proximity to New York City.

So, in early 2008, Ryan moved east and began working there. It was a real eye-opener to say the least. People were, well, just different—more liberal, more trusting of government than what he was used to, and very confident about their own opinions. To be sure, the people in the Midwest also weren't just like those from the Mountain West either but the people out East were even more different in their attitudes, generally speaking.

Nevertheless, Ryan was very careful not to reach any final judgment and, in particular, to not get defensive about his own opinions which had been influenced by his father and the people he grew up with in Montana. After all, part of why he left Montana and part of why he left a good job in Milwaukee and came to Connecticut was to learn and experience other attitudes and values.

One thing did surprise him, though. In 2008, Hillary Clinton and Barack Obama were vying for the nomination for president from the Democratic Party. The newsroom at the TV station and, indeed, the whole station, generally seemed to be rooting for either of them against what increasingly was looking like a McCain candidacy from the Republican Party. In particular, and especially as Obama began to gain an edge, there was near rejoicing at the prospect of a first black president. Of course, Ryan, too, felt a first black president would be a great thing but he carried that inside himself and, as he had been taught at DePaul, tried to stay objective. But it was clear that many of his colleagues were making no attempt to do the same and that to some degree it carried over into their reporting.

To Ryan, this was shocking and disappointing. At the previous two stations he had worked in the Midwest, he felt that the reporting was generally fair albeit with a slight leftward tilt at times. When he had considered that, it occurred to him that many of the people working at those stations were pretty young and he remembered the old saying, "If you're young and not a Democrat, you have no heart; if you're older and are not a Republican, you have no brain." The idea was that everyone is idealistic when they are young and so tend to be more liberal. But, as you presumably gain wisdom with age, one begins to see that many liberal/progressive ideals fail in reality.

Of course, nearly none of Ryan's Connecticut colleagues would admit that they were biased or even thought they were. When nearly everyone around you ranges from liberal to very liberal to socialistic, being "merely" liberal makes you think you are down the center. Then there were one or two that more or less admitted that they had a liberal bias but felt it justified because it was "obviously" the right way to be. One of them, not knowing Ryan's background, even made a remark to the effect of how dumb the people in the middle of the country must be. Ryan thought, "Aren't you supposed to be the people that are tolerant and respectful of all people?" but he didn't say anything.

From Ryan's observations, the bias he thought he saw was never in telling some untruth or making something up or anything direct. It was more in the stories that were chosen for reporting, the way the story was reported and the stories that were ignored even though, at least in his judgment, they had real news value.

Aside from a few conversations with the news director, Ryan didn't make an issue of any of this with his colleagues. He still felt like a newbie, especially in the East, even though he had now been in the business for a number of years. Then, too, there is always the desire to "fit in" which nearly everyone feels. He still felt he was learning and he wanted to give everyone the benefit of the doubt.

When Ryan had the opportunity to work with network reporters and producers, he found them to be similar but different. They were more serious people, people who had the power to inform and therefore shape opinion and so they wanted to be careful. Most of them felt they were objective although it was clear to Ryan that they suffered from the same malady as his Connecticut colleagues, mistaking *relative* objectivity for absolute objectivity. He felt like his Montana friends would have thought the network people *way* left and his Connecticut colleagues would have felt them slightly right. Therefore, Ryan concluded, they must be somewhat left. Ryan chuckled at himself for such a crude way to measure something so important.

So, during the course of the campaign, the people were fed a steady diet of what Ryan considered somewhat left of center reporting from which, at least some of them, would form opinions on for whom to vote. When Obama beat McCain in November, there was a near party atmosphere at the TV station in Hartford.

Ryan stuck around for another four years, observing 2012 presidential campaigns of Obama and Romney, the attacks on the consulate in Benghazi in September, and other events and feeling that he had seen enough of the East and how it covered the news. He had been pondering what his next move might be when Fortune raised her head and he got a call from an old friend and mentor at Channel 6 in Chicago. Would he be interested in coming back to the Windy City for a top general assignment job there?

Chapter 11

Ryan came back to Chicago to start work in late September 2012 and, in fairly short order, two things happened, one bad and one good. First, just a week after he returned and moved back into his old DePaul neighborhood, he met Michelle O'Reilly, a pharmaceutical sales rep with the north side of Chicago as her territory. That was the good thing. Second, also a week after he returned, he thought he noticed media bias again. It was much more subtle than what he had left back East but he thought it was there nonetheless. He was beginning to wonder about his profession. Now, he wondered, were his thoughts about media bias merely a reflection of his own bias? Is the problem just that other journalists see things differently than me and I have trouble with that or is there real bias in the media?

Ryan had literally bumped into Michelle in the best place for a man to meet women—the grocery store. They were in the same aisle and were both backing down looking for a particular product when their derrieres met mid aisle making them both jump just a little. When Ryan turned around, he saw a beautiful young woman well outfitted. She was tall and a little on the thin side. He laughed a little and with a mischievous grin on his face said, "Well, that was fun. Can we do that again?"

Taking the slightly suggestive remark in stride, Michelle smiled back and said, "Maybe another time."

Ryan said, "That would suit me. My name Ryan Johnston and he held out his hand.

After a moment of hesitation, Michelle took his hand and said, "Mine's Michelle O'Reilly. Nice to, um meet you, so to speak," and she laughed a sweet laugh.

"Nice to meet you," Ryan replied. "And I meant what I said. How about another time for coffee or a drink or maybe dinner this Friday?"

Again, Michelle hesitated, trying to size Ryan up. Normally, she would take a pass. But, she looked him over and liked his boyish grin. After a few moments, she said, "Okay. I'll meet you at Mon Ami Gabi at 6:30 on Friday."

"Ryan said, "I can pick you up," kind of half way between a statement and a question.

"No, that's fine. I'll just meet you there. And don't ever come back to this grocery store if you don't show up."

"Don't worry," he said. "I'll be there."

Ryan not only showed up but was there at 6:15. When she walked in, he whistled slowly to himself. She was a knockout. She had brownish blonde hair, a great figure with nice legs and a winning smile. Ryan jumped up and pulled her chair out for her for which she thanked him.

He sat down and looking across the table at her he said, "Wow! You look terrific!"

"Thanks again," she said, smiling.

"So, are you from Chicago originally?" he asked.

Michelle answered, "Yes, I was born and raised on the South Side. My mom was a clerk in a plumbing supply house and my dad was a butcher. I was the first one in my family that was able to go to college. I went to Illinois."

"Pretty and smart, huh?" said Ryan. Michelle just smiled.

"So what do you do now?" he asked.

"I'm a pharmaceutical sales rep and my territory is the whole city."

She went on to say that she didn't get hired directly from college, however. She had taken another, frankly lesser job but had made contact with the local manager. She kept after him and kept after him until she got an interview, then a trial and then an entry level sales position. A year later she was rookie salesperson of the year.

"So how do you like it?" Ryan asked.

"It's okay. The money is good but there's just too much to do for one person but the company doesn't see it that way. But, it's okay. It's a job. With this economy, I'm lucky to have a job."

"Sounds like you're a conservative," said Ryan with a big grin.

"Well, I'm conservative economically and more liberal socially; maybe even somewhat libertarian socially."

"Yet another reason I think we'll get along."

Michelle said, "So, how about you?"

Ryan gave her his story and when he was done, she said with just a little awe in her voice," I've always wanted to see the West. It looks so beautiful in pictures."

"It's always the way, isn't it? People in the country want to see the bright lights of the city. People in the city want the beauty of the country. It's the old grass is greener thing."

"You're right, but don't get me wrong. I love Chicago. I think it's the best big city in the country. But Colorado and Montana and Utah just look so, I don't know, almost spiritual in pictures. I just hope I can see them someday."

The rest of the evening went well and so they made plans to go out again the next week and, this time, she gave him her address and phone number. And the next weekend went well and then the one after that, too. They went out every weekend and then both nights every weekend. It turned out they were very much in sync on many things including politics.

Meanwhile, before the 2012 election, Ryan was noticing little bits of bias here and there, or so he thought. He wondered if that were possible. "Were we journalists not taught to be objective? To put aside our own feelings and just report the facts?" Of course, TV had changed a lot since he had first entered the business. National TV was more fragmented, the networks had lost a great deal of market share with the advent of cable and, particularly, with the growth of the Internet and social media. So many cable channels were liberal extensions of their network cousins that Fox had found a niche catering to conservatives. Ratings in an exploding media world were everything and deadlines demands were relentless.

So, Ryan started doing a little digging. Remembering the old saying when tracking down a business or corruption story, "follow the money" he looked up to see where high level journalists and other news types donated their money. He found that it was reported that in 2008, Obama received 88% of all political donations made by anchors, reporters, writers and other new employees of the three major networks. And he asked himself the question, "If I were doing a news story on political donations by network news types and came across this information, what would I conclude from that?" The conclusion was pretty basic and pretty obvious.

When he would occasionally talk to colleagues about this, they would generally say one of three things. First was simple denial. "I'm not liberal and my reporting certainly isn't tilted." Second was, "You're just saying that because you disagree on what some are saying. It's you that's biased." Or third, "I may be liberal but my reporting isn't."

For Ryan, however, the problem was like he had experienced back East. If everyone around you is skewed to the left, even if your aim is to be in the center, the center for you is still to the left.

As the winter of 2013 gave way to spring, Michelle and Ryan were definitely a couple, definitely in love and marriage seemed a certainty. It was only a matter of time. They were both working hard and enjoying their relationship. They talked about going out to Montana to visit the ranch which would be a double prize for Michelle—finally getting to see the West and seeing the Johnston Ranch in particular. Of course, she'd also get to meet Ryan's dad. Ryan seemed a little hesitant, however, but made vague declarations about going out West someday.

In May there came the news that the IRS had been targeting and harassing conservative groups who had applied for non-taxable status. It was a hot story for a couple of days but then the Obama administration line that it was just a couple of "rogue" employees in Cincinnati began to take hold and, pretty quickly, coverage on the networks pretty much stopped. Ryan talked with the news director at his station and he felt that there just wasn't any more to the story to report.

"How can they know that unless they investigate?" asked Ryan.

"Ryan, they just don't have the resources to investigate everything that you think they ought to."

Ryan was becoming disillusioned but wondered what he could do about it? Where could he go? He was a top reporter at a network owned station in one of the three top markets in the country. He was troubled by network reporting so he didn't want to go there. Heck, he'd probably get fired in a month. He didn't want to go to a small station where he'd be reporting on high school graduations and state fairs. Broadcast journalism was the only thing he knew. Well, that plus the fact that Michelle was going to be his wife one day.

2013 gave way to 2014 and, if anything, Ryan thought things were getting worse in the area of media bias. A solid majority of the country thought there was bias in the media but those in the profession were simply in denial or worse.

Ryan regularly talked to Michelle about his concerns over media bias. Like many Americans, and especially younger Americans, she had never really paid too much attention. She got most of her news from the Internet although once she knew Ryan she tried to watch him on TV but, of course, that was mostly local news. She always listened sympathetically but could offer little comfort and no answer to the problem. Ryan didn't want liberal reporters; he didn't want conservative reporters; he wanted neutral reporters and editors and producers. He'd clench his fist and say, "Don't they know about the harm they do to our profession and to the country?" Eventually, he concluded they cared more about their own opinions than anything else. Then, his rage was diluted with sadness.

Chapter 12

Julie was only about two when her mom died and so she only had vague impressions of the troubled time, not the more vivid experience of her older brother, Ryan. She and Ryan did talk about it a fair amount as they were growing up but neither of them understood why their dad acted the way he did. She took Ryan's word that Jerry was quite a bit different after their mom had died than before because she hadn't experienced the "before". All she knew was the "after" and she had always been somewhat perplexed by Jerry or at least his relationship with each of the kids. She knew he loved them all; he even said so now and then, but so much of the time it was more like people living in the same house but not related.

Even though she was closer in years to Colin she was emotionally closer to Ryan. He was her hero, her knight in shining armor. He had always been there to take care of her to comfort her and to protect her. Emily was great in those ways as well but there are times when a male figure does it better and it was most often Ryan who was there for her. As she grew older, all the boys knew you had better treat her with respect because if you didn't, you would have to answer to Ryan.

In spite of this potential obstacle, there were no shortage of interested boys and men who became interested in Julie. She had two things that in combination men find irresistible—good looks and a friendly, warm personality. Now, there are a lot of women that are good looking; but it's the ones that really aren't aware of it, aren't obsessed with it and to whom it isn't real important that really appeal to men. You can tell who they are because such a woman is happy to talk to anyone, regardless of how cool they were or how good looking, male or female. Of course, there's a bit of a Catch 22 because one of the reasons women are so interested in their looks is because that's one of the things men are interested in; maybe even the first thing. In any event, Julie had "it" and men and boys knew it.

Like Ryan she did a lot of work at the ranch and knew the operations pretty well. She was a favorite of all the guys on the ranch and at least one or two of the crew thought they were in love with her but didn't dare say anything about it. She did work a lot with the crews but, more than Ryan, she worked with Jerry. This was one of the things about her dad she found perplexing. She felt that he had her work with him even more than Ryan as a way of protecting her, although from God knows what. But he never said that or used their time together to really say anything that wasn't about the task at hand or the ranch more generally. It was like the love was assumed or imputed, not exactly the recommended ways of communicating personal emotions.

She always asked a lot of questions about cattle markets and how cattle are sold, what kind of marketing was done and all that sort of thing. She was young and in the middle of a changing world of communications what with a relatively new thing called the Internet. Jerry wasn't much help in those areas because he didn't know much about any of that. He grew up with the rotary dial phone so high tech was not his specialty.

Julie had many suitors in high school and several boyfriends but no lovers. She wasn't afraid of her father in most respects but he had given her the "talk" about sex and had made it very clear that she had better not allow anyone to go all the way with her. At first, she had found the fact that *he* had actually had the talk with her rather than delegate it to Emily or just leave it to the school surprising. But, after the talk, she thought she had figured it out. Besides the informational part about the birds and the bees, there was the opportunity, for Jerry the necessity, of laying out not just guidelines but hard and fast rules. So, even though the girls Livingston High schooled her about contraception techniques and one even mentioned abortion, her father still had plenty enough authority over her for her to even think about taking a chance on getting pregnant.

She knew her dad expected Ryan to stay on to help with the ranch when Ryan was a senior in high school because he would occasionally make a comment about it. But he never said anything to Julie about her future one way or another. Five years after Ryan had left and Julie was a senior, she had no idea what expectations her dad had for her, if any, and she was darned if she was going to ask. If her dad had wanted her to stay on he sure as heck would have said something by now and so she just figured he was indifferent at best. That being the case, she'd do what her older brother that she adored did, she'd go off to school and do something else with her life than work on the ranch. She was a little conflicted about it because she did like much of the ranch life and loved horses, especially her favorite, Honey, whom she called Honey Bear. She would have liked it if her dad had talked to her about staying even if she didn't plan on doing so. But, it never happened.

One thing that did please Jerry is that, unlike Ryan, she decided to go to Montana State and thought she'd double major in communications and political science. So, in 2003 she headed off to college at MSU in Bozeman, Montana. Now, by Montana standards, Livingston and Bozeman are next door to one another. It would have been physically possible to stay at home and attend classes in Bozeman but Julie wanted the college experience so she lived in a dorm until she joined one of the four sororities and then moved in to the sorority house. She took typical freshman classes and, as a sophomore, began to take more classes in her majors.

Even though she was going to major in political science, Julie had never considered herself particularly political. Like most of her friends in the Livingston area, she was relatively conservative and generally Republican because that's what their fathers and mothers mostly were. Therefore, during the 2004 presidential race between George W. Bush and John Kerry, she started out firmly in the Bush camp although if she had been asked on the street why she would have had to admit she wasn't 100% sure why. By the time voting day came, she was less sure about Bush although she still voted for him. Funny, she wasn't sure exactly why she was less sure although she knew what the source of some of the doubt was.

Most of the women who attended MSU were unlike most of the women who attended very private, very liberal colleges back East. But that didn't mean that there weren't some pockets of very liberal thinking and Julie had happened to stumble onto and into one of those pockets at her sorority. She had become fast friends with a woman named Nancy Fregosi who came from a rich family in California and who was very liberal, especially when it came to what was generally grouped as "women's rights." Why this rich, very liberal Californian had chosen to come to MSU was a mystery to which Julie had never found out the answer. But it was the fact that she was so different from Julie herself and most of the women Julie had ever known that had made her so interesting to Julie. For her part, Nancy felt Julie to be so "out of it," so behind the times, that she felt Julie needed her guidance to break out of the rube world she came from. Of course, Nancy never said that but she thought it; that was the essence of the attraction.

For a couple of years, Nancy the "instructor" took Julie the "student" under her wing and tried to teach her all the ways in which society in general and many men in particular abused women. From pay differentials to admission to country clubs to child support enforcement to alimony questions, Julie learned a lot about things she had never known. But it was contraception and abortion issues that would really wind Nancy up. Nancy felt contraception and abortion should be free and universally available to all women. When Julie asked Nancy about late term abortions, Nancy said that she had to admit that she had some misgiving about aborting a fetus that doctors would say was viable; but even that was OK if the mother's life was in any danger. The important point was that the choice was hers in consultation with her doctor, not some governmental authority run by men who just didn't get it.

Little by little, Julie's attitudes and her politics began to center around these issues and she gravitated to the Democratic Party. It felt a little odd much of the time because she generally had much to quarrel with Democrats over economic issues and other matters. But Nancy had her convinced that the women's issues were paramount. Julie began to attend political rallies and, in 2006, began working part time for the Democrat running in the 101st House District in the Montana State Legislature. She would assist the campaign communications director in writing press releases and other communications. She was so good at it that when she graduated, the campaign offered her a full time paid job as Assistant Communications Director.

During the home stretch in the fall, operatives from the national Democratic organization were in Montana, helping with some of the national races and they overlapped a bit with the local folks. Julie's skill and savvy at public relations and media messaging were noticed. A number of people had mentioned to Julie the possibility of doing something else in the political world after this race was over. She considered it just idle talk. And she wasn't sure what she would do after her candidate lost. Julie's candidate may have lost but the race was much closer than expected so the campaign team was credited with having done a very good job.

Julie had rented an apartment in Bozeman after graduation and now that the race was over she had to decide what to do next. She decided to contact the placement people at MSU and get their advice. When she called, they said they were glad she called because they had been contacted by a man named Tom Sanders who was a managing director with Capitol Strategy & Communications who wanted to talk with her. Julie remembered Tom as being part of the national Democratic team but she had had little interaction with him and couldn't even remember what he looked like. When she called, he asked if she'd be willing to come to Washington D.C. to interview for a position with CSC. Without a moment's hesitation she said yes and they set up the details for a meeting in a couple of days.

For the next day, Julie researched CSC and learned they provided consulting on strategy and communications for politicians, people wanting to know politicians, politicians wanting to know other people and, in particular, politicians who were in a contested race.

When the meeting did take place, Julie then remembered Tom Sanders. She was a little surprised she hadn't remembered him because he was a good looking man around thirty. He had apparently left the formal Democratic Party about a month before the election and had joined the relatively young firm which had been started by and was still headed by a former high ranking Republican in the George H. W. Bush administration named Pete Simpson. He had joined them for part of the interview and explained that CSC was a political and communications consulting firm and that their consultants were hired to achieve the goals of their clients. Therefore, their own beliefs were irrelevant. The only thing that mattered was achieving the client's goals.

"That's the *only* thing that matters?" Julie asked?

"What else is there," came the reply.

"What about the truth?" Julie replied.

"What about it? Look, let me be clear, we make our living here by meeting our client's political goals, period. That's what we focus on. We don't care what those goals are, what they believe or who they're screwing. Having said that, I personally don't believe there is one truth. Different people see things through different prisms and for them there are many truths. The world isn't black and white with some line that you cross that makes you right or wrong. We do what we have to do. Do you think you can live with that?"

Julie's hair on the back of her neck stood up. This definitely wasn't her dad talking; quite the opposite. She wondered what she might be getting into.

"Absolutely," she lied.

Chapter 13

It was late 2013 and Julie was approaching her sixth anniversary with CSC. She was now a managing director and she still worked for Tom Sanders who was now a principle with the firm. She now had a small team of her own but her main job was still to churn out communications strategy as well as actual writings for publications or for speeches. Of course, communication strategy was just a fancy way of saying "telling them the truth we want them to know, whether it was the truth or not." At least, that's how Julie felt about it.

CSC was definitely focused on meeting client's goals; so much so that half the time they were creating communications on different sides of the same issues. For one client you'd be creating a whole strategy about why taxes should be higher, especially on the wealthy; for another client you'd be creating a whole strategy about why taxes should be lower. There was no firm philosophy or general point of view. The founder of the firm didn't insist that his values be considered and sold. Any potential client of virtually any persuasion was told what they wanted to hear. The name of the game was revenue, not integrity.

Julie and Tom Sanders had been secretly dating for around four years although it was a very poorly kept secret. Most of the people in the office knew or had strong suspicions. But then half the office was fooling around with the other half, or so it seemed sometimes. Tom wasn't married so Julie felt that as long as she was OK with it, even though he was her superior and technically there was potential for sexual harassment and all kinds of other legal issues, at least it was better than the married folks who were fooling around.

One of the ironies of their work was that they often had to create proposals and later develop strategies regarding abortion.

Tom was ardently pro-life; he couldn't logically explain why, he was just raised that way and didn't question it now. Julie had mainly become pro-choice although she did feel that late-term abortions were a problem. So, when they were pursuing a client on one side of that issue or the other, one of them would be creating strategy and/or arguments that were contrary to their own beliefs. This happened all the time on a range of issues but the contrast was so stark in the case of abortion.

Julie and Tom each had their own apartments but, generally, Julie stayed with Tom at his place. It was closer to work and more convenient. She often wondered what Jerry would have said about the arrangement; actually, she pretty much knew what he would say, at least the general theme. But this was common practice in Washington D.C. and she was content to do the same as everyone else.

At least, she had felt that way in the beginning. Tom was an attractive man physically and, accordingly, she had been attracted to him from the very beginning. Most of his politics were in line with hers; especially because she had flipped to the liberal side of things since she had left Montana. He had wined and dined her in the beginning and she thought that he was pretty good in bed. Of course, she didn't have much experience in that area. She had not been a virgin when she and Tom first hooked up but she was close. She had had two lovers; both one night stands after a little too much to drink. Fortunately, she had not become pregnant either time but between the small number of lovers and the fact that she was somewhat inebriated both times, her ability to gauge the skill of Tom in bed was severely limited.

D.C was a pretty thrilling place to be especially for a young woman from Livingston, Montana. Given the nature of her work, she had met a number of leading politicians of both parties as well as staffers who wielded more clout than she had ever realized. Once, she had even been at a relatively small reception when the President was present. She didn't get to meet him but it was quite an experience for her.

But after a few years the glitter and the glamour began to wear off some. She began to turn down opportunities to meet famous politicians or powerful staffers unless it was related directly to CSC business. She had become tired of the same old B.S. that was discussed all the time and she tired of being hit on constantly, particularly by married men who seemed especially eager to cheat on their wives. D.C. was such a seamy place; everybody was out for themselves and backstabbing was commonplace. True friendships were few and far between and it was dangerous to take anyone into your confidence.

Even Tom had pulled a stunt on her a couple of times. There were two instances where CSC was competing with other firms for some prime business. At night, she and Tom had discussed the prospect and strategies to win the business. Then, when the next meeting took place regarding the pursuit of the client, Tom announced the approach that Julie had outlined to him but presented it as if it were his and not hers. Julie was in the room and was fuming but didn't feel it made any sense to call him on it publicly. The first time she chewed him out at home and he apologized. The second time she threatened to move out if he did it again. That threat, so far, had kept him from doing it again but it also made her less willing to share her ideas with him. "How screwed up is that?" she thought.

As the outer covering of power and prestige and politics began to fade away, what was left was not such a pretty picture to Julie. The "say anything, do anything" prime directive of the firm seemed awfully dirty when stripped of the sizzle that surrounded it. Julie began to wonder if she was losing her soul. "What do I believe in?" she thought.

When she thought about how her values and opinions had evolved from when she was in high school back in Montana to now, she thought that she should feel proud. After all, she had gone from being relatively conservative to relatively liberal and, at least at one point in time, she had thought liberals were the ones that cared. They cared about women's rights; they cared about the poor; they cared about equality. But now she felt like no one had the high ground when it came to those or any other issues. She had heard the true feelings of as many Democrats as Republicans who really didn't care about anyone but themselves. After all, most politicians are essentially narcissistic. Then there were those on both sides who truly had different ideas on how to handle things; different ideas on what would work; different ideas on which principles had priority. In short, no one had a stranglehold on caring.

One year began to tumble into the next and about the only thing that kept her going was the possibility of becoming a principal herself. Maybe then she could make some changes although she doubted it. Work slowly became drudgery with no way out. She could go to another firm but that would just be more of the same. She toyed with the idea of going into broadcasting but her discussions with Ryan on the idea were anything but encouraging. So she figuratively put one foot in front of the other and had her own death march, waiting for something to happen, waiting for something to change. Maybe a guy will come along and sweep her off her feet and change her life. A girl can dream, can't she?

Late in 2013, CSC had been pursuing one of its biggest prospects. As 2014 rolled in, the prospect was down to CSC and one other firm. At the end of January, each firm would be given a set of issues to analyze and prepare position papers for this particular prospect. The final presentations were to come in mid-February with the decision by the end of the month. This was a likely future presidential candidate and the revenue potential was very large. Julie and her team worked for countless hours analyzing the issues from different perspectives including purely political. There were many long nights of research. They did polling and statistical analysis and then analysis of the analysis. Then, they had to pull it all together into position papers which had to be written and then re-written and then re-written again.

The night before the final presentations, Tom and Julie were home making final checks on everything. Tom looked up and said, "Julie, maybe tomorrow you could wear that black dress that I got you last week; you know, the one that's kind of sexy?"

Julie looked at for several seconds Tom in disbelief. "Oh come on, Tom. I'm not going to try and win this thing by showing cleavage in place of capability. We've worked too long and too hard on this thing to pull that kind of bullshit now. What would everyone think? They know I don't wear that kind of outfit at work. I feel bad enough about what we do every day; I'm not going to prostitute myself to get this business. Besides, he might find it to be cheap and insulting."

Tom looked at her and with the weary tone of a man just following orders said, "Julie, Honey, this comes right from the top. The boss is positive that our prospect has the hots for you and he thinks this could put us over the top."

"Well, why don't I just proposition the guy before the meeting!" she yelled on the verge of tears. "I can't believe you guys are asking me to do something like this!" She starred at Tom for a long time. "What exactly did Pete say?"

Tom weighed whether he should tell the truth or not. This was going as badly as he had thought but then the boss had been direct. Finally he decided he didn't have a choice.

"He said something like 'Get her to wear something hot' or something like that, I don't know. Look, he's just trying to use every weapon we have."

"Well I'm not going to do it!" And with that, Julie ran off to the spare bedroom crying tears of pure anger all the way.

The next morning, Tom was waiting in the lobby of their apartment at the normal time that he and Julie left for work. He hadn't spoken to her since when she ran off and he didn't know what kind of mood she would be in. When the door opened, out came Julie in the sexy black dress and with a very unhappy expression on her face. Tom was at once relieved that the boss' wished were being followed but frankly afraid of the scowl Julie was wearing.

"What made you change your mind?" he asked.

"I don't want to talk about it. Lets' just go."

So they went. They went to the presentation and before, during and after Julie's presentation, she felt the eyes of everyone in the room, men and women, on her. Everyone knew what was happening, what she was doing. Most didn't know that she had been "ordered" to wear the sexy dress; most were surprised to see her in such an outfit. She felt like she was wearing the scarlet letter.

A week later, word came that CSC had won the assignment. There was much celebrating in the office. Tom was thrilled, thinking about the bonus he was going to get and how much more clout he would have in the firm. Pete came by to tell Julie what a great job she and her team had done. She wanted to puke. If hypocrisy were currency, she thought, there's be no national debt.

When they got home, Tom was riding high. "Do you know what this means, Baby?" You're going to make principal this year and I am going to run our whole department. There's no stopping us now." He noticed Julie looked anything but happy.

"Look, I know you had to do something that was disagreeable but I promise it won't happen again. Can't you be a little happy?"

"Damn it, Tom. It wasn't disagreeable, it was disgraceful! I humiliated myself, all for the glory of CSC. I can barely face the people in the office."

"I didn't hear anyone in the office say anything."

She looked at him with disgust as if to say, "You don't know what goes on in the office anyway."

"Look," he said. I'll tell Pete that we're taking the rest of the week off. We'll go down to the Bahamas and by the time we come back everyone will have moved on."

That was the first half way decent idea she had heard for around eight or nine days. At least she would be away from the office and all the looks and whispers. She doubted people would have "moved on" totally as Tom had put it but things might be better.

"Okay," she said joylessly.

The next day, Tom booked an expensive suite in an expensive hotel right on the beach a little outside of Nassau. He also booked a couple of airline tickets and they were on their way.

Julie recovered a little of her old self because she was in a different environment, out of what she now considered the cesspool of Washington D.C. She felt warm on the beach, another nice change. She slowly relaxed and actually began to enjoy herself, pushing out of her mind that soon she would be going back. So, for now, the hell with it, I'm just going to enjoy myself she thought. She had a couple of daiquiris right on the beach and was feeling good.

The hotel had a band that played every night, just one of the reasons why it was expensive; but, so what? It's only money. Tom got a very good table right on the beach for dinner. He ordered a bottle of Champaign to celebrate their great victory. Julie really didn't want to be reminded but that only made her drink a little more; it dulled the pain of what they had left. Tom thought she was finally getting past everything and, when they had finished the first bottle, he ordered a second.

After they had eaten the band was playing and they got up to dance. Julie was having a little trouble dancing to the reggae music but she didn't care. She didn't care about much right now. The band then shifted gears and played a slow song, almost like a waltz. Tom and Julie locked themselves together and danced slowly to the music. After a bit, they stopped moving their feet and were basically grinding on one another. Julie could feel Tom getting aroused. "Let's go up to the room," he said.

"Sure, why not?" she thought.

Without another word, they went up to the room and Tom was on her like hungry dog. It was mostly a one sided thing. Julie knew what was going on; she consented; she just really didn't care so what the fuck? "Hey, I made a joke," she thought.

The next morning, she had one doozy of a headache. In fact, they both did. It turned out that Tom had finished most of the second bottle by himself and Julie had never really had Champagne before and didn't know how to handle it. They stayed in the room all morning, finally venturing out about noon for lunch. Julie said to herself, "Perfect. Now I feel crappy on the inside and on the outside."

The next couple of days passed without noteworthy occurrence and then it was time to return to Washington which Julie was dreading. When they did return, she was surprised to find that people did seem to have moved on. She didn't notice any stares or whispers or hear any gossip even from her friends in the office. Maybe, just maybe things will be okay. A couple of weeks went by and she slipped back into the drudgery rut which wasn't good but better than the humiliation she had felt before the trip.

One morning in late March she awoke with a start. She sat up straight and tried to figure out what was going on. Like a slap to the face, it occurred to her that she had missed her period. She had never been one of those "regular" girls. Her period seemed to change every month, so maybe that was it although deep down she didn't think so. She waited another day and then went to the pharmacy and got one of those pregnancy tests that were not 100% reliable but still a good indicator. The test indicated she was pregnant. She went to see her OBGYN the next day and she confirmed that Julie was pregnant.

Up to this point, Julie had not said a word to Tom about any of this but she knew that was going to have to change, tonight. That night when they got home from work, Julie asked Tom to sit down, that they needed to talk. He thought it was going to be about some failure on his part to do something. He wasn't expecting what she did say.

"I'm pregnant," Julie said bluntly.

Tom's jaw dropped but for a moment he didn't say anything. Then, "Are you sure it's mine?"

Julie had never been in love with Tom but initially she had liked him quite a bit. That like had slowly dissolved over time into something akin to tolerance. Now, with a single question, he had moved the marker to disgust. "You asshole," she thought.

"Yes, I am sure," she said wearily. "I haven't been with anyone other than you."

"When? How?" he pleaded as if an explanation might somehow change the circumstance.

"How?!" she exclaimed, almost laughing in spite of her feelings.

"Okay, when?"

"Probably when we were down in the Bahamas. Our first night there; I didn't have my usual protection and as far as I remember, neither did you."

"You weren't using your diaphragm?"

"Not the first night. I was tired and drained and, frankly, wasn't thinking about sex."

"Are you sure about this?"

"My doctor confirmed it today. I'm due in December."

"Well, what are you going to do?"

"What do you mean?"

"Well," said Tom, "You're not going to keep it are you? I mean, maybe you should think about having an abortion."

"What! I thought you were the big pro-life guy."

"Well, I am," Tom stammered. "But, geez, Julie, I mean, what do you want to do? Do you want to get married?"

Not to you she thought. To Tom she said, "I don't know. I need to think things over. I just thought you should know."

"Look, Honey, I'm just not ready to get married and I don't think you are either. You're the one who is pro-choice. Why don't you just have a quiet abortion somewhere and make all this go away. I'll pay for everything and I'll support you every step of the way."

Julie really couldn't believe what she was hearing but she especially didn't want to talk about it anymore that evening. So she said, Let me think about it," and walked away.

A few more weeks passed and Julie was still thinking about it. Like asshole Tom, her first impulse had been to have an abortion but she just wasn't quite as sure now that it was the real thing as opposed to a policy position geared to election strategies. At around seven weeks of her pregnancy, she went back to her doctor and they did an ultrasound. She couldn't see much but she did see the heartbeat. Wow! She had never realized that there was a beating heart at such an early stage. She considered how most people look to the heart beating as a sign of life and here a fetus, or should she say baby, has one at seven weeks or maybe less. Seven weeks. Some people argue for abortions at seven months! She now was really conflicted over the whole abortion argument and over what she would do. Clearly, she had not planned for and, frankly, was not ready for a baby. Although she had not been to church in forever nor had she prayed about anything, now she made a little prayer that sounded like she was speaking to a friend. "Well, Lord, please give me a little help here. Thanks."

The next morning when she awoke, it somehow was all clear to her. As she and Tom were getting ready for work she said to him, "Tom, I'd like to talk to you about the abortion."

"Oh, good," he said. "Like I said, I will pay for everything and we can do it somewhere far away and quietly."

"No, Tom. I may have started the conversation poorly because you have the wrong impression. I'm not going to have an abortion; I'm going to keep the baby."

Tom sank down on a chair, looking at Julie in disbelief.

"What? Why"

"I'm really not totally sure, Tom. It's just something that I feel. Look, you said it, I'm pro-choice; I'm not really pro-abortion. Now that it's all close to home, I think I'm against abortion while at the same time I think it's a woman's choice, not the government's. I know others may see it differently; but anyway this is my choice."

"But Julie, I'm not ready to be married or be a father. I.."

"Don't worry," she cut him off. You don't need to be a part of any of this. In fact, I don't want you to be. I'll take care of everything. And, believe me, there won't be a wedding. In fact, I am going to move back into my own apartment."

"But Julie, why…"

Again she cut him off by putting her hands up in the air as a "stop" signal.

"Look, Tom, I'm not blaming you, I'm not saying you've done anything wrong or that you should have done or should now do something differently. Having this baby, this little person, inside me has changed the way I think and I'm not even sure how or why. As for you and me, our splitting has been coming on for a while; even you should have seen it coming. Let's just go our separate ways, except for work, and everything will be fine." With that, Julie went to Tom and gave him a peck on the cheek and a pat on the head and turned and walked out to go to work.

At work, everyone began to notice that Julie was pregnant but word had also filtered out that she and Tom were no longer living together. A few of Julie's closer associates asked her who the father was but she just said, "There's no need for anyone here to know."

By July, Julie began to feel better about everything because she knew she would be leaving CSC; she dreaded it there now, but she just wasn't sure how she would leave or where she would go. Then, one morning, she woke up and it hit her in the face. She picked up the phone and called her father.

"Hello," she heard Jerry's groggy sounding voice.

"Daddy, it's me."

"Are you okay, Julie? It's five o'clock in the morning. Is everything okay?"

"Everything's fine, Daddy. I'm sorry about the time, I forgot about the time difference. But I wanted to ask you something. I think I'm going to quit my job here and, if it's okay, I'd like to come home for a while. Would that be okay?

"Well, of course, Honey, but what's happened?"

"I'll explain it all to you when I get home. I'll let you know when I'll be arriving. Thank you, Daddy. See you soon." And she hung up before Jerry could ask any more questions.

Julie went into work and announced her decision. In particular, she went into Pete's office and said, "I just wanted to let you know that I am quitting as of today. And, for the record, the truth does matter. Those who do what we do are part of the problem and you and others like you are helping to destroy our country by the way you manipulate the truth so that ordinary people don't know what's really going on. I'm sorry I was a part of it but that ends as of right now."

She had no intention of getting into a discussion or letting Pete say his piece so she turned on her heels and marched out leaving Pete speechless. Julie enjoyed the irony.

Chapter 14

One might say that Colin was the forgotten child of the Johnston family. He wasn't the favored elder male and he wasn't the darling little girl that all fathers wanted; he was the runt to blame for the death of his mom. There was no truth to that statement but Colin sometimes felt that way. He believed his dad felt that way which was why he didn't spend time with Colin. It wasn't that Jerry never did anything with him or truly ignored him but by the time Jerry would quit working somewhere on the ranch and be home and maybe talk a little with Ryan or Julie, it was late and Jerry would be tired and barely able to muster a "G'night, Colin."

Emily saw all this and knew it wasn't intentional but also saw that it had an effect on Colin. She tried her best to make up the difference by spending more time with Colin than anyone. When he would have problems of one sort or another, it was Emily he would turn to, not his dad. She was truly Colin's mom and he loved her as much as he might have his real mom.

Like his older siblings, Colin worked on the ranch and, if the truth be told, he was better at the day-to-day stuff than any of them and it wasn't even close. He was on a horse before he could walk and was a champion in all the local rodeos growing up. He also was a natural in dealing with cows and steers and bulls. He almost never worked with Jerry which suited the crews just fine because he was a top hand even though just a young teenager.

He was allowed to carry a pistol because Jerry always felt it was better to have it and not need it than the other way around. But anyone who carried a gun on the Johnston Ranch had to undergo some form of safety training. And if you were caught "playing around" with a gun, loaded or unloaded, you were gone. Colin was often out on far reaches of the ranch and he felt safer with a gun. He not only took safety courses, he took shooting classes and in a very short time became a crack shot. Pistol shooting is totally different than shooting a shoulder fired weapon; Colin was OK to good with a rifle but unusually skilled with a handgun. In rodeos, in addition to riding events, he won a number of mounted shooting events and began to develop quite a reputation.

When Colin visited other ranches, sometimes he would get to ride a dirt bike because that ranch used them for herding and other chores. He was actually kind of glad that the Johnston Ranch still used horses, the traditional way even if it was not as efficient. But he enjoyed getting the chance to try a motorbike and, as with everything else, quickly became pretty good. He decided that he wanted to get a motorcycle of his own, not for the ranch; after all, a motorcycle was basically too big. But just to have and ride on the open road. But when he asked Jerry, he got a very quick and firm "No!" No explanation, no "maybe in a few years;" just "No!"

As he grew older, he became more and more tight-lipped. It seemed there was a proportional relationship between the gulf that separated he and his dad and how much or little Colin would have to say. And yet, strangely, instead of making Colin reject his dad, deep down he wanted ever so much to be just like his dad-- quiet, hardworking, tough and independent. It was a relationship that might have baffled a lot of psychologists.

When the September 11, 2001 terrorist attacks occurred, Colin felt a surge a patriotism inside. He was too young to join the service but the older brothers of a few friends were already in the service and he got to talk to a couple of them. When one of them died in the early days of the war in Afghanistan, rather than diminish Colin's patriotism and desire to serve, it increased it. But military service would have to wait until he was older. When the U.S. invaded Iraq in 2003, he told Jerry he was thinking about enlisting. Jerry "forbade" Colin from doing so even though technically, in a few months, there would be nothing that Jerry could do about it. "Just this one last time," Colin told himself, "I'm going to do what the old man wants." So, Colin went off to MSU to join his sister and to study agribusiness. Jerry was secretly quite pleased about that but, as usual, he didn't say much to Colin about it.

In 2006, a friend named Mike Hopper that Colin had met at MSU decided that college wasn't for him and he was ready for adventure. He asked Colin to accompany him down to the local U.S. Army recruiting office so that he could check things out. Colin did go with Mike for Mike's appointment; Mike decided to stay in school, Colin enlisted. Jerry blew a fuse.

"What in the hell did you go and do that for? And who gave you permission to do such a thing? What about school? What if something happens to you?"

On that last one, Colin was tempted to say, "What would you care?" but he didn't. Instead, he said, "Dad, I did it because I thought it was the right thing to do. I want to serve my country and I thought this would be a good way to do that. I don't need anyone's permission anymore for anything. I'm twenty years old and I can make my own decisions now. As for school, I can finish that when I'm out of the service and I'll have the G.I. Bill to help pay for things."

That little speech took some of the steam out of Jerry. Part of him felt Colin was being ungrateful regarding the opportunities that Jerry had afforded him with college and so on. Of course, Jerry hadn't talked much with Colin about the "and so on" but that didn't occur to him at the moment. On the other hand, it was pretty hard to not admire the commitment to serve one's country. And Colin did have the right to make his own decisions. But Jerry wished he would have spoken to him about it before actually enlisting. Then it occurred to him that he had said no once before. Further, it occurred to him that as a parent and counselor, he was lacking. "Why would he talk to me?" he thought to himself.

Nevertheless, he said, "Son, why didn't you talk to me about this?"

Colin just stood there with a look on his face that said, "You really want me to answer that?"

A little over a month later, Colin said goodbye to Emily and was headed to the airport for a series of flights to Fort Benning,

Georgia, home of the U.S. Army Infantry. Jerry drove and when they got to the airport, Jerry parked at the departure area. Colin reached for the door handle but before he could pull the door open, Jerry put his hand on Colin's arm to stop him.

Jerry looked at Colin and said, "Son, I'm proud of you."

A torrent of emotion ran through Colin's body but he managed to only show a bit of a trembling lip. He had so often so desperately wanted to hear words like that from his dad and now he was overjoyed that he did. At the same time, why did it take him leaving for the Army to say something? So many feelings and images flew past his mind it was like the "jump to hyperspace" from Star Wars. There was a long pause. Finally, Colin said, "Thanks, Dad." They looked at one another a long few seconds but no more words were spoken. Colin got out of the car and headed for the terminal. Just as he was about to go through the door, he couldn't help himself ; he turned and looked back and saw that Jerry hadn't moved. With one last look, but no gesture, Colin stepped into the terminal and took the first step to a new world.

Colin breezed through Basic Infantry Training and Advanced Individual Training at Fort Benning. He was in great shape; he was a better shot than all of his fellow soldiers of his training units and most if not all of the cadre. He took orders well, was well liked by his fellow trainees and was a natural leader. In short, he was a near perfect soldier in the Army's eyes.

After completing AIT, he was given orders to report to Fort Riley, Kansas. His new unit would be the first platoon of Alpha Company, 2nd Battalion, 4th Brigade of the First Infantry Division—The Big Red One. As luck would have it, the division pistol championships were just starting and somehow word of Colin's skill had made its way to Fort Riley. Colin's squad leader, Sgt. Gary Mahorn asked Colin if he'd like to compete. He said the company commander had bets with the other CO's of the 2nd Battalion and if Colin could help bring a victory it would be a very good start. Not only did he win for Alpha Company, he placed first in the entire division. While not part of the competitions, he was known for being a good and quick trick shot artist. He could shoot multiple targets at different heights and angles in rapid succession. He was promptly assigned to handgun training in addition to his duties as a rifleman in the 3rd Squad of the 1st Platoon.

In early 2007, Colin's unit was ordered to Iraq as part of the "surge" that took place. Colin was as good in combat as he had been in back in training in the States. Without really understanding why, he was very calm and cool in combat, keeping his head when others were rattled. Most men in combat are scared shitless even if they have had previous combat experiences. Colin was one of the few for whom everything slowed down in combat. He did experience fear but it was more than compensated for by a calm that came from some place deep inside him. He was quickly given more and more leadership roles and was promoted ahead of his contemporaries. His C.O. gave him permission to carry a handgun in addition to the standard issue rifle that he carried. Sometimes, in close quarters and/or to scare a local, he would use the handgun.

The surge proved a success and Colin stayed in the Army and kept re-upping. In the intervals between tours, he would visit Ryan and Julie but not his dad. He kept the intervals short and just claimed he didn't have time to go all the way west to see his dad. He did call each time, though. At the end of 2013, Colin came back from Iraq and was assigned to training duty at Ft. Benning. By July of 2014, Colin decided that he had done enough and been in the Army long enough and he was honorably discharged at Fort Benning.

Colin's whole military experience had been mostly good but having been in combat definitely had had an effect on him. He often thought to himself that before Iraq he had been a Boy Scout; now he was something else. He had a little swagger and a little anger and wasn't going to back down from anybody or anything. Fundamentally, he was still a "good" guy and he believed that when the baggage of combat faded a bit he would revert completely to good-guy status; but before that happened, he felt ready to explore his dark side. He was ready for a little bad-boy time.

During his first three years in the service and, especially during much of his initial time in Iraq, Colin had become very good friends with a fellow named Lucas John Herrelman, known affectionately as "Little John" to his comrades. Unlike the large fellow in Robin Hood lore, Luke Herrelman was actually a man of average height. Colin and he had helped each other get through a couple of close calls and had become close and very supportive of one another. John had left the service more than a year earlier. When Colin was planning on leaving the service, he tracked Little John down in California and told him he was leaving the Army. Little John told him to come out to California and join him, saying that Colin had earned some R & R. So, when Colin reached his Expiration of Term of Service, or E.T.S., he headed out to California near El Cajon, a little ways north of the Mexican border. John had a modest apartment there but he had an extra bedroom that Colin used until he found his own.

John sometimes worked at a nearby distribution warehouse but, near as Colin could figure, he spent most of his time hanging with a motorcycle club called the Honchos. It was a small group of a dozen or so headed by one Robert "Rocky" Newton. The club ran a mechanic shop and a bar that were combined in one building. The mechanic side specialized in motorcycles but could do also repair many makes of cars. Little John got a monthly dividend from the Club which seemed fairly generous to Colin for a mechanic shop and bar combination. Little John urged Colin to get a motorcycle of his own and 'hang around" with the Honchos. Getting a motorcycle appealed to Colin since his dad and not let him get one several years before. So, Colin went out and bought a 1200 Custom Harley Davidson. As for hanging with the Honchos, Colin was a little dubious but he had nothing else to do, so why not? What Little John failed to explain to Colin was that being a "hang around" was the first step in becoming a full patch member of the club.

After a week of generally doing nothing, Little John took Colin to meet Rocky, the head of the Club. So, Little John and Colin walked over to the mechanic shop & bar and through the front area to the back where there was a lounge just for Club members and an office.

Rocky was in the office, sitting at a desk leaning back in the chair with his feet up on the desk. Since he was sitting down it was a little hard to judge his height but he appeared to be a pretty big dude. He was muscular and his jacket was sleeveless so his large biceps were showing. Colin guessed that he must pump iron. His upper arms also had tattoos; the club emblem on one arm and an eagle on the other. Colin guessed there were probably a lot of other tattoos as well. He had long hair and a mustache and about two days' worth of stubble on his face.

"Rocky, I want you to meet Colin, the buddy I told you about," said Little John.

Rocky eyed Colin in what appeared to be a generally unfriendly way. "So," said Rocky, "you're the army hotshot that Little John has been telling us about." Those were the words that he spoke but somehow, it sounded more like, "So you think you're some big fucking deal just because you were in the army?"

Colin immediately decided that he didn't care for the greeting and that he didn't like Rocky which was rather remarkable on about three seconds of history. Colin and Rocky just stared at one another for several long seconds, neither one apparently intimidated.

"I was in the army" answered Colin, ignoring the hotshot remark.

"You ever kill anyone?"

Colin again stared at Newton for several long seconds. Then he looked over to Little John as if to say, "You put up with this shit?" Part of him wanted to get in Newton's face but he was aware that his friend, Little John, might suffer as a result and he didn't want that to happen.

Finally, he said, "I imagine so."

"Well, Hotshot, tell me how you did it?"

"Hey, Rocky," Little John cut in, "give him a break."

"Shut up, Little John! I'm not talking to you." Rocky glared at Little John who gulped a little and then looked down at his shoes.

Looking back to Colin, Rocky said, "So, what are your plans, Army? What are you going to do?"

"I thought he could maybe hang around with us," interjected Little John.

Rocky looked over at Little John with an annoyed look that he had again opened his mouth.

Then looking back to Colin he said, "If you want to ride with us, you had better show some respect."

Colin said, "I think I'm going to be going. You coming, L.J.?"

Little John looked over at Rocky who nodded his head in the direction of Colin as if to say, "OK, go with him."

Colin and Little John left the office and the bar and walked out into the bright sun. Once outside and out of earshot, Colin said, "What an asshole!"

"Oh, he's OK," said Little John. "You just have to get used to him."

Colin was a little disappointed in his friend whom he had thought a tough and capable soldier. He seemed to be under the thumb of Rocky for whom Colin now had more than one reason to dislike. Colin thought to himself, "This is the kind of guy that needs to have his ass kicked," and he wondered if he'd have to be the one to do it.

Chapter 15

Colin suspected that the Honchos were engaged in some illegal activity in addition to their bar and mechanic enterprises but he didn't know for sure. As a result, he rationalized to himself that since he didn't know for sure if they were outlaws and since he did know for sure that *he* had not committed any crime, riding with them for the time being was okay. Deeper down, he knew he was asking for trouble, riding with outlaws, but he was just trying to kill some time and decompress from the army. He had no intention of committing crimes. He never really knew what they did because anytime they had a meeting or wanted to talk "business" he was excused. Still, from stray comments here and there he assumed that illegal drugs and illegal firearms might be what brought in revenue to supplement, no to outstrip, the revenue from the bar and the mechanic shop.

He got a job at a warehouse in order to earn a little spending money and sometimes after work he would go over to the Honchos clubhouse. A few of the guys were pretty decent to him but most of them ignored him. He tried to avoid Rocky because he always had something to say that was really an insult or a challenge and Colin didn't like being on the receiving end of either.

On weekends, sometimes they would all ride somewhere, sometimes they would hang around the clubhouse. A number of them had girlfriends and there were always one or two girls that hung around because they found the idea of an outlaw motorcycle club exciting. Sometimes they would have strippers entertain them on and off the tables that served as mini-stages.

Colin learned that his hanging around was entirely different than the stray girls that hung around. Although he did not realize it from the outset, he was informed that as a 'hang around" he was taking the first step toward club membership. Upon learning that, he thought about quitting immediately although he had never, in his mind, wanted to be a member in the first place. But he stayed on because he knew that he was sponsored by his friend Little John and he didn't want to make trouble for him.

One weekend in late August, 2014, the Club went for a ride out into the California desert. Colin went along because it was a nice day and he wanted to enjoy a ride. They rode out to a place where they had apparently been a number of times before. It was off the highway a little and there were a lot of boulders around that formed a little canyon, almost like a little fort. In the afternoon, the "canyon" provided shade on one side and bright sun on the other so everyone could take their pick.

On this particular day there were eleven of the Honchos and a few girlfriends and stray girls; with Colin there were eighteen in total. They had brought beer and some snacks and most were sitting in the shade and enjoying the clean air and the cold beer. It reminded Colin of a few times in Iraq when his unit was technically "off duty" but still had to be semi-alert but also were allowed to enjoy a beer or two. Colin was sitting by himself but near some full patch members when Rocky came over, put his foot up on a big rock and leaned over toward Colin and started in on him and his army service.

"So, Hotshot, you never did tell me about all those people you killed."

"I never said anything about killing 'all those people'; that's your description."

"But you did say you killed people, right? So, who were they?"

"I don't know. Most of the time the shooting was at a pretty good distance."

"So, how do you know if you ever killed anyone?"

Colin realized this was going nowhere so he didn't answer, hoping Rocky would tire of it and go away. But Rocky had an audience of members and girls and was just the kind of guy who enjoyed making other people uncomfortable.

"Little John tells me you a pretty good pistol shot. Is that true?

Colin wanted to just get up and walk away but he could feel everyone looking at him and, once again, he was concerned for Little John if he pushed back too hard.

"I'm okay," Colin finally answered.

"Well, let's see what you can do, Hotshot. Let's see if you're worth of that nickname. Give us a demonstration."

"Rocky, I really don't want to---"

Rocky cut him off. "Get your ass up here and give us a show or we're going to kick your ass and then we're going to kick Little John's ass for bringing us such a pussy."

Well, there it was—fight, run or comply. Not much choice with Colin against the rest. Reluctantly, he got up and walked over to where Rocky was now standing, brandishing a Glock 9mm. He had the girls take nine of the beer cans and set them up in the rocks but not in a nice, straight line. They put the cans at different heights and spaced several yard apart so that the nine cans in total were as much as thirty feet apart.

"Okay, Hotshot, let's see what you can do. Let's see how long it will take you to hit these beer cans and how many you miss."

Colin took the pistol and ejected the magazine and observed that there were nine rounds in the magazine. Rocky had given him just enough, no more. He pulled back the receiver and loaded a round into the chamber. The safety was built into the grip so that when gripped properly, the safety was off. He looked at the beer cans and noted their positions then he looked back at Rocky and gave him a short but intense stare as if to say, "Fuck you, asshole." Then, in a flash, Colin turned and crouched into a competition shooting stance and fired nine perfect shots, blowing away all nine beer cans within a couple of seconds. Colin heard a couple of the boys say "Holy Shit" and a couple more say of "Damn". He then stood straight, looked at Rocky with the same look of contempt, tossed him the gun and walked back to where he had been sitting, drinking his beer.

Rocky watched Colin walk back to his place and nodded his head with a little grin. "Not bad, Hotshot, not bad. We may have use for you yet."

Some of the guys that ordinarily ignored Colin came over and congratulated him on his skill and on the demonstration. Colin quietly said thanks but was really thinking how guys were always impressed with good shooters. What was it about boys and their gun toys? He had always been taught by Jerry that it was a tool to be used properly, not a toy and, hopefully, not a weapon. Obviously, the Honchos thought differently.

Colin knew he had to leave the Honchos sooner rather than later. He was more than familiar with Jerry's harsh code "Ride with and outlaw, die with him" and he knew it was only a matter of time before something bad would happen that he would be caught up in. Part of the problem in not leaving sooner was that every day made it just a little harder because there would be more resentment when he left; maybe retaliation on Little John.

In the meantime, he had heard from Julie and knew that she was pregnant and planning on moving back to the family ranch. He wondered how that was going. He and she had always been close even if they hadn't seen each other much over the past five or so years. He'd really like to see her and her baby which was due in a few months.

Chapter 16

It was getting late now in the summer of 2014 and it occurred to Jerry that he hadn't spent much time with his "adopted" son, Austin. So he headed out to the area he knew Elmer and his crew would be working that day. When he found them, he asked Elmer if he could borrow Austin for a couple of hours and Elmer, of course, said yes.

Jerry had ponied an extra horse that was carrying a couple of shovels and a couple of picks, water and other supplies. He and Austin set out for a spot a mile or so away where the cattle had trampled an irrigation ditch to the point that it was leaking even though the level of the water was pretty low. The job was pretty straight forward; dig out and re-shape the ditch so the water would flow through the ditch and not leak out. Jerry unlashed the picks and shovels, grabbed one of the picks and handed the other to Austin, and began to loosen the trampled earth that was in the middle of the ditch. Soon, they were both dripping with sweat and Jerry was the first to take a break.

"So, Austin, how's everything going? How are things with your family?"

"Everything's going pretty good, Mr. Johnston. Things with the family are okay."

"You know," Jerry replied, "you can call me Jerry."

"Oh, my dad wouldn't approve of that, Mr. Johnston," replied Austin. "He was a real stickler for showing respect for your elders; I mean for people older than you; I mean for those that should have your respect." Austin was tripping all over himself because he was afraid it sounded like he was calling Jerry old.

Jerry laughed, "That's okay, Austin, I am your elder and not afraid to admit it!"

Knowing that Austin had a somewhat negative feeling about his dad, Jerry said, "You see, your dad may have some issues but he sure brought you up right. Respect for elders would be a good thing for everyone in the country to practice."

"Yes, Sir," replied Austin.

They worked for a while in silence and once again the sweat began to flow freely. After a while Austin asked, "Mr. Johnston, can I ask you a question?

"Fire away," answered Jerry.

"Did you ever think about doing something else besides cattle ranching? I mean, I know this is your family ranch and all, but I was wondering if you always wanted to do this or if you thought about trying something else?"

Pausing to think and formulate his answer gave Jerry the opportunity to stop and wipe his sweaty brow. "I not only thought about it, I tried a couple of other things for a fairly short time and decided, for better or worse, that ranching is where I should be."

"Really?" queried Austin. "You actually did some other kind of work?"

"Sure did, "Jerry answered. "When I was about your age, I had the same kind of questions that you probably have. I wondered if raising cattle was what I wanted to do. Did I really want to work that hard all my life? Did I want to spend all my time in Montana? What about some big city somewhere were the girls were all pretty and, well, you know, shall we say more independent? Well, anyway, I didn't go far, never worked in a big city, but I went to Billings and worked at a kind of general store that sold ranch supplies. I started in the office helping the man who did the purchasing. I checked inventory, helped decide how much of something to order and did special orders and so on. This was before computers, remember."

"Did you like it?" asked Austin.

"Well, at first, I loved how easy it was physically. I was working seven-thirty to five- thirty which was a lot shorter than the hours on the ranch. And yet I got paid overtime for the hours over forty hours.

After about six months, I switched to selling feed and fencing and all kinds of outdoor ranch stuff. That was nice and I got paid a base salary and a commission so I was making even more money. I liked being outside more and not sitting at a desk. Things were going pretty good; there was even talk of me going to the corporate headquarters in Omaha."

"Wow," said Austin, somewhat wide-eyed. "So, what happened?"

"I'll tell you, but first tell me why you're asking?"

"Well, Mr. Johnston, I'm kind of thinking about whether ranching is what I want to do. I mean, there's a whole world out there and all I know is dealing' with a bunch of stinky cows. Maybe I should at least try somethin' else."

"That's what I thought," said Jerry. I'm sure as heck not going to tell you that you shouldn't try something else. I know a lot of people who say they wish they had tried to do this or had done that. You don't ever want to find yourself sayin' that."

"So what happened? If it was all going pretty good why didn't you stick with it?"

Again, Jerry stopped working and thought about his answer. He hadn't thought about this time in his life for a long time and it brought back a bunch of memories, good and bad.

"I guess there were two reasons. First, I found the work to be reasonably enjoyable but not particularly satisfying. It was pretty easy and I was making decent money but I was only working to make money. The work itself didn't give me any particular satisfaction. And the same was true for my co-workers. No one was there because their dream job was working at a store."

"Oh, I get it," said Austin, "that old thing about following your dreams."

"Yes," replied Jerry, "but I don't think everyone can do that. It's hard sometimes just to know what you want to do; but the real thing is sometimes life just gets in the way. Something happens and next thing you know you need to work, not pursue a dream you're not even sure about. And over time, that working for someone else, doing stuff day after day after day you're not particularly interested in can wear a man down a little each day; like the way a prairie wind will erode the land."

Austin pondered that for a moment. "So, you're sayin' you shouldn't necessarily follow your dreams?"

"Heck, no, I'm not saying that," Jerry answered. "I'm sayin' go ahead and follow your dreams if you truly know what they are. But for lot of people, their dreams don't have anything to do with what they do as much as what they want out of the rest of their life; work is just a means to that end; or they never know dreams, they only know real life.

I wouldn't exactly say that ranching was my dream; I'm not sure what my dream work would have been. But ranching was what I knew and I made a choice to stay with it because it makes me a better person, a better man."

Austin was completely puzzled. "How does it do that?"

Jerry chuckled a little. "Partly because of the culture of ranching and the people of the Mountain West and partly because of what you can't do out here that you can in the city. That gets into the second reason I quit the store. Near the end of my time I had a week's vacation coming to me and I went to New York City and spent the week there. I saw all the sights and all; did the whole tourist thing."

"Wow!" exclaimed Austin. You've been to the Big Apple! What was it like?"

"Well, that's the thing. Like I said, during the day, I did the tourist thing. At night, well at night, I found a few watering holes where the women were intrigued by seeing a real cowboy. It didn't take much to be able to hook up with someone almost every night. So, nearly every night was with some gal and drinkin' and, well, you know. A couple times I was offered drugs, one time was marijuana or and another time it was somethin' I didn't even know what it was. I stayed away from the drugs because I was scared of passing out and getting robbed."

Austin seemed impressed. "Man! Mr. Johnston, I had no idea you had done stuff like that!"

"Well, I might ask you to keep this all to yourself. No need to let the world know."

"Sure, no problem," said Austin. "But why did doin' that stuff make you want to go back to ranching?"

Well, the first few nights of raising hell were great although I kind of knew it was somehow a little wrong, more than a little self-indulgent."

"What does that mean?" asked Austin.

"It means being so focused on doing what you want, especially regarding pleasure."

Looking at the quizzical look on Austin's face, Jerry started to laugh. "I know, I know. You're thinkin' to yourself, 'What's wrong with that?' But have you ever eaten too much of something you really like and gotten so full or even sick that you didn't want to eat that food again for a while? That's the problem.

Then my dad called to check up on me and although I didn't tell him the specifics, I told him enough and we was arguing about it and he called me a hedonist. I had to go look it up. A hedonist is a person who believes that the most important thing in life is the pursuit of pleasure. At that moment, I just didn't see what the problem was.

But after a couple of more nights, I really started to question whether this was bringing out the best in me. I admit, I thought about what my dad would say had he known the details. But, more importantly, I just knew this would tear me down over time. It wasn't purely a choice between good and evil but it was kind of like that. I envisioned myself years down the road a fat old drunk that had been with a lot of women but either wasn't married or had a bad marriage. That man, me, would have not liked himself and would have been miserable. I didn't like that vision and so decided to go home, leave the store and come back to this ranch. I chose the harder way but, I thought, the better one. The city was made by man and was full of temptations; the ranch was spiritual, some even say divine."

Austin laughed just a little and said, "You kind of make it sound like a religion or something."

That made Jerry laugh. "Yeah, I guess it might sound that way; and although I wouldn't call it a religion, there is a religious element to it in the sense that you're choosing a way of life that isn't the easiest or the one where you make the most money. Instead, you're choosing a way that's good, a way that has some nobility to it precisely because it's not the easiest."

Austin leaned on his shovel and tried to process what he had heard. He felt like he had just listened to someone who spoke English but with a very heavy accent. He had heard all the words but they were a little foreign to him and the way he was used to thinking.

Finally, Austin asked, "So, what do you think I should do?"

"Ah," Jerry said while laughing, "that's for you to figure out. I can't do that for you. But I can tell you that you need to figure out what you want out of life, what kind of man you want to be and then go from there."

Austin stood still with his mouth open, pondering the enormity of these new questions.

"Come on," said Jerry, "lets' finish this ditch work so you can get back with your crew."

Chapter 17

Austin left to find his crew and Jerry went home and surprised the heck out of everyone, including himself, by deciding to take rest of the day off. After all, the cattle were well taken care of, the grass was still high, water had been good and, by golly, he just wanted to. The men on the crews took note because none of them could ever recall Jerry taking a time off except for some kind of emergency or a doctor's appointment for one of the kids or when he would go to Scottsdale to visit his dad or something like that. But to take time off just for the sake of it, well, that was new and different.

Jerry felt like, at least to some extent, his life was now new and different and he knew it was because of Jan. He wasn't about to think or believe that he was in love. It couldn't happen that quickly, could it? But he did know that she had had an effect on him that he hadn't expected. He wanted to change his routine today, wanted to let this unfamiliar feeling continue to develop. Most of all, he wanted to enjoy this little, positive buzz that he felt even if he didn't fully understand it. It had been a long time since he had felt any buzz except the generally worthless and temporary one from booze.

Added to all that was that his little chat with Austin had been a bit of a surprise to Jerry himself. Here he was saying all this stuff and he wasn't sure where it had come from. He had come up with some of those thoughts on the spot. He thought they were right and proper but wondered if he really believed them as much as he had made it sound to Austin. He started to think about his own life and how it stacked up to the one he had described to Austin when he heard the sound of someone coming into the kitchen.

Emily came in with a couple of sacks full of groceries and almost jumped when she saw Jerry sitting in his reading chair but not reading, just kind of staring.

"What are you doing here?" she said. "Are you okay?"

"I'm fine. I just decided to take half a day off."

"Lord Almighty, stop the presses!" shouted Emily. "What has gotten into you?"

"Can't a guy take some time off now and then?"

"Of course, but not you! You live in your work; you hide in your work. I can't remember you ever taking a day off just to have it off, so what is the reason for this?"

"No reason."

"It wouldn't have anything to do with that lady you've been dating, would it?"

"What makes you say that?"

"What do you think?"

"So I had a couple of dates. What's the big deal?"

"Is it a big deal?"

Jerry and Emily had been together too long for Jerry to be able to lie effectively to her. There was no romance and no sex but they knew each other almost as well as husband and wife. Jerry looked at Emily for a few seconds, not knowing how he would answer; not because he was trying to make something up but because he wasn't sure what the real answer was. Finally, he said, simply, "I don't know."

"Well, I'll be," said Emily softly.

She went over to the refrigerator and started to unload the groceries from the sacks. Jerry ambled in quietly and started to help her which was a new experience for her. She looked at him with a little smile on her face as if she was looking at her 12 year old son who had his first crush on a girl. Jerry smiled back, knowing that whatever Emily was thinking, she was a friend, someone he could trust.

"Well, tell me about her."

Jerry told Emily all about Jan, at least as much as he knew which he realized wasn't a whole lot. He talked about how they met and their date and what they talked about including his "ungrateful" kids. He mentioned that Jan didn't exactly seem to agree that his kids were ungrateful.

"Jerry, you've got three of the sharpest, sweetest, best kids a man could want. Just because they didn't want to come back here and be under your thumb the way you were with your dad and him before that doesn't make them ungrateful," Emily said, exasperated because she had made the same or similar speeches so many times before. "I'm not surprised that your lady friend didn't buy into your definition of ungrateful."

Jerry figured he might as well get it all out. "Also, she invited me to go to church and then breakfast but I told her that I didn't have much use for God but that I'd join her for breakfast. She, uh, took a pass."

"Oh, brother! Did you have to waive your 'I'm mad at God so I have no use for Him' flag at her the first date?"

"Well, it's the truth!"

"Well, that's the only thing that attitude has going for it. Maybe you need to rethink things just a bit."

Now Jerry did feel like he was twelve and had just been scolded by his older sister or something. Had he messed up? Were these fatal mistakes? He stood quietly trying to make the calculations. Emily saw the concern and softened her expression and her tone of voice became conciliatory.

"Well, don't worry about it. Most women are smart enough not to take everything a man says at face value. Heck, we tend to discount just about everything men say anyway."

"So you don't think my ideas about the kids and about God will be a problem?"

"I didn't say that. There's no way of me telling without having met the lady and without having been there. I'm just saying those thoughts probably didn't *automatically* kill the deal."

"Well, is it wrong to be truthful about those things?"

"Of course not; but first of all, you don't have to bring it up so early; give her a chance to get to know you a little before you start badmouthing your kids and the Good Lord. More important, however, is that you're wrong and stupid and stubborn on both counts."

"Okay, okay," said Jerry, holding up his hands. "Let's not get into that stuff now." Jerry paused for a few seconds and then said in a way that conveyed he was asking for Emily's help, "Em, I think I really like this lady. What should I do?"

Emily couldn't help but smile at Jerry's relative helplessness. It was so contrary to the way he had acted and had been all the years she had known him. Jerry—unsure? She was laughing on the inside but with him, not at him.

Out loud she said in a soft but firm voice, "Jerry, you're a good man and you have a lot going for you. Your decent looking, your belly doesn't hang over your belt"—she leaned over to take a closer look and was satisfied that there was no belly overhang—"you're in a good place financially and, aside from the two things we're not talking about, you've got good values. All you need to do is be yourself. Now I'm not sayin' that will guarantee success, but if you just be yourself and treat her right with proper attention, your chances are good."

"How aggressive should I be?"

"That's a tough one; women are all a little different in that regard." Thinking she might get some clue regarding the answer to his question, she asked, "What is it you like about her?"

"Well, the usual things. You know, she's good looking, not overweight, smart"—here Jerry paused trying to pin down even for himself what the source of attraction was; he thought about it for several seconds and finally continued—"and I guess the really unusual thing about her is how independent she seems. I mean, most of the women I know, women somewhere around my age, are, you know, kind of dependent. They want to lean on a man and have him be in charge. Jan's just got this air about her that kind of says, "I don't need anybody for anything. She seems totally capable and acts that way."

"There's your answer on how aggressive to be then," said Emily. If she's independent and not needy, take it slow. If you push too hard she probably won't like you being very aggressive.

"Do you think this is a little crazy at my age?"

Emily's shoulders slumped a little as she considered how lost she felt Jerry was and how much of life he had missed. "Jerry," she said in a very quiet, gentle, loving way, "I don't have any idea where this relationship is going. But that you would ask me if it's crazy at your age, at our age, to find someone special, to maybe fall in love, is more than a little sad to be honest. I've never tried to push too hard on why you didn't date after Jackie died or why you spend sixteen hours or seventeen hours a day working where there is so much more to life or why with all the women around here you didn't just once pick up the phone and call one. I figured that's your business. But you need to understand that life without love is like, I don't know, cake without the frosting. It's still good, but you're missing the best part. Only love can make you truly happy. How happy have you been for the last twenty-eight or nine years? You've been missing the best part! Hell no, I don't think this is crazy."

Jerry noted her use of the word "hell." That was about as rowdy as Miss Emily ever got.

He then said to her, "What about you? You've been content to be alone all these years."

Emily replied, "I wouldn't call it content; I've just accepted what God apparently had in store for me. I've never stopped looking. I've dated several men around here but it just didn't work out. But I tried and I still keep looking."

"Really? I had no idea that you ever dated anyone around here. Who were they?"

"Never you mind. Just know that I practice what I am preaching to you."

With that, she walked over to him and they hugged; they hugged for quite some time and Emily thought she felt Jerry's body jerk a little once or twice. Was he crying? No matter. Finally, they released one another and without a word, Emily headed toward her room. Just before she got to her door she heard, "Emily?" She turned around and Jerry had, indeed, been crying. "Thanks, Em."

She went through the door into her room and wished yet one more time that Jerry could somehow move beyond the aftermath of Jackie's death. He just seemed to be stuck in the past and Emily was dubious that would ever change.

Chapter 18

When Jerry returned from visiting his father, Joe, he called Jan and during their chat she asked him a question about the ranch. He suggested that she come over the next Saturday for a tour and then they could go to dinner.

So on Saturday, she came over around three o'clock in the afternoon. Jan had on jeans and a long-sleeved Western shirt. Jerry thought she looked great in the jeans. About the shirt, Jerry said, "I bet you bought that shirt in the last two weeks. I doubt they have those back in Illinois."

Jan just laughed and said, "You might be surprised, but you are correct, I did buy it recently. If I am going to live in ranch country I need to dress the part." This pleased Jerry.

Jerry decided to use an ATV to get around because he wasn't sure if Jan was comfortable riding a horse and because they could cover more ground using the ATV. First, though, he showed her the main ranch house which was old in age but modern in terms of fixtures and convenience. Emily was there and Jerry introduced them to each other.

Jan said, "It's very nice to meet you, Emily. Jerry tells me that he couldn't get along without you."

"Really," said Emily. "Funny but I never quite pick that up from what Jerry says to me," she said with a sidelong glance at Jerry. "So, I gather you have moved here, how do you like it?"

"So far, very much," Jan answered. "Part of what I like is how nice everyone is. You must be exceptional to have been with Jerry all these years." She and Emily continued to chat while Jerry just sat back and observed. He could tell that Emily liked Jan right away which surprised Jerry just a little. Emily was usually a little slower to warm up to people.

Then Jan and Jerry headed out to see the ranch and find the herd. It took a while to get out where the herd was so along the way, they talked about her move and the town but avoided the children and religion.

When they got to the herd, Jerry introduced her to Cooper and the other hands that were close by. Cooper got down from his horse, took off his cowboy hat and said, "Howdy, Ma'am; very nice to meet you."

Jan replied, "Well, thank you; it's nice to meet you, too. Jerry tells me that you're his top hand, that you're really important to the ranch."

At this, Cooper blushed a little and just said with a shy smile, "Well, I don't know about that."

"And he also tells me that your father is a doctor and wanted you to be one as well but that you decided that you'd rather work in ranching. Is that right?"

"Well, yes, Ma'am," answered Cooper, glancing over at Jerry.

Jan continued, "Tell me why you made that choice; I'd love to know."

Cooper said, "Well, it's kinda hard to explain to someone who hasn't lived the life. There's just a feelin' about it that beats just about anything I know. Every day I go to bed tired but content and I sleep like a baby. It's my impression that people that work in an office in a big city don't experience that. I do and I love it."

Jan smiled a big smile and simply nodded. She continued chatting with Cooper and the other boys and Jerry just kept quiet and observed. He knew his crew and was a little shocked at how easily she interacted with them and how they seemed drawn to her.

He realized he was falling in love with her. Actually, he thought, he was in love with her but was just now coming to grips with it. It had been relatively quick but there was no doubt in his mind.

They continued looking at more of the ranch but eventually headed home for dinner. Jerry was enveloped in this long forgotten feeling of being in love. He felt good but also nervous.

When you love someone, if it doesn't work out or something goes wrong, there can be pain.

Jan eventually said, "You're awfully quiet. What are you thinking about?"

"Nothing," answered Jerry, not wanting to give a hint of what he was thinking. "Just wondering what's for dinner."

At dinner, Jan commented that Jerry had mentioned something about weaning calves and she asked how they did that.

Jerry laughed. "Well, like everything else about cattle ranching, you can get about ten different answers from ten people and they'll all be sure that their way is best. We like to wean'em as early as possible so that the nutritional content of the pasture grass is still good. The first consideration in weaning is the cow, not the calf. You want'em to be able to put weight back on so they get ready to be bred back and so that they're ready for winter."

Jan asked a question in the form of a statement. "With all the pasture, it wouldn't seem like it's hard for them to put weight on."

Jerry replied, "Lactation really puts nutritional stress on a cow. They need more feed and more protein than any other time—even when their pregnant. They will lose weight as the grass has less nutrition. That means you either have to supplement their feed or let them be thin which puts their next calf crop at some risk of being thin themselves."

Jan was impressed with how Jerry seemed to be thinking in terms of the animals' needs. She noted how he loved to talk about his ranch and the business of ranching; really anything connected with ranching. There was something about his devotion to it all that she found very compelling.

"So how is the weaning actually accomplished?" she asked.

"There's a bunch of different ways you can do it," Jerry replied. "There's natural weaning where the cow kicks off last year's calf just before she drops a new one. I don't think that's a good way. Then there's corral weaning where you put'em in a corral by themselves. Problem with that it's stressful for the calves and, believe it or not, that can lead to health and other problems. Pasture weaning is better but you still have some of the same problems. Fence line weaning is pretty good. You put the moms on one side and the kids on the other so that they can see and smell one another but the calves can't nurse. We usually do a lot of fence line weaning."

"This year, we've been trying something a little new. It's called nose flap weaning. You run the calves through a chute which is good 'cause then you can give them some booster shots. Then, you stick this stick this flap on'em and it hangs over their nose and mouth. They can't nurse but they can eat and drink. So far, we think it works pretty well."

"Whew," said Jan, "I didn't realize it was so complicated. It seems from the outside like ranching is a simple thing with simple animals but I guess that isn't so."

"No, indeed, it's a lot more complicated than most people think."

Jan looked at Jerry and was trying to get a handle on what her feelings for him were. She more than liked him but to what degree? She really didn't want to think about that. So, after more than a few moments of silence, she asked, "So, have you heard from your children at all?"

"No," answered Jerry.

Jan hoped he might say more or amplify his answer in some way but Jerry just looked into his water glass and stayed silent.

Jan was a little disappointed but didn't show it. When dinner was done, Jan said it was late and she needed to head home. She gave Jerry a simple kiss and thanked him for the tour and the dinner and drove off.

Jan and Jerry courted this way for much of the rest of the summer. She would sometimes stay with him at the ranch. They were good with each other and fit together well. They each had fallen in love—Jerry knew it, Jan knew it subconsciously but wouldn't admit it. They talked about so many things and generally agreed on all things except his relationship with his kids and his attitude toward God and religion.

Jerry thought he knew where things were headed. Jan wasn't so sure.

Chapter 19

Jerry and his crews were working on fattening up the calves for sale. The market prices were pretty good in the fall of 2014 and it looked to be a banner year for the Johnston Ranch. The only fly in the ointment, or maybe it was something worse than a mere fly, was that the food company who for so many years had bought the Johnston Ranch cattle on a handshake notified Jerry that this would be the last year they could continue that arrangement. Apparently, they had had trouble with some new government regulations, had had some fines over some technical matters and were revamping everything from top to bottom in the hopes of getting the government regulators in Washington off its back.

Jerry's only concern was that it had been so long since he had had to sell anything, he wasn't sure how it was done in this day and age of social media, websites and all the stuff that he was vaguely familiar with but not knowledgeable about. But there was time to worry about that next year. For this year, the usual deal was in effect and that meant getting the calves fattened up and ready for sale.

One day in September, Jerry was riding with Elmer's crew and he saw Austin riding over to where Jerry was looking things over. "Mr. Johnston, can I speak with you a minute?" he asked.

"Anytime," answered Jerry. "What's on your mind?"

"Well, you remember that conversation we had a while ago about doing somethin' other than ranching?"

"Sure do," answered Jerry.

"Well, I think I am going to do what you did and try something else just to see what it's like."

"What are you going to do, Austin?"

"The family of a friend of mine from college has an insurance brokerage and he said they are always looking for good, new salesmen. He says I only have to work five days a week, no weekends; my hours are nine to five with an hour for lunch; and I'll make more than I do working here."

"That all sounds pretty good," answered Jerry. What do you think about selling insurance?"

Austin hesitated and then said, "Well, I don't really know but I guess I am willing to give it a try. I mean, how bad can it be if it has all those other advantages."

"Where's this outfit located?" asked Jerry.

"San Francisco. I guess I'll get my taste of the big city, see what it's like. Tomorrow will be my last day here, so I just want to say thanks for everything. I really appreciate all your advice and help."

"We'll miss you, Austin," Jerry replied. "You stay in touch; and, if things don't work out, there'll always be a place for you here."

"I appreciate that, Mr. Johnston. Thanks a lot." With that, Austin rode off. As Jerry watched him, he felt a little bit of emotion, a little sadness that he hadn't expected. In a way, he was glad that Austin was courageous enough to try something different; but he also hoped that Austin wouldn't like it. Either way, he realized that he would miss him.

Chapter 20

His sense of loss was soon compensated for by the arrival of his daughter. One day, out of the blue, Julie showed up. Out of the blue might be overstating her arrival since it was known that she was coming; but she gave no warning that she was coming on a particular day. Jerry came in from work and she had already moved into her old room and was in the kitchen talking with Emily. Of course, Jerry saw immediately that she was pregnant. He also saw her as a grown woman for perhaps the first time. She hadn't been his little girl for some time. And even though there had been visits within the past couple of years, this time Jerry saw her differently, as a woman beyond his ability to order around as he once might have.

She saw his jaws tense just a bit and there was a brief hesitation, then, "Hello, Sweetie, how are you?" And he walked over and gave her a kiss on the cheek and a big hug. Julie was shocked at how good the hug felt. She held on for a little longer than either was expecting, long enough for one little tear to roll down her cheek. When they released one another, she wiped the tear away and to show it didn't mean weakness said, "I'm fine, Daddy, and, as you can see, six months pregnant." Julie figured she might as well get right to it.

"Yes, I see." Pause. "Well is there a father I'm going to meet? Has there been or will there be a wedding? Or did one of your liberal girlfriends convince you to try artificial insemination?" Jerry said just a little sardonically.

"Oh for heaven's sake," said Emily.

"Well, anything's possible in this day and age."

Looking at Emily, Julie said, "I guess not much has changed, huh?"

Emily threw her hands up in the air, shook her head, turned and walked out.

Looking back to Jerry she said, "No, Daddy, it wasn't artificial insemination; there is a father but there will be no wedding and you won't meet him. I really don't want him in my life."

"Well, who is he?"

Julie hesitated, wondering if she should get into the detail with her father, not sure what he might do when all she wanted was to leave everything back East back East. Finally, she said, "Daddy, if you'll promise to not interfere, to not try and do anything, to not call anyone, I'll tell you whatever you want to know. But I want to put it all behind me and I won't be able to do that if you start making a ruckus."

Jerry looked at Julie long and hard and was again amazed at how much more grown up she seemed, not just physically but especially in how she talked, than even the last time she had visited the previous Christmas.

"Okay, I promise."

So Julie told her dad the whole story, told him about Tom Sanders and CSC and how she didn't like it too much and how she got pregnant. As she talked, Jerry considered that, all things considered, she hadn't acted so badly. He wasn't concerned about Julie's attitude toward premarital sex; even Jerry understood that times were different, *very* different than when he was growing up. He kept hoping she might say something about coming back to the ranch permanently but she didn't and he wasn't about to bring it up. He stubbornly clung to the notion that she should ask him.

"So what do you want to do?" he asked, hoping that maybe she would say something now about the long term.

"Well, Julie said just a little hesitantly, "if it's okay with you, I'd like to stay here long enough to have my baby and to figure out what I'm going to do next. Right now, I have no idea what that might be. I'm due in just a few months and I'm really focused on that."

"Of course it's okay with me," Jerry replied, thinking that at least she'll be here a few months. It wasn't exactly what he wanted. After all, she had come home because of her being pregnant, not as a return to the ranch as a long-term home, and she even indicated that it wouldn't be permanent. But he was happy nonetheless.

"Thanks, Daddy." Then, after a little pause and with a twinkle in her eye, Julie said, "Emily tells me that you've been seeing a lady, a lady named Jan." Julie had just a hint of a grin showing at the corners of her mouth because she was certain that her dad would be a little uncomfortable about the topic and anytime he was a little uncomfortable in front of his kids was entertaining.

"Seems like everyone thinks it's important to announce that news to anyone they can and as soon as they can. But, yes, I have been seeing her and I like her a lot. In fact, she's coming over here for dinner this Saturday."

"Well, how serious is this?" asked Julie, again with just a little grin.

"Young lady, you just worry about your baby and I'll take care of my relationships," he said somewhat seriously but then showed a little grin himself. "Now, I've got a couple more things to do before dinner so let me get to them and I'll see you at dinner."

The next day, Julie phoned a doctor, a general practitioner that Emily recommended to get set up for general health purposes down the road and to get a referral to an OB/GYN her immediate care. The OB/GYN was a woman named Marilyn Hollande. Julie was pleased that she could have a woman as her doctor. Interestingly, Dr. Hollande's nurse was a man, a young man whose name badge said Smith. She noticed that he was quite good looking but also seemed to be on the quiet side. She wondered about having a male nurse but assumed that Dr. Hollande must have it all figured out. Probably, the nurse did the routine stuff and the doctor did the more intimate work. Anyway, she wasn't going to worry about it now.

Saturday came and Julie went with Emily in to town to do some grocery and other shopping. Julie was a little surprised at all the changes in Livingston in just a few short years. There were new stores and some of the streets had been widened and there was a new municipal parking garage. When they went into the stores, the clerks said hello and asked if they could help with anything. Julie had forgotten what friendly customer service was.

Emily and Julie came home in the late afternoon with four bags full of groceries. They put them on the kitchen counter and, as they were unloading the bags and starting to put things either in the refrigerator or the pantry, Julie asked "So what's this Jan, um, what's her name like? Do you like her?"

Emily laughed and said, "No way, I'm not going there. You're going to have to make up your own mind about Ms. Jan Martino."

"Hmm, Martino, eh? Well, the suspense is going to kill me," Julie responded with a chuckle. "What kind of women would appeal to Dad after all these years?" Julie queried to no one in particular.

"Does it bother you that your dad is dating someone?"

"Heck no," answered. "I wish he had done it years ago. Maybe he wouldn't have been such a problem all these years."

"Now, Julie, your dad's a good man. It was rough on him when your mom died."

"I know. I was there, remember? I mean I may have been a toddler but I felt it."

Emily tried to be diplomatic. "I know he didn't do everything right, but I know he tried. It was just so hard because he loved your mom very much."

"I know, I know," Julie said wearily as if to say 'Spare me the excuses.' "I've heard it all before. It was rough on him but it was rough on us, too." Julie went quiet for a time, thinking about that few years after her mom had died.

"Well," said Emily, "I've never had to go through such a thing so it's hard for me to know what to think. Anyway, you go get ready and I'll finish up here. When you're ready, maybe you can set the table."

"Sure thing," said Julie and she went off to clean up and change.

Promptly at 6:30 the doorbell rang and Julie went to the front door and opened it. There stood Jan with flowers in one hand and a bottle of wine in the other and a big smile on her face. "Hi," she said enthusiastically, "you must be Julie."

"Yes I am," Julie answered, "and you must be Jan." Julie started to put her hand out to shake hands and then realized that both of Jan's were full and so a handshake was impossible. She pulled her hand back and both ladies laughed, not awkwardly but warmly. "Come on in."

Jan came in and walked right to the kitchen. Obviously, she's been here before, thought Julie. After Julie put the flowers in a vase and Jan put the wine on the counter, Jan and Julie sat down in the living room.

Jan said, "I'm so happy to get to meet you. Jerry's not the most talkative guy when it comes to his kids and getting information out of him is like pulling teeth. I hope we'll have a little time before dinner so that we can get acquainted."

"Ha-ha," Julie laughed. "I'm surprised Dad's even told you he has children. You must know that he's not particularly happy with us."

"Oh?" I get the impression that Jerry loves you all very much. I do know he wishes you were here at the ranch instead of, where was it? Washington D.C"

"Yes. And that well, that may be true, but it's hard to tell sometimes. And though he hasn't said anything, I know he's not happy about this," she said, putting her hand on her swollen belly.

"Is there some reason he shouldn't be happy?"

"Well, I'm not getting married to the father and, in fact, I don't want the father around at all; so I'm going to be a single mom, I don't have a job, and I'm not sure what I'm going to do after I have the baby. That's probably not the formula Dad would draw up for me."

"If he hasn't said anything, how do you know what he's thinking?"

"Experience. I generally know what he thinks."

"Well, I'm still working on that skill. I've only known Jerry for a few months and, as I say, he's not very talkative in some areas; of course in others he'll talk you ear off."

"Like politics?"

"Yes," answered Jan and, again both of them laughed. The laughter was not nervous laughter but a kind of bonding laugh where each side begins to sense that there is common ground and so potential for friendship.

Dinner was ready and everyone helped get everything on the table. Even Jerry, who normally didn't do much in the kitchen, was on good behavior and filled the water glasses. Emily joined the three of them at dinner so it was Jerry against the three ladies. They had great fun at his expense. Julie talked about her time at CSC and what she did and some of the people she met and interacted with. Emily and Jan seemed somewhat impressed as people always are when you can drop a name or two that people recognize. In Julie's case, she wasn't name dropping, though. She was just telling them the straight dope and that included some recognizable names. Julie also described the highlights or, rather, the lowlights, of her relationship with Tom Sanders. Very briefly, she recounted the circumstances which led to her pregnancy.

Jerry remarked, "He sounds like a first class jerk to me; but Emily, let's make sure there's no Champagne in the house."

Julie stuck out her tongue at Jerry; Emily and Jan rolled their eyes.

"Well?" said Jerry.

The rest of the dinner conversation was about current events and a little about the ranch. With each utterance out of Jan, Julie felt she liked her and that Jan was a good person. We might become good friends, she thought.

Then, Jerry spoke up. "Oh, there's something I forgot to tell you. The company that has bought our cattle on a handshake for I don't know how many years has told me that they can't do that anymore. They're having some problems with government regulators over something and, well, they just said they can't do it anymore after this year. So, I guess I'll have to bone up on sales and marketing and all that stuff."

Julie asked, "Do we have a website, Daddy?"

"Nope; never needed one."

Julie said, "Maybe I can help."

"Sounds good to me," said Jerry. "Sales was never my strong suit."

Jerry got up and said, "Would you ladies excuse me for a minute? I need to check on one of my horses. I'll be back in a few minutes."

Emily then got up and started clearing the dishes and when Jan and Julie started to get up as well said, "You two just stay put. I'll take care of this."

Julie was glad to have a little time alone with Jan. She had formed a good first impression of Jan but it was just that. She decided to explore the pre-dinner conversation a little more and see if there was common ground. So she asked, "Do you mind if I ask what *you* think of my situation? I hope you won't mind my pointing out that you are of my dad's generation and I'd be interested in your point of view. It might help me with him. Please be candid."

"Well," Jan answered, "if you're asking if I am making any judgments, particularly negative judgments about your situation, the answer is "No." First of all, I generally don't judge women at all. After all, we have to put up with the male of the species and that's enough to make any woman behave in ways she didn't intend." Again, they both laughed, this time the sisterhood laugh. "Second, I don't know the details of how you became pregnant so I'm in no position to reach any conclusions. And third, even though I am, as you put it, of your father's generation, I've been single for many years and for a time was, shall we say, romantically active. So at least for a number of years, though not now, I could have found myself in the same situation as you. No, Julie, to me, life is too short to judge good people for an occasional mistake, even a big one, if that's what this is. No, I'd like to reserve my judgments for those who are bad, who are evil, and who hurt people."

Julie smiled and decided at that moment that she liked Jan.

Just then Jerry came back and said, "Well, did I miss anything?"

Jan and Julie looked at one another and laughed and said in unison "No!" while acting like they had a secret.

"Well," Jan said, "it's getting late and I am going to early Mass tomorrow so I need to get going. Thanks you all for a very nice evening."

Jerry might have protested but he was already yawning. He and Julie walked Jan to the door and said goodnight. As Jerry went to his bedroom, Julie went out the front door and trotted a few steps to catch up with Jan. "I just wanted to say how much I enjoyed meeting you," said Julie.

"Oh heavens, me, too."

"Maybe we could have coffee or something sometime?"

"I'd like that very much," Jan said warmly. "Let's make a point to do it."

"Wonderful," said Julie. "Good night."

Good night, Julie."

Chapter 21

One evening in the late summer of 2014, Michelle and Ryan were out to dinner at the restaurant Tuscany and Ryan was railing about the media and bemoaning the bias in his own profession. Michelle said, "Honey, why don't you think about quitting?"

Ryan looked at her like she was a mind reader and said, "Actually, I have been thinking about it. But where would I go? What would I do? Broadcast journalism is the only thing I know."

"There is one other thing, or, really two," Michelle said.

"Like what?"

"Well," she said very mischievously, "I can think of one thing you apparently know that you showed me last night."

Ryan immediately smiled as he recalled a night of particular passion they had enjoyed the previous night.

"Okay," he said, "but I don't think I could make a living out of that."

"Oh, I think you could." Then she quickly changed her expression and tone to a more serious and business-like tone, "But I wouldn't want you to."

"So, what's the second thing?"

"Didn't you tell me that you knew a fair amount about cattle ranching?"

"Yeah, but that would require me to go home and ask my dad to take me back and I'm not ready to do that."

Michelle said, "So, what's the answer?"

Ryan reached across the table and took both of Michelle's hands and held them. They looked intently at each other, searching for some solution to the difficult problem.

Finally, Michelle said with a little burst of enthusiasm, "Well, you could quit and I could support you."

Ryan smiled appreciatively. "For how long? I mean, we couldn't do that for a long time; so the issue is, if I were to quit this great job that I have, what would I do then?"

Michelle laughed and then said jokingly but only half joking, "Well, if we got married, I could support you forever. I make pretty decent money."

She and Ryan had talked about getting married; actually the proposal had been made and accepted. The hang-up was Ryan because he was uncertain about his future. He didn't want to get married and then in a short time want to quit without a replacement job lined up. Quitting his profession early in their marriage would not be good. Wanting to quit but being married would be worse. So, for the time being, he pleaded with Michelle for patience. He assured her this job thing was the only issue, nothing to do with them.

Michelle didn't fully understand Ryan's thinking. To her, it was mainly male pride. The important thing was being together, to be married and together. A job was just a way to pay the bills. Heck, they could live anywhere and he could dig ditches and she could do dishes and she'd be happy because they'd be together. But men saw things differently and she would just have to bide her time.

Of course, Michelle had her own issues, too. It was true that she made a pretty good salary and bonus but she really didn't like her job. After doing it for a number of years, she found selling pharmaceutical drugs to be boring. She had to constantly cater to busy, often cranky nurses, receptionists, physician's assistants and others whose main job it seemed to her was to keep her away from the doctors who were her real customers. Her days started early, trying to get in before the first patients consumed the doctors' time; and they ended late, trying to get in a pitch while the doctor was still there but usually distracted by the many things he or she had to do. The city was often tough to get around with traffic snarls and then of course parking was always an issue. Lunch? Forgetabout it.

On the home front, she had moved in with Ryan and had even let the lease on her own apartment lapse. She was committed and believed he was as well. But the clock was ticking; he was thirty-five and she was thirty-two. There was plenty of time to have several children, which was her wish, but it seemed like yesterday that she hit the magic thirtieth birthday. Though it made no absolutely sense, she began to feel like forty was just around the corner.

So Michelle and Ryan each plodded through each day, each week, each month, waiting for some game-changer that never seemed to occur. Ryan explored a few things. Maybe he could teach? But he had to admit that teaching just didn't appeal to him. He looked at going back to school for a new career but nothing really appealed to him. So, he just kept on doing TV news where he was highly regarded.

In the previous October, Ryan had marveled at the disastrous launch of Obamacare. How many years and how many hundreds of millions of dollars spent to create a working website and then to have such a clusterfuck as the result? This time, there was plenty of coverage and it was pretty negative. But, Ryan thought, even now it's not the gleeful pounding that Bush took when things went badly for him. It wasn't the relentless insinuation of malfeasance. It was merely poor management. The coverage of Obamacare was negative but what else could it be? Even the press couldn't make a silk purse out of this sow's ear.

By the end of October of this year, Ryan had decided to use one of his vacation weeks to go home and visit Julie. It had been some time since he had seen her and, if the price of seeing his sister was to put up with his dad for a week, well, he'd just have to do it. He called Jerry and said he's like to come and visit, he didn't add the word "Julie" after the word visit, and asked if that would be okay. His dad said "Sure, that's fine" in what to Ryan's ears sounded like agreeing on an appointment time with the dentist. Nevertheless, the visit was now set.

When he told Michelle, he knew that she would want to come as well; she had told him several times that she would love to see the family ranch. But he just didn't feel the time was right. "Look," he said, "I don't know what it's going to be like. Especially with Julie being pregnant, I don't want to make things more complicated than they have to be. I'm only going to be there for a two or three days and then I'll be back and we'll make some decisions, okay?"

Michelle wasn't happy but she nodded her head.

So one day in early November, Ryan took a couple of planes to Livingston and then picked up a rental car to drive to the ranch. He didn't want to get picked up because he wanted a vehicle to escape the ranch if that became necessary. When he got to the main house, Jerry had just come in from the field and was talking with Julie and Emily in the kitchen. To Ryan's surprise, Jerry gave him a warm hug and said "Welcome home, Son." That's all it took for Julie and Emily; there were hugs and even a few tears.

After they settled down they all sat down and, with a bit of a crooked grin and as only an older brother could, Ryan asked, "So, what the hell happened, Little Sister? Didn't those sorority girls at MSU teach you anything?"

"Very funny," Julie replied, knowing that Ryan was just teasing her.

She told him the whole story and when she was done, his focus was more on her job and the people and that she essentially "spun" the truth for a living as opposed to her pregnancy, although he didn't say anything. Nevertheless, she seemed to read his mind.

"It wasn't a pretty job in many ways. But in the beginning it was so exciting to be around such powerful people; it made me feel important and like I could make a difference. But, in the end, it was dirty and I'm glad to be out of it."

"So, what are you going to do after you have the baby? By the way, do you know whether it's a girl or boy?"

It's a boy," Julie answered and I have no idea. I'll stay here for a while. I'm going to help Daddy with marketing, websites and that kind of stuff. But enough about me; what's going on with you? When are you and Michelle going to get married?"

"Well," Ryan said with a big sigh, "that's a long story." Ryan proceeded to tell them all about his frustrations with the media and his uncertainty about his future. "You should read a book I read on the way out here by Sheryl Atkinson called "Stonewalled" and then there's a subtitle about obstruction and other bad stuff in Washington. She was a reporter for many years including for CBS News. She's won a bunch of awards. And she basically confirms all my fears about liberal media bias all the way to the top of the networks, government lying and obstruction and the media's covering it up, and about the government hacking into her computers. I mean, it's really frightening. Anyway, I think I may need to find something else to do. This isn't what I was taught in journalism school."

They all pondered what Ryan said for a few moments after which Julie broke the silence.

"So, what about you and Michelle?

"Well, we have basically agreed to get married but I'm holding off until my future is a little more certain."

At this, Julie erupted and exclaimed, "You big jerk! You're going to make the love of your life wait because of uncertainty? Brother, life itself is nothing but uncertainty. You need to quit worrying about jobs and careers and do the deed before she decides to move on."

"I'm pretty confident that that won't happen; and, trust me, I don't want to wait much longer and I know damn well that she doesn't want to either. Whoops! Sorry, Emily, I didn't mean to use the "d" word."

"That's okay," said Emily, "but your sister is right."

Ryan pondered the situation for a bit.

Julie said, "I'd love to meet the woman that snared my big brother. Why don't you have her come out and spend a few days while you're here? She can see the ranch and meet everybody and we can all give you our opinion." Julie chuckled a little at the end.

Also laughing, Ryan said, "Thanks but no thanks on your opinions but it's true she really wants to come out. In fact we talked about it but I thought I would only be here for a few days. Maybe I'll take a little more vacation, have her come out and really try and relax a little. I'd sure love to get some riding in."

Ryan never even thought about asking his dad because whatever else, Jerry loved having people around. So Ryan called his boss and said he'd like to take an extra week which was no problem; he had plenty of vacation time accrued. Then he called Michelle and left her a message asking if she wanted to come for a visit even though he already knew the answer. She called a little later and was thrilled with Ryan's invitation.

"I had to tell my boss that there was a bit of a family emergency," she said, "and that's kind of true. Anyway, I don't care. I'll be out on Thursday. Can you pick me up?"

Ryan picked Michelle up on Thursday and during the drive to the ranch, Michelle was just gushing about how beautiful it was. He said, "You haven't seen anything, yet."

There are beautiful places all over the world and the U.S.A. has its fair share of them. For whatever reason, people are drawn to different types of physical environments. Some people love water and beaches. Some love wide open spaces. And some people love the mountains. The Johnstons all loved the mountains and Michelle was about to join the club.

The mountains in the American West are so jaw-droppingly beautiful that one never gets tired of looking at them. And actually living in them creates a spiritual feeling that strongly implies a supernatural being. They aren't by any means the biggest or tallest mountains in the world but they were certainly among the prettiest. They change every day in small ways and every season in major ways.

The air is very clear because of little pollution and because the elevation makes the air thinner. As a result, the colors are more vivid; they are like the jump from standard TV to high definition TV. On a clear day, the sky is a deep, rich blue and in the mornings there may not be a cloud anywhere. The mountains themselves are a blend of light and darker greens. If there has been an early snow at the higher elevations, a dazzling white blanket covers the top. And, the best is when, in October, the aspen trees turn a brilliant gold and the scrub oak turn a rusty orange and red. The resulting, very vivid Joseph's coat is enough to make one drop to their knees.

Michelle was drinking all this in as they drove to the ranch. She had been so happy to see Ryan but was now totally distracted by the divine artist's canvas which stretched before her. She had only been in Montana for a few minutes but she was already wondering why she had lived in the big city all her life. What had she missed? She was totally consumed by the environment that she wasn't able to focus on what Ryan had just said. Finally, trying to concentrate, she said, "What, Honey?"

Ryan laughed and said, "Did I lose you there? I said 'I'm sorry but we have to go back. I was supposed to stop at the grocery store.'"

"Okay, fine," and she fell back into her semi stupor.

Ryan and she went into the grocery store and he quickly got the items that Emily had requested. Michelle noted that the clerk was helpful and smiled, something she wasn't really used to.

Finally, they got to the ranch house and that sealed the deal. To her, it was a little slice of heaven. She wanted to drink it in so much that she sat in the car for several moments causing Ryan to laugh and tell her, "Come on!" Getting out, she took a deep breath and savored the fresh air like an oenophile sampling a great wine. She listened for several seconds to the silence and was astounded; there's no such thing in the city. The silence wasn't a nothing, some void; it was a real note, with a sound but different from every other kind of sound. Michelle was overwhelmed and felt like she was ten years old.

Inside the spacious ranch house, she met Emily and Julie. Like women so often do, even as strangers, they all hugged as if they were family but then said, paradoxically, "It so nice to finally meet you both. I've heard so much about you."

"I'm afraid Ryan has been pretty taciturn about you," Julie said with a cross-wise glance at Ryan. "So, what do you do back in Chicago? How did you guys meet? Is this your first time out west?"

"Yes, it's my first time west of Iowa, actually."

"Well, what do you think so far?"

Michelle took a breath as if to speak and then couldn't find the words. Finally, she said just that. "Oh my gosh! I just can't find the words to tell you how beautiful everything is. You think tall buildings made by man are impressive and then you come out here and, oh my, the mountains and the colors and, well, I just love it so far."

"Well," said Emily, it's a little different in winter; but even though I've been out here for some twenty-seven years, I never get tired of the beauty."

Looking at Julie, Ryan said, "Maybe you can do a download about that other stuff tonight." Then, turning to Michelle he said, "There's still a little time before dinner. Would you like to see a little of the ranch?"

"Oh, yes," she said. "Let me change and I'll be ready in a sec."

For the next couple of hours Ryan showed Michelle some of the property and facilities that were reasonably close to the ranch house. As they were coming back in for dinner, they ran into Jerry who was just coming in himself.

"Hi, Dad,"

"Hello, Son," Jerry replied.

"Dad, this is my girlfriend, Michelle. Michelle, this is my dad, Jerry."

Michelle said, "It's so nice to meet you. I've heard so much about you."

Jerry hooted just a bit and said, "I bet you have. Well, it's my honor to meet you, Ma'am."

At dinner there was lots of family kidding, mostly between Ryan and Julie with a little of Emily in the mix. Michelle was too new to either have much ammunition or to make fun of on such short acquaintance. Jerry was mostly quiet during dinner, studying Ryan, noting the changes since they had last seen one another. Afterward, Michelle helped with the dishes and the bonds of female companionship were formed.

Sleeping arrangements hadn't been discussed but Ryan said that he and Michelle lived together in Chicago and that wasn't going to change in Montana. Jerry was a little troubled by having two people not married in one bedroom in his house but was too tired to argue over it so he just kept quiet.

The next day, Ryan saddled up a couple of horses including one he was assured was the most gentle of the remuda, the herd of horses. He brought water, a couple of sack lunches and wore his pistol. The back country is just that and sometimes the only thing that might save your life is being armed. On horseback, even at a walk, they were able to cover more than twice as much ground as they could on foot. They spent most of the day riding from one beautiful canyon or valley to another. Michelle was a trooper, if she was stiff or sore anywhere, she wouldn't admit it.

Saturday they looked around a little more and then went into town in the afternoon. Ryan had to do a little more grocery shopping for Emily since they were having another big family dinner. Jan was coming over for dinner as she had been for a number of weeks. Jan protested that the entertaining was all one sided and that she should have them over some time but neither Jerry nor Emily would hear of it.

Promptly at 6:30 the doorbell rang and it was Jan. She came in and gave a kiss on the cheek to Jerry and hugs to Emily and Julie. Then she and Ryan and Michelle were introduced to one another. Jan turned to Jerry and said, "Jerry, this young man is so good looking. Are you sure he's yours?"

Ryan was pleased to see that Jan was willing to tease his dad and wasn't, apparently, a 'Whatever you say, Dear' type.

To Michelle, Jan said, "Michelle, you and Julie make a pair of gorgeous young women. It's going to take all my will power to keep from being supremely jealous." There were smiles all around.

During dinner, Ryan and Michelle became more acquainted with Jan. Michelle gushed about how beautiful she found everything. Jan replied that she had had the same reaction on her first visit. "All the locals say 'Yeah, let's see what you say when winter comes.'"

Michelle said, "So, I know you teach school here. What do you do on weekends?"

"Well, Saturdays during the day I grade papers or do lesson plans for the following week. Saturday night, I either mooch off of Jerry and Emily or sometimes get Jerry to take me on a hike." Everyone laughed except Jerry who cracked a bit of a grin and shook his head but remained quiet.

"On Sundays, I go to Mass and I've been helping out with things at the church."

Michelle said, "I take it your Catholic then?"

"Yes, I am."

"Well, so am I and if you're going to Mass tomorrow, I'd like to go with you if that's okay."

"That would be lovely," replied Jan.

"Maybe I'll go, too," said Julie to the surprise of Emily and Ryan and Jerry.

"Michelle, I can see you're already having a good influence on Julie," said Emily.

Jan turned to Jerry and said, "How about you joining us, Jerry, and making it a foursome?"

Jerry laughed in a mildly derisive manner and said simply, "No way."

Jan knew his feelings about God and church but was nevertheless disappointed. She thought it sad that having his daughter and possible future daughter-in-law volunteer to go wasn't enough to overcome his anger toward the Almighty.

Ryan said he'd go but that he just wanted to sleep in the next day and, anyway, it would be nicer to make it "Ladies Only."

Arrangements were made for Julie and Michelle to pick Jan up and go to church. And with that, the dinner was over, Jan left, everyone helped Emily clean up and then they all went to their respective rooms.

Once in their room and the door closed and in Ryan's boyhood bed, Michelle, turned to Ryan and said, "I really like your family and I like Jan a lot, too."

For the next week, Ryan showed Michelle as much as he could about the family ranch, about Livingston and about living in the mountains. She drank it all in like it was coming from a fire hose.

"Ryan," she said one day, "I feel so alive out here. How did you ever leave? Don't you miss it all the time?"

"I do miss it a lot but I have enjoyed seeing other parts of the country, too."

Michelle said, "If I lived here, I'd never leave."

But leave they did, a few days later, returning to Chicago. It was clear to all that Michelle felt worse about it than Ryan.

Chapter 22

Julie had surprised nearly everyone, even herself, by going to church with Jan. She hadn't been for a number of years and really hadn't thought about it too much. Upon entering the church building, she felt a little strange and even a bit guilty. But once she got over the initial feelings of unfamiliarity, she began to feel not just comfortable but relaxed. There was something right and good that she couldn't quite put her finger on.

The priest who said Mass was the same one who had been there for a number of years including the last time Julie had been to church, Father Jeff as everyone called him. During the Mass, Julie was thinking ahead to when everyone filed out and Father Jeff would be there to greet everyone. What might he say? Would he ask her about her pregnancy? About the father? After Mass, he did approach her but with such a big grin and open arms that Julie's earlier concerns instantly dissipated. They hugged and he kissed her on the cheek.

"Julie, it's so great to see you? How many years has it been? You have really grown up!"

"It's good to see you, too, Father Jeff; it's been a while."

The priest stole a glance at Julie's swollen belly. "So, Julie," he said, "I know it's always dangerous for a man to ask this but knowing how you're always in such great shape, I assume you're pregnant, right?"

"Yes, Father," she said. "I'm due in just a few weeks."

"Do I know the father?"

"Well, Father, if you'll pardon the pun, I have to confess that not only do you not know him you won't ever know him because he's back in Washington D.C. and out of my life. I'm having the baby on my own."

"Julie, it's not my place to make judgments and I didn't mean to embarrass you. If I did, I apologize."

"No apologies needed, Father." Then, as she was running off to catch up with Michelle and Jan, she said, "I have to run, Father. Maybe we can talk sometime."

"I'd like that," he said.

She caught up to Julie and Michelle and got in the car with them. As they were driving off, Julie turned to Jan and said, "Jan, if you don't mind my asking, have you always been religious?"

Jan said, "Not really. I mean I was brought up Catholic but then like so many, I kind of fell away a little. But, then I had some experiences back in Illinois that prompted me to re-examine my faith and the basis for it."

"What kind of experiences?"

"One of the things that someone once said to me was that Jesus Christ was the only major human figure to have claimed to be God. And he either had to be delusional, lying or truly the Son of God. There's no other logical possibility. No one has ever made a reasonable claim that he was delusional; no one has ever had any real proof or even solid evidence that he was lying. On the contrary, there's lots of proof that he was telling the truth. So, that leaves only one conclusion.

But believe me, my faith gets tested every day and I have doubts that creep in now and then. It's not like you can just say, 'Okay, I believe' and then coast from there. You have to work at it and pray every day."

Julie fell silent, letting those thoughts bounce around in her head. Meanwhile, Michelle and Jan chatted happily. They dropped Jan off and went home.

The next day was Monday and Julie had an appointment with her new OB/GYN, Dr. Hollande. When she checked in at Dr. Hollande's office, she had her weight, blood pressure, heart rate and other vital signs checked by Nurse Smith. After taking off the blood pressure cuff he said, "Well, everything seems pretty good, Ms. Johnston."

Julie said, "Wow! That's awfully formal. Can't you call me Julie? And, if I may be so bold, what's your name?"

He blushed a little and answered, "Christopher."

"You don't sound like you're from around here," Julie said. "Where are you from originally?"

"Well, he said, "I was born and raised near a little town in Georgia called LaGrange. But when I was nine, we moved to Washington D.C. because my dad was in the Air Force and worked in the Pentagon." When Christopher said nine, it sounded like "nahn." I lived there until I went off to college and then nursing school. After nursing school, I decided to move out West because I like the outdoors." He blushed again and Julie thought he was awfully cute when he did. "I guess I answered more question than you asked," he said, laughing a little boyish, nervous laugh.

Julie said, "I spent about five years in D.C. I liked it at first but later decided it wasn't for me. So, now I'm back here where I started."

"What do you do here?" asked Christopher.

Julie laughed and said, "Right now not much except have this baby. I live at the Johnston Ranch; Jerry Johnston is my father."

Christopher didn't say anything but did steal a quick glance at Julie's left hand to see if there was a wedding ring.

Julie saw the glance and said, not unkindly, "If you're wondering, the father is back in Washington and out of my life. I'm having this baby on my own."

Christopher looked ashen. "Oh, no, Ms. Johnson, I mean Julie. I wasn't thinking about that at all. It's none of my business. Really, I'm sorry if I somehow gave you the impression…"

Julie raised her hand to cut him off. "It's okay. You didn't do or say anything wrong. I just thought I'd get that out there. I'm completely at ease with what I'm doing."

He looked down at his feet, a little embarrassed and a little uncertain over what to do or say next. Julie noticed his discomfort and, somehow, found it endearing. Without really thinking about it she blurted out, "Would you like to, maybe, have coffee some day?"

Christopher was astonished and looked as surprised as if she had asked him to marry her. He looked at her without saying anything; trying to be sure he had really heard what he thought he did. He said, "Did you say coffee?"

"Yup," she answered now giggling quite openly at his discomfiture.

"Well, yes," he said, still a little uncertain. "When?"

"I'll call you," she replied.

"Great," he said, still in a bit of a daze. "I'll see if Dr. Hollande is ready for you." Christopher went to the door of the little room and looked back at Julie who was still smiling because she was having so much fun with a man so different than the ones she had known in Washington. He still was trying to digest what had happened although he did know it was good.

Chapter 23

A couple of days later, Julie called Dr. Hollande's office and asked for Nurse Smith.

"This is Christopher Smith," he said.

"Hi, Christopher, this is Julie Johnston. How are you?"

"Oh, hi, Julie, I'm fine. How are you?

"I'm fine and the baby's fine. Now how about that coffee we discussed,"

"Well, I was wondering," he said, "we're only working half days on Fridays. It might be a little easier if we had lunch on Friday instead of trying to have coffee. I never know when I'm going to be free when dealing with patients."

"Ah, yes," Julie said, "those pesky patients."

Again, Christopher was afraid he had said something wrong and started to apologize.

She cut him off. "Christopher, I'm kidding. Friday for lunch would be great. I'll drive in and pick you up at, what, noon?"

"Make it 12:15 just so I don't keep you waiting."

"I'll see you at 12:15 on Friday.

When Friday came, Julie drove into town to pick him up. It was a little difficult because her belly stuck out and pushed against the steering wheel so she had to sit further back than normal and her arms were straight out; but she managed.

At lunch, she came to believe that her first impressions were spot on. Christopher was intelligent, unassuming, polite and a gentleman. Must have been that LaGrange upbringing she thought. Why couldn't you find this kind of guy in D.C.? Everyone there was like Tom Sanders or should I say asshole Tom Sanders, she thought. So many men were like asshole Tom Sanders. The problem with men she thought was that they really didn't generally mature, at least vis-à-vis women, until somewhere in their forties or maybe even fifties. There were exceptions and Christopher seemed to be one of them.

For his part, Christopher began to relax around Julie and discussed his job, nursing school, his family and such topics. He found Julie to be intelligent, beautiful and full of confidence. He could only shake his head at her description of her life in the nation's capital. He told her a little about his family. His parents had had him at a relatively old age so that even though he was only thirty, his dad was seventy-two and his mom was sixty-five. Unfortunately, his dad suffered from early dementia and was confined to a home; his mom spent most of her time with his father although she had a number of physical ailments of her own. He had just visited them at Thanksgiving and things were not good.

Julie and Christopher had lunch every Friday for the next few weeks and quickly became good friends; both were aware that there was the potential for much more than friendship. Julie's due date was coming up and it was getting more and more uncomfortable for her to do anything so they deferred nighttime dating until after she had her baby.

In the early morning hours of December 8, Julie's water broke and she started having contractions and Jerry and Ryan and Emily all piled in a couple of cars and raced off to the hospital. They took her right up to the maternity ward and got her prepared for delivery. For Julie, it was all a fairly painful blur; but in the end, she forgot about the pain when she produced a fine looking and healthy baby boy. She named him Alexander Joseph Johnston. Everyone was thrilled and celebrated. Even Jerry was a proud and as happy as could be and he surprised everyone that night by cracking open a bottle of Champagne that he had, somewhat ironically, bought for the occasion.

One thing Julie had wondered about regarding her budding relationship with Christopher was the effect having a baby might have. She wondered if it might scare him off; that he would not want to go further with a single mom with a baby that wasn't his. It was one thing to be pregnant; it was another to have a real, live baby that has to be taken care of night and day.

THE RANCHERS

Julie returned home on the 12th and found flowers and a note from Christopher. It read, "Congratulations! I hear everything went fine. I won't bother you this Friday but, if okay, I'll swing by on the 21st. My only concern is that now I'll have some competition for your affections." It was signed simply, "Christopher." On the 21st, he came to visit, held her hand and even held the baby a little. Unlike many men, he was very comfortable around babies. I guess it was part of his training she thought. Anyway, she was more than a little pleased to see him.

A thought popped into her head, she said to him, "What are you doing for Christmas?"

"Well," he said a little uneasily, "nothing right now. Probably just staying at home and watching football."

"Well, you can watch football here. I want you to come over and spend Christmas day here and have Christmas dinner with us that night. No arguments, okay?"

Christopher smiled at Julie giving orders but now it was not a nervous smile but a happy smile.

"Yes, Ma'am," he said and punctuated it with a salute.

Julie thought, "This may be a better Christmas than I thought."

Chapter 24

Michelle and Ryan had returned to Chicago and both found themselves unhappy. Ryan was still struggling with bias in the press he felt was obvious; Michelle, having finally seeing the West, realized she had merely been tolerating her existence in Chicago as a sales rep.

One night over dinner, she said to Ryan, "What a horrible day. I had four appointments with doctors today, each of which had canceled previous appointments. The first guy kept me waiting for almost an hour so that by the time I got to the second guy he said he didn't have time to see me. I saw the third guy for about three minutes and accomplished nothing. Then the traffic was so bad I couldn't get to the fourth guy until late and he had left to go to the hospital. Plus, I spilled part of my smoothie on my dress. Sometimes I really hate this job."

Ryan responded, "Well, cheer up, things are no better on my end either. Every time I see something on how other media outlets are covering something and I make a comment or suggestion, I get nasty looks or worse from many of my co-workers. They just don't see it or don't want to."

They ate in desultory silence, wallowing in a shallow bath of unhappiness.

Finally, Michelle remarked, "You know, I really like the ranch and everything that comes with it. I even found Livingston to be pretty neat."

"Well, I'm glad, answered Ryan."

Michelle suddenly sat up straight with a hopeful expression on her face like she had just had a brainstorm.

"No, Ryan, I mean I really, really, really like it there," putting more emphasis on each successive 'really.' I've never asked you for anything but now I know what I really want. I don't know why I didn't think of it before. I want to ask you to do something for us. Tell your dad that you want to go back and stay there permanently. Then, we can get married and we can live there and get on with having a family of our own."

"But," said Ryan, "you've only been there a couple of days. You might change your mind after a few weeks or when winter comes or when you haven't been shopping on Michigan Avenue for a while. Don't you think this is a little quick?"

"Ryan, I've never been so sure of anything in my life. I felt this way the first day I got there but I kept quiet. I felt it when you and I rode around but I kept quiet. Now having had a week there and meeting Jan, and then coming back to my job and life here, there's no doubt in my mind that this is the right thing at the right time. This is the game-changer we've been waiting for. And, most importantly, it's the place you and I can settle down and have a family and make a life for ourselves."

Ryan looked at her and saw the determination on her face and knew he had to at least try.

He took a deep breath and said, "Okay," he said, "I'll talk to my Dad. My only caution is that I don't know what he'll say but it's possible that the talk may go very badly."

"I understand and I don't want you to be miserable. But we're both miserable here. I know it's a little hard for you but you'll do your best, right?"

Ryan nodded but was concerned that while it made sense in so many ways were they rushing into it. He also hated having to ask his dad for anything.

Ryan didn't sleep very well and was up early. He knew Jerry would be up early and he called to catch him before he would go out to work. Ryan felt like he wanted to get it over with so right after saying hello and how are you, he said, "Dad, can I talk to you about something?"

"Uh-huh."

"Dad, I was wondering what you would think about me coming back there full time, permanently?"

Jerry didn't say anything at first and Ryan wondered if he had heard him. Then, "So now you want to come back. Why now?"

Ryan responded, "Well, as you know, I am kind of fed up with my job, or really my career, and Michelle likes it there a lot and, well, if we moved there we could get married."

"I see," said Jerry simply. Ryan squirmed a little in his chair, not knowing what his dad was thinking or would say next.

Finally, Jerry, said, "Okay, we'll figure something out."

These were not exactly the welcoming words Ryan might have hoped for and they told him nothing about what he would be doing. It seemed like there should be further discussion but his dad said he had to get to work.

"Thanks, Dad," Ryan offered.

Jerry said very simply, "Okay."

When Michelle got up a little later, Ryan told her about the outcome of the discussion with Jerry without getting into the nuances of what exactly was said or how. Michelle gave Ryan a big kiss and hugged him tightly. "Thank you, Dear, thank you so much."

Ryan replied, "You're welcome. I'm glad it worked out and we can start making wedding plans." She hugged her head tightly to his chest and so she couldn't see Ryan's face. If she had been able to see it, she would have seen a look of concern. Ryan was hoping he hadn't made a big mistake.

Chapter 25

One evening in early December, Colin was at the club bar along with most of the rest of the Honchos. Rocky came out of the office of the bar and came right over to Colin.

"I'm glad you're here. We've got a little job to do tonight and you're the perfect one to help us out. Come on."

Everyone started to head toward the door. Colin didn't have a good feeling about what was happening but, in the midst of so many of them, he didn't feel he had much choice. Maybe it wouldn't be any big deal, he hoped. They all got on their bikes and headed out of town.

On the outskirts of town, there was an old abandoned Mexican restaurant and that was the destination. Colin couldn't imagine what they would be doing there. They went into the restaurant and then into what was the kitchen and storage area at one point in time. In the back there were a couple of more Honcho members with work lights that lit things up quite brightly. Colin looked around and saw there was still some semblance of a kitchen with shelves and bowls and a few other items that the owners or operators had apparently not bothered to take away. Then, as he came around one of the shells, he saw a man on the ground, his face bloody from a beating, who was having some trouble breathing. His hair was totally mussed and bloody and one eye was partly shut. He was groaning loudly from the pain.

"This, Hotshot, is Rolando Garcia, one of the top guys of Los Doble Diablos. They've been cutting into our territory and we've warned them and yet they just wouldn't listen. So we caught Rolando here and we need to teach them a lesson that they won't forget. And you get to do the honors, Hotshot.

Execute him. Put a bullet in his fucking brain!" He handed a pistol to Colin.

Colin looked at Rocky in disbelief. "Right here? Right now?"

"Why not? You want to be a part of the club; this is what you gotta do!"

Colin knew he was cornered, but in a larger sense he knew this was a pivotal moment. He had finally been led to the "line," the one his dad had always talked about when you have to decide what kind of person you are, what your values were. He knew that this was an execution of a rival but also a test of his loyalty and obedience to the gang and the truth was he had neither. He had been hanging around the edges of the gang for a while but not because he felt a kinship with them or even a desire to be a member. He just hadn't been ready to settle down to a normal, civilian life.

He looked around and saw nine or ten faces looking at him intently, looking to see what he would do. Colin had faced death a number of times in Iraq and he was ready for it then and he was ready for it now. He would kill if he had to but not on their terms, not at their bidding. He would not cross that line. He just wasn't sure how he would get out of this predicament; or if.

They pulled Rolando to his feet and brought him over to Colin, leaned him up against a shelf and then backed away so as not to be splattered with blood and brains. Rocky gave Colin the pistol. Just like he did when they were out in the desert, Colin checked the magazine. "Thank God you're not so bright, Rocky," thought Colin. There were ten rounds in the magazine. Colin yanked on the receiver and chambered a round. He then grabbed Rolando and turned to Rocky and said in a low voice, "Rocky, let me take him out of here and deal with him my own special way. I learned some things in Iraq that are worse than death." Colin doubted he would be allowed to do so but he had to try.

Rocky took several steps forward, away from the rest of the gang to get within six inches of Colin. He put his nose inches from Colin's and said, "Kill him or you're a dead man. We'll fuck you both up and then kill you both."

Colin was calm and felt no fear. He looked right into Rocky's eyes and put the muzzle of the gun against Rocky's stomach, Rocky had been so close that the other gang members couldn't really see that what was happening. Then, Colin spoke in a near whisper and said so quietly that only Rocky could hear, "Rocky, there are ten rounds in the chamber, enough for you and most of your boys here. Now, I might not get them all but you'll never know. Because if you don't let me take care of Rolando my way, I'm going to blow a hole in you so big that you'll be dead before you hit the floor. They glared at each other for just a moment and then Colin said, "What's it going to be?"

Rocky looked down at the gun up against his stomach. Then he looked back up at Colin and said, "You'll pay for this, Asshole."

"Oh," said Colin with a grin, "I'm not Hotshot anymore?" Then, deadly serious, "Okay, Rocky, you come with us, and make it look good."

Then Rocky turned to the gang and said, "Okay, Boys, you stay here. Hotshot here and I are going to take Rolando and give him some special U.S. Army treatment."

Colin grabbed Rolando's vest by the throat and pulled him toward the door but kept the gun pointed at Rocky. Some of the members who were furthest away from where Colin and Rocky had been thought this was all legit and so didn't know what was really happening. Some closer had suspicions about what was happening, and they were armed, but they knew they could barely shoot straight and they had all seen what Colin could do. No one made a move to stop Colin. When they got to the outside, Colin let Rolando loose and pointed him to his motorcycle. Colin kept one eye on Rocky and the other on the front door but no one wanted to test him after his desert demonstration.

"Don't kill me," Rolando pleaded.

"Shut up!" answered Colin. "You get on my bike and I'll ride in the bitch seat and I'll blow your head off if you try anything."

Rocky said, "I always figured you weren't legit. How long do you think it will take us to catch up with you?"

"Rocky," Colin answered, "just remember, if you come after me, you'll always be the first to go. I'm going to ride out of your life and my advice for you is to let it go." Colin began to walk toward his chopper where Rolando was waiting. "Now, I am going to take care of Rolando just like I said."

Colin and Rolando rode back toward town and went to a spot where Colin knew they would be alone and undisturbed. As they rode, Colin now felt the nerves and shivers of what a bad situation he had just been through. He thought about the lifestyle he had been living and, surprisingly, what his dad would say. He felt good about staying on the good side of the line and decided it was time to start acting the way Jerry had expected of him. He almost laughed out loud, thinking that, in spite of everything, his dad still held sway over him.

They got off the bike and Colin grabbed Rolando by the collar and marched him into a spot where they couldn't be seen by anyone. He put the gun to Rolando's head and made like he was going to shoot.

Again, Rolando started pleading, "Don't kill me. I've got a wife and two kids. Please, let me go and I'll do anything."

Colin looked at him and tried to make some kind of appraisal of the man's character. "What the hell are you doing living this kind of life with a wife and two kids? Do you think this is the right and proper way to live your life? What the fuck, man! Why don't you go straight?"

That was about the last thing that Rolando expected to hear and the look on his face said the same thing. "What are you talking about, man?"

"Why are you into whatever illegal stuff you are doing? You have a family to take care of. Do you think selling drugs or guns is a proper way to make a living? Do you want your kids to grow up in this culture? Do you want your kids to see you in prison?"

"Man, I just kind of fell into this. I came back from Afghanistan and fell in with a bad bunch. I was having trouble finding a job and needed to make some money. One thing led to another and I was in this gang. I'm just trying to get by, man."

"You were in the Army?

"Yeah. I was with the 4th Infantry Brigade Combat team of the First Infantry Division"

Colin didn't say anything about his service but he had empathy for a fellow G.I. "You said if I didn't kill you would do anything, right?"

"Anything, Man. Anything."

"Okay, go home. Get your wife and kids, pack up and go somewhere else. Get out of the gang; get out of doing bad stuff. Get whatever kind of job you can find and go straight."

"Are you serious?"

"I couldn't be more serious. You keep doing this and you'll be dead and your kids will wind up doing the same thing with the same result. You go on home and then head out of here; anywhere."

"I don't have my bike, man."

"That's all right; I'll drop you wherever you need."

Rolando looked at Colin and said, "Why are you doing this?"

Colin answered, "Let's just say I'm a good guy."

"If you're such a good guy, why are you mixed up with a motorcycle gang?"

Colin let the question register for a moment. "Very good question," he said.

Rolando told Colin where he could drop him and promised he would go straight. Colin thought the odds of that were slim but at least he tried.

Then he had to hustle and get back to his apartment and load up all of the important stuff that he had before the Honchos figured out that they might catch him there. He had bought an old but good running pick-up truck. He went to his apartment and, to his relief, there was no sign of anyone else. He didn't have much so it didn't take long to pack everything up. The lease was month-to-month so he wasn't out anything. He blasted out of town and then started thinking about where he might go.

"I'd like to see Julie," he said out loud. "I'll just put up with dad as best I can, "and he pointed the truck toward Montana and hit the gas pedal.

Chapter 26

Colin cruised up I-15 all night through Las Vegas and into Utah. As he was approaching Cedar City, Utah, he suddenly felt so sleepy he could barely keep his eyes open. He pulled over and found a motel and got a room and quickly hit the sack. He was asleep before his head hit the pillow.

The next morning, mid-morning, he stumbled to a nearby diner for breakfast. He sat at a table by the line of windows and enjoyed the view on a crisp, cool Utah morning. Like his dad, he was a bacon and eggs man and the bacon had better be ultra-crisp. After placing his order, he savored the strong coffee and surveyed nearby fields. A movement caught his eye and he spied a horse trying to find something to eat in a field that was totally eaten down and half dirt to begin with. The horse looked to be or five years old with a good conformation but it was quite thin. Its ribs were prominent and it just looked gaunt. Colin loved horses and it pained him to see one that maybe was being mistreated.

The cook himself brought Colin's order to the table. Colin asked him, "Do you by any chance know who owns that horse?"

The cook bent down to look out the window and, pointing, said, "You mean that scrawny thing over there?"

"Yeah," said Colin.

"That's old Ed Ogier's place. His wife died a few years ago and that was her horse. Ed kept it but I'm not sure he's got the money to take care of it proper. He's gotta be about seventy now and his health is failing. Not sure he'll be around too long."

The cook looked at Colin as if to say, "Got what you need?"

Colin said, "Thanks."

After breakfast, Colin got in his truck and drove down the road he hoped would lead to the residence on the property where the horse was. It took a bit of driving around but he finally found

166

a little drive leading to a house. The yard was overgrown and it looked like the house could use a few repairs and maybe a coat of paint. Colin got out of the truck and looked around but didn't see anyone. For no reason other than instinct born of training and experience, he was on alert in case anything unexpected happened. He went up to the door and didn't see a bell so he knocked on the door. There was no answer. He knocked again but more loudly. This time he heard, "Hold on, hold on, I'm coming!"

The door opened and there stood an old man who looked even older than he probably was. He had on a work shirt with the sleeves gone from where they joined the shoulder seam, blue jeans that were too big for his skinny, old-man build that were held up by a pair of suspenders. He squinted down a pair of wire rim glasses and said, "Yeah, what can I do for you?"

"Well, Sir, my name is Colin Johnston and I was having breakfast at the diner down there and I noticed your horse."

"Yeah, what about him?"

"Well, he looks a little thin. I don't mean to stick my nose into your business but I was wondering if he was getting enough to eat?"

"Well, it ain't your business," he barked. He glared at Colin who looked back without expression. Then, as if confessing, the man said, "But to be honest, I'm on a fixed income and sometimes I get a little short and I'm afraid Cinnamon there gets a little less food than he should."

"Well, maybe I can help," said Colin. I just got out of the service a little while ago and I still have some cash that I saved. If you would, Sir, maybe you'd let me buy him some extra food."

Ed Ogier peered at Colin for a long time, wondering what his game was.

"Maybe you'd better come in. You want some coffee?"

"Sure," said Colin, "you can never have too much Joe."

They went inside and Colin noticed the inside was in about the same condition as the outside. In addition, the place was pretty messy, clothes all over, dishes in the sink and crumbs on the counter. Ogier noticed Colin noticing the mess. He poured a couple of cups of coffee and motioned to Colin to sit at the small kitchen table.

"So, you were in the service?"

"Yes, Sir" answered Colin.

"What branch?"

"Army."

"Oh, God, we Marines were always bailing you guys out. Half the army would have been gone if it weren't for us," he said with a satisfied grin on his face. Colin recognized this as the usual inter-service rivalry and trash talk that was so common in the military.

"Where were you stationed?"

"I did basic and AIT at Ft. Benning, then I was assigned to the Big Red One and then went to Iraq for a couple of tours."

"No shit. I was in Vietnam myself." They toasted one another by clinking their coffee mugs.

Ogier again saw Colin looking at the mess. "Ever since my wife died," he said, "I haven't had the motivation to do much of anything. It's a hell of a thing to lose your wife. We were married for forty-nine years, had big plans for our fiftieth anniversary and then one day she just keeled over and died. You're together day after day for over fifty years, counting the time before we were married, and then all of a sudden one day, she's gone. The only time we weren't together was when I was in Vietnam and that was three years. I've been lost ever since she died. You can't imagine what it does to a man to lose the love of your life."

Colin's mind immediately flipped to his dad and mom. What Ogier said was true, he thought, I really can't imagine it; I don't know what it's like to be married or with a woman for a long time. I guess it was tough on dad, but it's no picnic for the youngest child, I can tell you that.

"I appreciate your offer, Colin, one combat veteran to another, but I couldn't just let you buy food for Cinnamon; that's his name by the way. I'll probably just sell him to someone around here."

Colin asked, "Has he been started? Has he had any training? Has anybody ridden him?"

"Oh, yeah, we had a top notch trainer get him started and give him some real good training. My wife used to ride him all the time but no one has been on him since she died. I don't think it would take much to get him back in shape. He's a really good horse."

"How about I buy him?"

"What would you do with him?"

"I'm going up to a ranch in Montana and I was going to get a horse anyway."

"I'm not sure Cinnamon is quite ready for ranch work. He's going to need some time to regain his strength."

"Don't worry," said Colin, "I'll give him plenty of time to get fit and strong." Colin remembered seeing a one horse trailer in the yard just off the driveway. "I assume that horse trailer out front is your, too. If you don't need it, I'll buy that from you, too."

"Are you sure you want to do this? A horse requires a lot of care."

"Yes, Sir, I'm very sure," answered Colin. I grew up with horses and I missed them when I was in the Army. Now I can have one again."

"Okay," said Ogier I'll sell you both for, um, how does a thousand dollars sound to you?"

"It sounds too low, " replied Colin. He pulled his checkbook out of his jacket and began writing. When done, he handed the check to him.

"Two thousand dollars! That's way too much. I was stretching it at a thousand." He held the check out to Colin to give it back."

"No, Sir," Colin replied, refusing to take back the check. From my perspective, I'm getting a great deal. I just have a hunch that Cinnamon and I are going to be great pals."

Colin got up to leave and went to the door; Ogier followed him. At the door, Colin turned and said, "It's been an honor and a pleasure to meet you Mr. Ogier." Then, with a broad grin he said, "Semper Fi".

Colin took a look at the trailer and it was in pretty good condition and clean inside. He hitched it to his pickup and drove back down toward the highway. He stopped at a feed store and got a big bucket for water, a halter, a bale of hay and a feeder bag for the trailer. He cut the baling twine and took a flake and put it in the feeder back and hung it in the trailer. Then he filled the bucket three quarters with water. Finally, he went back to the Ogier place and got Cinnamon and led him into the trailer. There was no hesitation on the horse's part and he quickly was at the hay. Colin stroked him for a little and said softly, "Yes, you and I are going to be good friends."

Colin hit the highway again, now with a heavier load but a happier state of mind. He thought about what Ed Ogier had said about losing a wife. Maybe he had been too harsh in his judgment on his dad. Maybe he had gone through something more emotionally painful than any of the kids could imagine. Hard to say but Colin still felt like his dad could have handled it better but maybe he would have to re-think things a little.

Colin was very pleased with himself with how he had helped out an old man and a veteran at that. The horse and trailer were probably worth about eight or nine hundred dollars so the extra was, in effect, charity. Ed Ogier knew it and Colin knew it but so what? In many ways Colin felt fortunate and he was happy to make someone else's life a little better.

Colin drove a little slower with the horse and trailer in tow. He made it to Pocatello, Idaho the next day and was within easy range of getting to Livingston some time the next day. He found a place outside of town where he could stay and where there was a corral and food and water for Cinnamon.

The next day he was up early to shower and shave. When he had been hanging with the Honchos he had grown some facial hair, mustache, a bit of a goatee and a soul patch. Now he decided that it would be easier at home if he was clean shaven and, besides, that was more in keeping with his personality anyway. And it was another way to put those wasted months with the Honchos behind him.

He grabbed a coffee to go at the diner because he was anxious to be on the road early, making good time. Including one stop it took a little over five hours to get to the outskirts of Livingston. It occurred to Colin that maybe he should get some kind of baby gift for Julie so he found a clothing store and parked the truck and trailer in the spacious lot a good distance from the front door. He didn't bother to lock the trailer. "Wasn't horse thievery still a hanging offence?" he chuckled to himself.

Going in the store he was directed to the infant department and headed over to the counter where there was a cash register and a young woman doing some kind of paperwork; and it was an attractive young woman at that. As he approached the counter, he had the feeling that he might know her but he wasn't sure, partly because she was looking down and he couldn't see her face.

She looked up and said to him, "Well, hello, Colin Johnston, long time no see." Seeing that he was searching for a name, she laughed a delightful laugh and said, "Don't you recognize me? It's me, Patty Neal."

Colin was stunned. "Holy crap!" he said to himself. Patty Neal had been a freshman in high school when he was a senior. She was the younger sister of a classmate and one of his better friends. Because of his friendship with her brother, they were friendly but not really friends in part because of the age difference. She always looked up to Colin though he had more or less treated her like a kid. In high school, Patty Neal had been pretty skinny with brown hair, glasses and braces on her teeth. The woman standing in front of him with a big grin on her face had long blonde hair, had generous curves in all the right places and no glasses. Colin simply couldn't believe his eyes.

"My God, Patty, you've changed. I mean, you look terrific."

She was still laughing. "Yeah, I get that a lot. I have to admit I look a lot different than I did when you last saw me. My braces came off my sophomore year in high school. Then I got contacts. And then in my senior year in high school, all of a sudden, I just developed I'd guess you'd say." After a little pause where both of them just looked at the other she said, "Well, how have you been?

You look terrific yourself. I heard you went into the Army and were in Iraq. Is that right?"

"Yes," he replied, still a little stunned at the beautiful woman in front of him. "I was in Iraq but I left the Army a little while back and I'm going home for a visit. My older sister Julie just had a baby and I wanted to get a gift for her."

"Well, you're in the right place. Did you have anything in particular in mind?"

"No, not really. I mean I don't know too much about this stuff. She had a little boy and I was thinking about a couple of outfits."

Patty helped Colin pick out a couple of outfits and they went back to the counter where they had first been talking so that she could ring him up and gift wrap the outfits.

"So," said Colin, "what have you been up to since high school?"

"After high school, I went to the University of Montana and got a degree in retail marketing. Then after college, I looked around for a job but there weren't a lot of jobs at the time. I finally got a job with this chain and so I am spending a couple of years here and then, maybe, I'll get a promotion and move to another store somewhere else."

Colin was processing the information especially about moving somewhere else.

"And, if you don't mind my asking, you never got married?"

"No."

"Having gone to MSU, I always knew those Grizzlies were none too bright."

Patty smiled at the indirect compliment. "I do have a boyfriend," she said. Colin's heart sank. "But it's nothing serious." His heart jumped back up, perhaps even a little higher because he sensed she was sending him a message. Another customer, a middle aged woman, approached the counter and Patty had to finish with him and wait on the new customer.

Colin said, "Well, if there is any problem with these gifts, maybe you should give me your number so I can make an exchange or something."

"Patty smiled and so did the other customer. She wrote her number on a piece of paper and handed it to him. "Here you go. It was great to see you, Colin. "I'm glad you're back."

"Likewise," he said. "Thanks for your help."

Outside, Colin looked at the front entry of the store and there were the hours of business and a telephone number. He looked at the piece of paper that she had written the telephone number and he could tell it wasn't any number connected to the store. Excellent!

When he got to his truck, he checked on Cinnamon and everything seemed to be fine. He piled in and headed out of town toward the Johnston Ranch. His mind was swirling over Patty Neal. He just couldn't get over the physical change. He knew some of what he was feeling was pure lust. Men generally have a specific face and body type of woman that they think is the most attractive from a purely physical standpoint. Patty, as transformed, just happened to hit Colin's entire checklist. But he also remembered that the little girl he had known in high school was pretty sweet. Of course, sometimes that changes as people get a little older but in the brief encounter in the store, she seemed pretty much the same from a personality standpoint. He thought to himself, "Well, depending on what happens, this might definitely be worth putting up with dad for a while."

Soon, Colin was coming up the main drive of his family's ranch. He stopped near the barn where there were a bunch of horse corrals and put Cinnamon in one of them. He went over to the hay barn and got a flake and gave it to Cinnamon and made sure that the water trough in that corral had water. After making sure Cinnamon was doing okay, he headed for the house with his gift packages under his arm.

He went inside the house expecting to surprise everyone, someone, but to his surprise there was no one there. He wondered what to do. It felt a little strange to be in his own house, at least the one where he grew up. Even though everything was nearly exactly the same, somehow it all seemed strangely different in a way he couldn't identify. The rooms were the same but felt different to him; like his dad's study, where Jerry had denied that Colin was responsible for his mom's death but in a less than convincing way. His recollection of these rooms as a youngster was a lot different than now. "What was it," he asked himself. "What's the difference? I don't feel like a little kid anymore. I've been in the Army, I've been in combat and I'm not intimidated by much. I'm not going to let dad frighten me or make me feel bad. The hell with him. If he can't treat me right, I'll tell him where to get off." Colin paced around for another fifteen minutes, getting all worked up, imagining behavior from Jerry that hadn't happened.

Finally, he heard a car come up the drive and he looked out a window. It was Julie and Emily who had apparently been grocery shopping because they each had a couple of bags of groceries and Julie was carrying her baby in a carrier. Colin took a seat in the kitchen, thinking that would be a good place to surprise them. He heard the front door open and heard the ladies headed toward the kitchen and heard Emily say, "I don't know whose truck that is."

At about that same moment, Julie came through the door into the kitchen and saw Colin sitting with a big grin at the counter. "Colin!" she exclaimed, gently put the baby carrier down and then threw her bags on the table and ran over to him and gave him a big hug. "When did you get here? Why didn't you tell us you were coming? It's so good to see you!"

Colin returned the hug and gave her a kiss on the cheek. "It was just a couple of days ago that I decided to come and visit and I decided I wanted to surprise everyone. And, it postponed my having to deal with dad."

Emily came into the kitchen and was already smiling having heard the explosion from Julie. "Colin, it's so good to see you," she said. Colin and Emily then hugged. Emily said, "Is that your truck outside?"

"Yes, it is," he answered. "And that's my new horse in the corral. He's a little on the skinny side right now but I think once I get him in shape he's going to be a good horse."

"Does that mean you're going to stay here a while?"

Colin said quickly, "Well, I'm not sure how long I'll be here."

Julie refused to think negatively. "I'm just happy you're here now."

After a brief pause, she asked, "So, what have you been up to since you got out of the service?"

Colin gave an edited version of what he had been doing and, in particular, described a motor cycle club as opposed to an outlaw motorcycle club. Naturally, he didn't refer to any of the potential unlawful activities or the episode with Rolando Garcia. He went on to describe how he had acquired Cinnamon, omitting the part on how he had overpaid for the horse and trailer. When he finished, he said, "How's dad?"

Julie replied, "Oh, you know, he's the same old dad we know and love."

"Great," said Colin, "like I said, it may be a short stay." Then, after a pause he said, "So, let me see the baby? What's its name?"

Julie said, "It's a boy and his name is Alex."

In spite of the excitement of the adults, Alex was asleep so Julie and Colin went into one of the spare bedrooms that served as a nursery and spent some time just looking at Alex and talking quietly.

"So, how did all this happen?"

Now it was Julie's turn to tell the story of her life in D.C. and working for CSC and about Tom Sanders. She pretended like she was feeling a little shiver and said with a bit of emotion, "I hate to even think about him."

"Well, I've got to say that it takes a lot of guts to come back here and do all this on your own. Speaking of coming back here, how was Ryan when he visited? He texted me and said he was making a change from Chicago back to the ranch but that it might only be temporary. What's going on?"

Julie said, "He got frustrated in his job and his profession, really. Michelle likes it here and she talked Ryan into coming back here to give it a try."

Just then, Julie and Colin heard voices coming from the kitchen and realized it was Jerry talking with Emily. Julie went first and stopped at the interior doorway to the kitchen and blocked it, keeping Colin out in the main room. Julie announced,

"You're never going to guess who's here." She then stepped out of the way so that Colin could enter the kitchen.

"Hi, Dad," he said and, after a moment of gauging Jerry's reaction, went over to Jerry and they hugged stiffly.

"Hello, Son," said Jerry. "Welcome home. This wasn't expected."

They were the right words thought Colin but the tone was very subdued and Colin couldn't help but think "Same ol' Dad."

"How long are you here for?" asked Jerry.

"Not sure," replied Colin. "That's to be determined."

Jerry said, "I'll be right back; I was right in the middle of giving some meds to Rocket in the barn. Back in a minute or two."

After he was out the door, Julie said, "Colin, I hadn't had the chance to tell you but Daddy has a girlfriend."

Colin felt a funny rush, thinking about a woman other than his mom being with his dad.

Colin said, "What's her name? What do you guys think?"

Julie said, "Her name is Jan, Jan Martino and I like her a lot." She looked over to Emily and she was nodding in agreement. "I think she'll be good for Dad."

Colin queried, "When do you think I might meet her?"

Emily said, "She normally has dinner with us on Saturday but since Christmas is next week and she's coming for Christmas dinner she's not coming this Saturday. I guess you'll have to wait until Christmas to meet her."

"So be it," Colin answered. "Well, I am going to unpack and get a little settled," and he went off to his old room.

Over the next week or so Colin spent time working with Cinnamon. He had the vet the ranch used come and give him a thorough examination. The vet said the horse was fine just needed to get his weight up and his strength back. The vet suggested that Colin get some weight on the horse and do some ground work with him during that time. Then, in a few weeks, he could start riding him, a little at first and then gradually building up. He dewormed Cinnamon and gave him vaccinations. Colin had also arranged for the ranch farrier to shoe Cinnamon.

Shoeing the horse turned out to be a bit of a chore because he hadn't been shod in so long he had apparently grown unaccustomed to it. But Colin knew that, like most horses, he would settle down over time. Finally, he went into town and bought presents for everyone for Christmas.

Come Christmas morning, everyone gathered in the living room and exchanged their presents. Colin felt very odd, participating in this most family oriented activity when he just wasn't sure about the whole family thing to begin with. Of course, he loved and had no problems with Julie or Ryan or even Emily for that matter. It was his dad. He loved Jerry but the hurt he had long felt suppressed the love. Deep down, he wanted a normal, loving relationship with his dad but he wasn't going to beg for one which is what he viewed asking to work on the ranch would be. And since his dad was, well, stubborn about their relationship and who should make a move to fix it, Colin just figured it would always be what it was now—awkward. And so here he was, sitting with family members but the lead family member felt to Colin like something else, something a little alien.

He wondered about Jan. He wondered what kind of woman his dad would be interested in and vice-versa. What woman would find his cool-hearted dad someone worth a relationship? And by all accounts, it was a serious relationship. Colin was pretty sure that he wouldn't particularly like her.

When Jan arrived for dinner, she knew everyone except Colin and that introduction was handled by Ryan.

Jan said, "Colin, it's so nice to meet you. I've heard a lot about you from your father."

Colin laughed a little derisively, "I bet." Ryan laughed, too.

"Well, your father is very proud of you. And I would like to thank you very much for your service to our country."

Colin thought that he wished his dad would tell him he was very proud of him. And, also, he was pleased that Jan had thanked him for his military service. Though he knew it was an oversight with all the commotion, no one else in the family had thought to do so. Maybe it was hard for them to think of their little brother and son a combat veteran, but he was.

When dinner was ready, there was a buffet set up in the kitchen and everyone but Colin helped themselves. He was already sitting at the dining room table but just wasn't hungry at the moment. He was still finding this whole family thing a bit disorienting and it was sapping his appetite for the moment. He did put a meager amount on his plate just to avoid commentary but his plan failed. Jan was second to last out of the kitchen and was supposed to sit across from Colin. She had put her plate down at her place and was still standing when she saw his plate and she said, "What's the matter? Don't you like turkey?"

"Oh, yeah," he said, "I like it all. I'm just feeling a little lazy at the moment but I'll go get more soon."

Hearing that lame excuse, Jan looked at him and knew it wasn't laziness that was at work. She went over to his side of the table and bent over and put her arms around his neck from the side and behind and hugged him as best as one can from that position and said, "You poor boy. I'm going to get you a proper plate." She then picked up his plate and went into the kitchen.

Colin looked around and everyone was looking at him as if they were thinking, "Wow! Special treatment!" He noticed the looks and wore a goofy little grin. He felt so good about what she had just done and said and, generally, just the attention she gave him. He calculated that he felt better than others might over a relatively simple gesture but he wasn't sure *why* he felt so good about it. But he did and now he ate with gusto, even getting seconds. It was certainly nicer than the previous Christmas meal he had had in Iraq.

The next day, Colin slept in just a little, at least by his standards, and was eating a bowl of cereal a little after eight o'clock. The phone rang and Emily answered and said, "Yes, he is; just a moment." Then she walked over to Colin and handed him the phone.

"For me?" he mouthed the words, wondering who might be calling him.

"Hello, Colin, this is Jan. I gambled that you would be up. How are you?"

"Fine, thanks," he answered, wondering why she would be calling him.

"We didn't get much chance to talk yesterday. I was wondering how you're finding civilian life?"

"Oh, it's fine. It's not as exciting but I get to sleep later in the morning." He was still wondering what the purpose of the call was.

Jan kept asking him a number of questions about his service in the Army, his thoughts about the Iraq war, and if he had any idea what he was going to do now. He answered them all as well as possible and still he waited to hear why she had called. After several more minutes, she repeated that she had wished they had been able to talk more the day before and so that's why she called. She said goodbye and hung up.

Colin put the phone down and tried to digest what had just happened. Someone had called just because they were interested in him. They didn't need anything, didn't ask for anything, just wanted to get to know him a little better. He then realized that the day before had been the same but amplified by a healthy dose of tenderness, something he was not sure he had ever been on the receiving end of. Oh, sure, Emily had done her best when they were growing up but she had four people to take care of and there was only so much time. He had had a favorable opinion of Jan but based on a nebulous sense that she was a nice lady. But now the esteem he felt for her was off the charts. Somehow, on very short acquaintance, she was providing him with a treasure trove of positive vibes. His mind took a leap when he wondered if she could have a positive effect on his dad.

"Could she turn him into the father we'd all like to have?" he wondered.

Chapter 27

A couple of days after Christmas, Jerry was having breakfast and Colin came in and said there was a guy named Austin Harris at the front door asking for Jerry. Jerry jumped up and headed straight for the front door. There, indeed, stood Austin Harris.

"Hello, Austin, " said Jerry warmly. "What brings you here?"

"Well, Mr. Johnston, I was wondering if your offer of me being able to come back to work here was still on the table?"

Jerry peered at Austin, as something about his appearance of facial expression would tell Jerry what was going on.

"Well of course it is," answered Jerry. "Why don't you come on in and tell me about it." He motioned Austin to come in and led him to the kitchen where they sat at the big table. "Would you like some breakfast or coffee?"

"No, thanks," Mr. Johnston.

Jerry said, "So, tell me about it. What happened? Didn't like the insurance business?"

Austin looked down at his feet. "Yes and no," he said. I mean, I found some of it very interesting and I learned a lot about something that I knew nothin' about. But I didn't always like to operate the way they wanted me to."

"Like what?" asked Jerry.

"Well. The main thing is that the whole place was geared to selling people as much insurance as you could, not selling them what they needed or wanted. There were times when someone came in and pretty much knew what they wanted but our job was always to sell more. I mean, I don't know if that's really wrong; I mean, no one was forcin' nobody, but somehow it just didn't seem right. What do you think, Mr. Johnston?

"Austin," he began, "have you ever heard of the cowboy code?"

"Yeah, I guess so."

"Back in the old days, there wasn't much law out in the West and so the pioneers just made up rules of behavior that became the cowboy code. But it was really the way most people lived. Of course, some didn't, but most did and it kind got baked into the culture of the West.

You ever heard the expression, 'A man's word is his bond'"?

"Yeah."

"What's it mean to you?"

"I don't rightly know; I never thought about it that much."

"Well, you know a bond is something you give, money or goods, to show good faith and to give assurance to someone that you will perform whatever you are supposed to. So, think about it? The cowboy code is saying that a man's word is his bond. If a cowboy gives his word, that's all that's needed.

The code also implies fair dealing and treating people fairly. So sure, no one's forcing anyone to buy anything but you knew inside that trying to get people to buy more than they needed somehow just wasn't right."

After a bit of a pause, Jerry asked, "What did you think of San Francisco?"

Austin laughed and shook his head a little and said, "Well, it sure was different from here. I mean, it was pretty exciting, lots of energy and all but really different. The people seemed a lot different. They were a lot more liberal for one thing, not that there's anything wrong with that, I suppose. But everyone seemed to be arguing over what they wanted everyone else to do when it seems like if everyone would just treat everyone else in a respectful and fair way they wouldn't have to pass a million laws tellin' everyone how to behave. They just need a simple guide instead of a million rules"

"You mean kind of like the cowboy code?" Jerry said, grinning.

Austin grinned back at him. "Yes, Sir. I guess that's right."

"Austin, I might be overstating it, but I don't really think I am. The cowboy code is not just for cowboys or ranchers. It's pretty simple and it applies to everyone and it would be great if everyone followed it. It's not complicated stuff and, if you had to boil it all down, it starts with the golden rule, follows that by the character and values that make up a real man or woman, and then with the ideas of doing your work, taking responsibility, not unnecessarily depending on others, and finally ends with honesty and loyalty. It's simple stuff, but it just shows that you don't have to have, as you say, a million rules tellin' everyone how to act."

Austin nodded, then he took on a serious face. "I have to be honest with you, Mr. Johnston, I don't plan on workin' here forever. I'm hopin' to save enough money, maybe get a little backin' and get my own place, run my own operation." Austin sounded a little tentative, like he thought Jerry would be upset with that.

"Well, that's fine, Austin. Heck, maybe I'll be the one to back you."

"That would be great," a surprised Austin said with a smile. Then he got serious again. I just thought I should be up front with you as to what I am thinking."

"There you go," said Jerry. You're following the cowboy code already."

Jerry stood up and gave Austin a slap on the shoulder. "Good to have you back," he said. I'll call Elmer and tell him he's got an experienced hand joining him."

"Thanks again, Mr. Johnston."

Austin left and Jerry sat back down and thought about their conversation. Jerry hadn't ever articulated those beliefs so completely even though he held them. It was a moment he would always remember and helped him understand why he was a rancher and not something else.

Chapter 28

Jerry and Jan had been dating for going on six months. It wasn't what you would call whirlwind but things had progressed nicely. They saw each other regularly and talked on the phone one or two nights a week plus Jan came over to dinner every Saturday at Jerry's insistence. They went to a lot of parties and dinner parties and everyone liked being around Jan. But Jerry was still trying to sort out why he felt about her the way he did.

He had been asking that question of himself from the first day he met her when the balloon nearly crashed into his house. Unlike most of the women that Jerry knew in and around Livingston, Jan was very independent; the other women were generally needier. Perhaps it was that difference that was particularly attractive. Then, again, over time he learned that her values were above reproach. She enjoyed the finer things life had to offer but also could live without them, and she certainly didn't put having them high on her list of what she thought was important. She clearly wanted a man she could respect because of *his* values. He was certainly happy that she apparently felt that way about him; but that still didn't give a clear, concise answer as to why he had fallen for her when no other woman in three decades had even come close. There was just some spark, some special something that he was still trying to discern that he found compelling.

While he didn't fully understand all the whys of his attraction to her, there was no doubt that the coup de grace for Jerry was the occasional brief moment when she would, probably inadvertently, show her vulnerability, show that she needed him. Deep down, he discovered, she had the same uncertainties and emotions as the rest of us; it's just that not many got to see those conditions in her. As those emotions and vulnerabilities began to appear in the middle stages of their romance, Jerry began to think about marriage. By Thanksgiving, there was no doubt in his mind that that's what he wanted.

During the week between Christmas and New Year's, Ryan and Julie and Colin had several impromptu discussions and realized they had all separately come to the same conclusion; namely that Jan was the best thing that had happened to their dad in a long time and could be a great addition to the family. There was concern, partly based in reality and partly based in comedic banter that their dad would somehow screw it up. The most popular theory of how that might happen was that he would continue to date her but never ask her to marry and she would tire of that and move on.

For New Year's Eve in a bit of role reversal, the three kids plus Michelle and Christopher opted to stay in, maybe watch the ball drop but basically just hang out. Meanwhile, the old folks, Jan and Jerry were going out to a New Year's Eve party at the Wilsons. Generally, New Year's Eve parties populated by people age sixty and up celebrate New Year's an average of two time zones to the east. In other words, at the party in Livingston, Montana, the celebration would be as if they all lived in New York City which meant ten o'clock in Montana.

Jan and Jerry had a nice time at the Wilson party, kissed at Adjusted New Year's or ten o'clock and not too long afterward they left and Jerry drove Jan to her apartment in town. Jan invited Jerry in for a nightcap and they settled down on her couch with a fire roaring that Jerry had built while she was getting a couple of glasses of wine.

Jan said, "I must say, I think your kids are terrific. You must be really happy that they're all home."

"Well," he replied, "they didn't come home to see me. They just came home because it was convenient."

"The point is they are here and they probably could have gone anywhere. Aren't you at least a little happy about that?"

"I guess so; but you know I'd really be happier if they would say they were sorry. Besides, we've been over and over this many times before."

"Sorry for what?" Jan persisted.

"Sorry that instead of staying on and helping their dad, who, by the way, paid for all their college educations, they went off and none of them really found something worth sticking with."

"But, Jerry, don't you think it's natural for kids to want to go out and explore the world and see what else is out there besides what they know?"

"I don't know. I mean, I didn't do that. I know my father expected me to take over the ranch and that's what I did."

"Did you ever have a desire to do something else?"

"No; well, mostly no. I briefly tried something else but learned that ranching is what I wanted to do."

"Well, there's the difference. Evidently, your kids wanted to try other things. I think that's very natural. And then they will figure out what *they* want to do."

"Well, I think there are other things besides just what you want to do. There are obligations and gratitude and respect. It seems to me that my kids showed me none of those things but when it's convenient or they're in some pinch, then they come home. I mean, I am glad they're here but I just wish they had come under other circumstances."

"You say that you wanted them to stay or at least come back after college. Did you ever talk specifically to them about that?"

"I did with Ryan, at least after he said he was going off to Chicago to study journalism. After Ryan kind of bailed on me, I didn't want to go through that with Julie or Colin so I probably didn't say much to them. But I think they knew that I wanted them to stay."

"Oh, Jerry, you can't assume people know what you feel or what you want. It sounds like you waited too long to talk to Ryan; he had started to formulate different plans before he knew what you hoped for. And why would you expect Julie or Colin to stick around if you didn't make it very plain that you wanted them to."

"Damn it, Jan, I say the kids knew what I hoped for; they didn't need to have it all laid out. No one ever laid out my future for me but I think it all worked out pretty well."

"I just would like to see you get along better with all of them, especially Colin. He's such a fine young man. If you would make a gesture toward them instead of insisting that they give you some kind of apology, I am certain that your relationships with all of them would improve."

Jerry felt the heat rising inside of him; frankly, he didn't like an outsider, even Jan, telling him how to deal with the kids.

"Look," he said, "you haven't been around here all that long. You didn't see them growing up or all the things that I gave them and did for them. I don't think I am out of line for expecting a little something in return."

"It's not a business investment, Jerry. You don't do things for your kids with the idea of getting something in return."

"I just don't see the problem in wanting a little bit back for all that I did for them. I just want them to be here to say, 'Thanks, Dad' instead of 'Hey, Dad, I'm pregnant and I want to come home to have my baby.'"

"What I am trying to tell you is that you do the things you do because you love them, not because you expect to get something in return. That's not the way it works."

"How would you know?" Jerry said, now visibly upset. "You've never even had kids."

Though true, the argument that she didn't have kids and so couldn't or wouldn't know the basis for why parents do things for their kids was not true. Moreover, there was an element of meanness in making the statement. When logic or the truth are not there, attack the opponent. Jan felt it was an attack and, though she had long since been reconciled with not having children, she didn't like Jerry throwing it up at her in the middle of an argument into which the discussion had plainly evolved. She felt he was out of line but because things were getting heated she decided not to make an issue out of it.

"That's beside the point. I do have some understanding of relationships of all types and it's pretty clear that parents do things for their kids out of love and not for the kind of reasons you talk about."

"Jan, maybe it would be best if you would just butt out of my relationships with my kids."

"Jerry!" Jan exclaimed. She couldn't believe he said that.

"Let's change the subject."

Fire or no fire, that brought an unaccustomed chill as well as an awkward silence to the room.

After what seemed like many minutes, Jerry said, "So, how's the teaching going?"

Jan replied, "Oh, it's going just fine. The kids are pretty good except for the usual one or two problem kids; and the parents are generally involved and that's one of the most important things in education."

"Yes," Jerry said, "you mentioned that before."

More silence.

Eventually, Jerry said, "Well, I should probably be going."

Jan asked, "I know I'm supposed to come for brunch and watching football tomorrow, but what time should I come?"

"Anytime is fine. The football starts early and we'll probably have the food out mid- morning."

"Oh, good," Jan replied. "I'll have time to go to church in the morning. I don't suppose you'd care to join me?"

"Now, you know I have no use for God and you know why. And I don't hear any good explanations."

"Well, I certainly don't have the right training to know or say why such things happen but maybe if you would come to church or at least talk to someone connected to the church you'd get some answers."

"Nope, I prayed to God when Jackie was giving birth and the problems right after. I told Him I would do anything if He would just let her live and He turned me down. That was the end of it for me. Hell, this whole thing with all religions is likely just a big fantasy. How can anyone believe that stuff? If my Christian God couldn't give the one thing I asked for, why should I give Him anything?"

Very quietly, Jan said, "Okay." Then, after a long and awkward pause, "I'll see you tomorrow."

Jerry drove home just a little upset. He and Jan saw eye-to-eye on most everything-- the values people should hold, politics, travel, where to live-- except on his kids and God and, naturally, those were the two topics that ended an otherwise great evening. He hoped that things between them didn't backslide any. He hated to conclude the evening on two basically sour notes but at least he was being honest. Well, there would be the brunch and football the next day. And, Jerry had something up his sleeve that would make this New Year's Day the best one he had had in years. As Scarlett O'Hara would say, 'Tomorrow is another day.'

Chapter 29

The day started great with everyone, even Jerry, in the kitchen helping to get a terrific spread ready for later in the morning. Then, they all went into the TV room to settle down and watch some football. All three of the ladies, Michelle, Julie and Emily liked football just as much as the men. Jan loved football, too, and Jerry realized that was yet another thing he loved about her. What a difference from way back when women hardly knew anything about sports. Jerry rejoiced in that difference from earlier days.

They all were intently watching football on multiple TVs. Family favorite Notre Dame had beaten LSU a couple of days before and they were awaiting the Ohio State-Alabama game. While all the kids and partners stayed to watch, Jerry suggested to Jan that they go into the living room. Jerry got a couple of cups of coffee and they went into the living room and sat on the couch.

Jerry started things off. "I just wanted to say I'm sorry about how the last of the conversation went last night. I hate for an evening to end that way."

Jan said, "That's all right, Jerry, I know that's just the way you feel. We've talked about those things enough times but I guess I just always hope things might change."

Jerry noted a bit less emotion, a bit less steam in her comments. He wondered if there were more.

"You seem a little disturbed or quiet or something. Is anything wrong?

"No, I'm probably just tired. There's been a lot going on lately. And we were up late last night, at least by my standards."

Jerry pondered for a moment about whether she had answered or dodged the question; too hard to tell. He then proceeded. "Well, I thought maybe we could talk about us for a little bit, what we're doing, where things are headed."

Very tentatively Jan said, "Okay."

"Jan, we've been seeing each other a lot since July. I guess you know you're the first woman I've really dated since my first wife died. And, well, the truth is that I'm crazy about you. In fact, I love you and I don't want to lose you, ever."

Jerry paused partly because it was hard to say those things to a woman after so many years and partly because he wanted to see if there was any reaction from Jan. But she had a blank look on her face or, possibly, was there a little look of fear?

"Anyway, I know I'm not perfect and you could probably do a lot better, but what would you think about spending the rest of your life as my wife?"

For a couple of seconds, Jan's expression stayed exactly the same. Then, her hand went up to cover her mouth, her face contorted and she fought unsuccessfully to hold back tears.

At first Jerry wondered if these were tears of joy; but quickly it became apparent that they were not.

"What's wrong?" he asked. "Is marrying me such a horrible idea?"

Jan struggled to talk through her tears. At the same time, it was hard for Jerry to see any woman cry but, particularly, Jan because she always seems so strong; he had never seen her cry before.

"Oh, Jerry, it's not a horrible idea and, yet, at the same time it is."

Obviously, this didn't answer anything so Jerry just waited for Jan to offer more. She cried for just a bit and then as she started to regain her composure, she actually laughed a little and said, "I'm sorry, I can't imagine what you must be thinking."

What Jerry was thinking was that although he had heard 'No' he wasn't convinced that it was final. He had that state of mind, different from an actual thought process, that if I can just get clear on what the problem is I'm sure I can talk my way through it.

When she had finally settled down enough to talk she said, "Of course the idea of marrying you is not horrible. I'll admit, I've thought about that prospect a lot myself. But last night, I realized that it wouldn't work for us. I can't be married to a man that is, well, estranged from his family. I love your family. I think your kids are terrific and I think the world of Emily. But if I became your wife I would have to choose sides. You have strong feelings about them and, while I disagree, I know you feel strongly. And my job as your wife is to support you. But if you're at war with your kids, where would I fit in? I don't want to be in that position. I would want the whole family to love and respect one another. I could fit in to that kind of family but not one like yours is now. Yours is the way it is mostly because of you.

And then there are your feelings about God. I don't know what to say. I know a lot of people feel the way you do but I happen to think differently. I believe in God. I believe in Jesus Christ. I believe in what churches teach even if the churches themselves are wrong or worse. And you've got such anger about the whole thing. You're right, in so many ways we're a good fit. I was hoping you might change, at least a little, but it doesn't seem like that's going to happen. I just don't see how it could work."

Jerry looked at Jan and knew this was going to be his only chance to change her mind. "Well, as far as the kids are concerned, I could tone down my comments a little and hold my feelings back. You know, try to make a better atmosphere, one that would be pleasant for you and for everybody. You wouldn't have to take sides because I wouldn't force you to. You could do or say whatever you want regarding them.

As for the God thing, I don't know that I could totally change but you mentioned last night that if I went to church that I might just change my feelings. I'd be willing to do that. I'd go to church with you every Sunday. How would that be?"

"Jerry, don't you see? You're talking about changing things at the surface level, changing the appearance of things. If you don't change how you really feel, I don't think just changing how things appear is really going to work in the long run."

"Jan, tell me what I can do or say to make you change your mind. Please, I'll do anything."

She said, "Jerry, it's not a matter of me changing my mind. It's a matter of *you* changing, you changing who you are by changing how you feel about two deep-seated, important cornerstones of life—God and family. You can't just decide to change because it's convenient at the moment; you have to commit to it; you have to live it. I don't think you're ready to truly do that."

Jerry felt the knot in his stomach; he was starting to feel nauseous. He knew he was losing and had little else to say or offer. He looked for a long time into her eyes and she looked back at his. He searched for something magical to say but came up empty.

Finally, he said, "Well, will I see you this weekend?"

"Jerry, I don't think we should see each other anymore," came the words he didn't want to hear.

"But, Jan, let's not throw this all away. We can work on it. I can change."

"Jerry, I've been trying to get you to change or at least consider it for a while. I don't think it's in you. All we would wind up doing is hurting each other even more than now and I don't want to do that. I'm sorry."

Jan leaned over and gave Jerry a kiss. "Goodbye, Jerry." With that, she got up and went out the front door and left, apparently for good.

Jerry couldn't believe the turn of events over the past eleven or so hours. He had gone from loving a woman whom he thought was going to be his wife to having her reject him and having her walk out on him. Jerry had always had a bit of a defense mechanism kick in when bad things happened. He didn't feel the effect of something that hurt him right away; it came over time. So, he knew that as bad as he felt at the moment, it was going to get worse. That night was going to be a rough one. He normally wasn't a drinking man but tonight he just might be.

Ryan and Julie came into the room laughing about something. "Where's Jan?" Julie asked.

Jerry looked up still in a little bit of shock. "Oh, it turned out that she had something she had to do today. She said to tell you goodbye."

Ryan and Julie looked at one another in disbelief but said nothing.

Jerry said, "I don't feel very well. I'm going to lie down for a while," and went to his bedroom.

Chapter 30

Everyone noticed the change in Jerry but it wasn't the one that Jan had wanted. He was even more taciturn than before but that change was only incremental. The real change was that he didn't seem to care about the ranch anymore or what was going on. Instead of fourteen hour days he stopped promptly at five o'clock or even before, went home and had several glasses of wine. He was quiet and brooding and even Emily couldn't really get through to him. His directions to his crews, even to Ryan, were vague and not always helpful. Fortunately, everyone knew the drill well enough that in spite of his funk most things got done as they were supposed to.

But there was nothing they could do or say about Jerry and Jan. It was evident that something had happened between him and Jan but no one wanted to even ask him about it and no one thought it their place to get in touch with Jan. Even though the kids adored her, they thought this was one place where there were boundaries and they were on the side where they weren't allowed to play. They thought if they reached out to her they would be intruding on their dad's personal life. If Jan were to get in touch with them, that would be a different story but that didn't happen.

In the first few days after her rejection of his marriage proposal, Jerry himself tried to call her but she never answered. He left messages, hoping she would at least call but she never did. After a few days, it became clear that it really was over. Jan was gone and had apparently already moved on. She didn't even want to speak to him.

Before he was generally taciturn; he was now bordering on surly. There were plenty of moments when Jerry felt embittered and mad at the world. Being caught in the middle of all that was enough to make a man cry and privately, alone in his room at night, he did more than a little crying.

One day merged into another, and then became a week and then two weeks. Nothing changed over that time. Jerry tried calling a few more times but, after not receiving an answer after leaving a dozen messages he considered it pathetic to continue. He even went to church a couple of times to the 9:30 Mass that she had told him was the one she always went to hoping to "bump into her" but she wasn't there. He wondered if she had moved away but he was able to confirm that she was still in town. But as far as he was concerned, she wasn't. He didn't want to just go over to her apartment because he felt that would not go well. No, he had to "accidentally" see her, whether fake or legitimate, to have a reasonable chance of success. But how to make that happen?

Emily decided enough was enough. She said, "Jerry, I know you're feeling bad about Jan but it's time you stopped moping and time you started bein' nicer to people."

Jerry looked sternly at Emily and seemed about to argue with her but then he took a deep breath and asked in a whiny tone, "Well, dang it, Em, why does bad stuff like this always happen to me?"

Emily replied, "Oh, Jerry, for heaven's sake. First of all, it doesn't always happen to you and it doesn't happen to you as much as it does to a lot of people." She looked at Jerry for several long seconds. "What exactly happened anyway?"

Jerry thought for several seconds and answered, "I asked her to marry me and she turned me down."

"That's what I figured," replied Emily. "Did she say why?"

"She said she didn't want to be in between me and the kids and have to take sides; and she doesn't like that I don't believe in God or at least that if there is one, I blame him for Jackie's death."

"Jerry, I don't know what to say anymore. How many people have to tell you that your attitude about your kids is messed up and your attitude about God is worse? You're one of the most stubborn people I know about some things."

"Well, I offered to tone things down a bit with the kids and I offered to go to church with her."

Emily responded, "That sounds like you making minor accommodations to change her mind rather than you really changing."

"That's basically what she said."

"And she was right. Jerry, you're a good man but you've got a wall around those two areas in your life that keeps people away. And you're stubborn as can be. It's no wonder she turned you down."

"Thanks for the words of comfort," said Jerry sullenly.

"Well believe it or not, I'm trying to help you; I've been trying to help you for a lot of years but you just won't listen to me."

Emily continued lecturing Jerry but her comment sent Jerry back in time to when he had first met Emily, shortly after Jackie's death. It had been her marriage misfortune that had caused her to show up just when Jerry had needed help. As he found out somewhat after that first meeting, Emily had had two near marriages.

The first time, when she was twenty-four in 1965, she had been dating a gentleman by the name of Jason Cody who had enlisted in the Army and was awaiting his orders to report. They saw each other continuously for about six weeks when the order came and off he went. They corresponded furiously while he was gone and their relationship deepened as much as possible under the circumstances. When he came home on his next leave, he was busting with pride and bursting with love for Emily.

His pride was over the fact that he had been assigned as a rifleman to the 1st Battalion of the Seventh Cavalry Regiment or, as it was referred to by its members, the 1st of the 7th. More importantly, this was the unit once commanded by General George Armstrong Custer, who was famous in U.S. Army lore and, at least to some historians, infamous for his bravado and stupidity.

Jason proposed and Emily readily accepted. They considered a wedding before he left but they both concluded their families would be disappointed with such a quickie celebration and so they decided to wait until he came home in a year. They promised to write each other every day and they did.

In November, 1965, the 1st of the 7th was helicoptered into the Ia Drang Valley in South Vietnam and became involved in one of the most intense battles of the war. Roughly 450 Americans surrounded by 2,000 enemy soldiers. Jason's company was the first one in and he was in a platoon that got cut off from the rest of the company. When the battle was over, the carnage was monumental. Jason Cody was killed in action.

Over the next twenty years, she had probably dated a hundred men, a few of whom were interested in marriage, many of whom were interested in a "honeymoon." She wasn't opposed to sex outside of marriage but was uncomfortable with casual sex. In the period after Jason's death, she did not want to get married. Later, when she was open to the idea, there were a couple more serious romances but things never got as far as marriage.

What became her last chance to marry came when she was forty-four. She was living in New York City and met a man named Brad Williams who was some kind of big shot in advertising. They dated occasionally at first but then began to see each other all the time. Brad was also forty four and had never been married which Emily had found a little strange but didn't think much about it. He wooed her incessantly and eventually proposed. Deep, deep down, Emily wasn't sure she loved Brad; in fact, there was a little seed of a doubt about his character. But, she was forty-four and men weren't knocking on her door the way they had done when she was twenty-four.

So, they set a date a few months out and Emily notified her family and close friends. She spent much of the next months organizing the wedding, the wedding party, the church, the reception, the flowers—all the things women usually handle. She was pleased that she was going to be married more than happy about marrying Brad but she found it hard to admit that she might be making a mistake. Frankly, she wasn't sure what women should feel when getting married, maybe this was normal. Besides, she was so caught up in the preparations, she just didn't have the time to think about how she felt in the deepest recesses of her being.

About two weeks before the wedding, there was a knock at the door. When she opened it, there was a young woman holding a baby. The woman said, "Are you Emily?"

To which Emily replied, "Yes, yes I am. Who are you?" The woman said, "I am the mother of Brad Williams' baby and I intend to hold him to his promise to marry me!"

Her feelings for Brad, whatever they were, dissipated almost before she was able to close the door. Needless to say, the wedding was called off and Emily was embarrassed and disappointed. And, yet, there was a subtle yet powerful sense of relief that she had avoided disaster. Brad was nothing to her now. She discovered she was only disappointed that she wouldn't, finally, be married. Moreover, she now believed that it just wasn't meant to be. Somehow the men she attracted weren't really right or maybe the gods had other plans for her, but she resigned herself to being a spinster, a word she hated but knew that the word was worse than the reality.

But, she didn't want to stay in New York any longer—she had never really liked it all that much and now there was this very bad experience that too many locales in the City reminded her of. So, she had no idea where she might go but one day opened up a map of the U.S., twirled around in a circle with her eyes closed, and plopped her finger somewhere on the map; somewhere turned out to be Livingston, Montana. The thought of moving there both excited and scared her for the same reason—it was a total unknown. She had never been out in the Mountain West and assumed that everyone was not as sophisticated as the people she knew in New York City, Of course, she had to admit, New Yorkers generally think everyone else is less sophisticated than they are. And maybe, a little less charm and sophistication than she had once thought Brad Williams had would be a good thing.

She packed up and moved to Livingston, staying in a hotel in town and began looking for work. There were a number of job openings, but they all were either things she wasn't right for or things she wasn't interested in. The, one day she saw an ad in the paper for a nanny and housekeeper. "Recently widowed man needs nanny and housekeeper for three children. Good salary. Room and board provided." It struck her that she could be almost married; she would live in the same house as a man, she'd have three kids to take care of, and she'd keep a house. If she wasn't going to be really and truly married, this might be the next best thing.

She called Jerry up and they agreed to meet the next day in town near her hotel. Of course, Jerry was more used to hiring cowboys and the like and really wasn't sure how to go about interviewing a woman for a housekeeping and nanny job. He started off a little awkwardly.

"So, how come you're available for this job and not tied down with other obligations?"

She smiled at the strange first question. "You mean how come I'm not married and with a family of my own?"

"Yeah, I guess so."

Emily smiled a little and wondered if this were in the corporate world and back in New York if a lawyer would have told her that this was grounds for a lawsuit. Of course, she had intentionally had left all that behind and didn't think Jerry was being disrespectful, just a little ignorant. So, she told him her story and about Jason and Brad and how she had come to Livingston.

When she had finished, he said, "Are you sure this is something you want to do? You know, moving here permanently and all that? I'd like to have someone who will stick around."

"Emily answered, "I can't give you any guarantees but I'm not a teenager who flits here and there. I've made the decision to move here and so far I like it a lot. If I go to work for you, how long I stay will depend a lot on you and your children. I'm applying to be a nanny and a housekeeper, not a maid and servant."

Jerry sat back, satisfied because he liked the direct answer. He told her she was hired and they worked out the details.

She moved out of the hotel the next day and into the house and lives of the Johnstons. She immediately fell in love with all three children, Ryan, Julie and Colin, the newborn baby. She knew their mother had died giving birth to Colin—that much Jerry had told her, but she didn't know much else. Over the next couple of months or so, here and there from friends who might stop by and whisper to her while Jerry was out of the room or store clerks she became friendly with, she would pick bits and pieces of the story of Jackie dying and how it changed Jerry and, in turn, the kids.

The "job" for Emily became a new life, her life, which she quickly cherished. Having never been a birth-mother, she had never realized how much she loved children and how much she enjoyed being around them. She raised his kids and cared for them and loved them, and they loved her. She was as much a mom to them as if she had given birth herself. At the same time, it pained her that there wasn't a real, complete father in the picture and over the years she had made sure to tell Jerry her feelings on the matter. Emily had been an independent, blunt speaking person all her life and her stint in New York had only sharpened her verbal edge. On more than one occasion, she had given him both barrels over something he had done or failed to do, particularly with respect to the kids. His usual reaction would be to just take it silently, wait until she was done, and then amble off.

"...so it's high time you reconsider your opinions on these things," Emily said, apparently having been speaking the whole time. Jerry had not heard a word. But having remembered her love stories that didn't work out, he realized that other people have misfortune, too. But he wasn't ready to acknowledge that.

"Well, if you insist, Mom. I'll give it all some prayerful thought," said Jerry, hoping she appreciated the sarcasm.

This time it was Emily who turned and ambled off with a wave of her hand, shaking her head.

Chapter 31

Jerry went off by himself on Rocket quite often taking only Puck, his faithful mutt, as a companion. It had been an unusually warm winter so far and there wasn't very much snow although both conditions were likely to change at some point. But, for now, it was relatively pleasant to go out on horseback and hope that the crisp air and beautiful countryside would soothe his soul. Jerry had the farrier remove Rocket's shoes. Even though it was warmer than normal, there was still snow and ice and horses did better without shoes in those conditions.

He purposely stayed away from places he thought he might run into one of his crews. He wanted to be alone and didn't want to have to talk to anyone about ranch business or anything else. In spite of stating otherwise, he wanted to consider the things about which Emily had spoken. He wanted to figure out how to deal with his kids. And, in particular, he wanted to feel sorry for himself over why bad stuff always seemed to happen to him.

Relative to how he felt when he was in the house with people around, he felt pretty good getting out to places he normally didn't. In many years the snow would have been too deep and the air too cold to go where he was able to now. Puck had no trouble getting around and his presence was a good palliative for how Jerry felt. Puck didn't ask for anything; instead giving complete loyalty.

Jerry decided to take one of his sojourns one day in mid-January, partly because the weather forecast was that normal winter was about to return with much colder temperatures and a big snowstorm. He saddled up Rocket and put some hay in a large saddlebag. He got Emily to make a little lunch and brought along something for Puck and some water. He had on several layers of clothing, a scarf, although he wasn't wearing it, and he strapped on his .45 pistol like he always did when he was out on his own.

There were some pretty good trails that the elk had made over the years that lead to the higher elevations. Jerry always liked to be at high elevations; sometimes he thought he might have been a bird in a former life although, of course, he didn't believe in former lives. He worked his way up the mountain side that was on one side of his ranch and home until he got to where he had a real nice view across the valley. It was another sunny and pretty warm day for January with cloudless skies and he was content to park himself there for a while.

As always, Jerry was awed by the scenery. He even admitted to himself that there must be some kind of divine being to create what he was looking at. The angle of the sun, obviously different from the summer, along with the white snow and skies bluer than blue, created yet another interlude that Jerry had enjoyed so many times.

He tied Rocket's reins loosely to a tree branch and gave him the hay. He gave Puck the food he had brought for him. Then he got out a little portable stove and attached the gas canister to it, poured water into a metal cup and set it on the stove in order to heat water to make coffee. He found a flat rock where what little snow there had been had melted which made for a great seat. It didn't take long for the water to boil and he made his coffee which he drank black, no sugar and no cream. He laughed to himself, thinking he could have just brought a thermos. But this was so much better. Brewing his coffee, even using a tiny gas stove, seemed closer to nature than using a thermos. He sat munching on his sandwich, drinking his hot coffee, accompanied by his favorite horse and his loyal dog and looked across the sunlit valley to another mountain with nothing but blue sky in between. For just a little, he forgot how miserable he was.

He had just finished his sandwich and coffee when he looked over and saw Rocket starting to fidget. Rocket's feet were dancing and he was moving his head back and forth; clearly, something was bothering him. Jerry looked around but didn't see anything. Jerry started to walk over to Rocket to see if he could determine what was bothering him when Puck started barking. Now Jerry knew something was up but he didn't know what. Rocket jerked his head back and pulled the reins off the tree branch and took off running. Jerry cursed himself for being so negligent as to tie reins loosely to a branch. He knew better.

He still was trying to figure out what had made Rocket bolt and had Puck barking when he spotted him—a large male black bear about fifty yards away. In the back of his mind he remembered that sometimes when it was warm, bears came out of hibernation to look for food. He knew there was debate about whether bears were hibernators at all. He knew that young males were more likely to be predatory than the "mother with cubs" possibility. He tried to remember whether with black bears you were supposed to submit and play dead or fight back. All these thoughts flashed but at the back of his mind. At the front of his mind he was thinking, "Oh, shit!"

He started to back away as slowly as he could get himself to which was fast enough to seem like he was fleeing, which he was. The bear began to charge and Jerry saw that the bear was closing quickly. He drew his gun not knowing whether it would be effective or not but it was all he had. Just as he was about to take aim he tripped over a root and fell on his back and the gun fell out of his hand on the ground a few feet away. "Oh, my God," he thought, "I'm screwed." The bear was about twenty yards away and coming fast.

All of a sudden, out of nowhere, Puck jumped on the bear and began biting it about the face and snout. The bear was surprised for just a second and then threw Puck off like human brushes away a fly. Puck let out a yelp from the force of the bear's powerful arm. The bear then turned back to his prey and began another charge when Puck again jumped on the bear and again began to bite him. This time the bear swatted Puck to the ground and with one great swipe with his huge paw and long claws gashed open Puck's side and chest which caused Puck to emit a mortal cry of anguish.

With the moments that Puck had bought for him with his heroic attack on the bear, Jerry was able to reach his gun and get into a kneeling position to shoot. He had no idea if his gun would stop the hungry bear but if he was going to go down, he was going to go down fighting. "Get control of yourself," he thought. "Make every shot count."

The bear had just begun his final charge and was only about fifteen yards away. Jerry knew that most people were bad shots from as short a distance as ten yards. And while he had been a good shot once, he hadn't done much shooting over the last twenty years. "Where should I aim?" he thought. As he took final aim he thought, "Anywhere will do; just start shooting and hope to get him somewhere."

The bear was now only a dozen yards away and running right at Jerry. Jerry fired two quick shots with apparently no effect. He fired a third and a fourth and a fifth and the bear kept coming. It was now just a few yards away and Jerry could see his eyes and teeth and heard his growls.

They say when a man is about to die that his life flashes before him in an instant. Nothing flashed for Jerry. Instead, time relative to him slowed down relative to real time. Each tenth of a second in real time was like a minute to Jerry. Instead of a re-run of his whole life, he saw the most important people in his life—his father and mother, Jackie and his children. He saw his children one by one and felt acute sadness that he was going to die while his relationships with them were strained. He saw Jan and thought how senseless it was for him to have let her get away. Wasn't there any way to avoid death and have a second chance with her and his kids? "God, help me!" he heard a voice cry.

He aimed his last shot for bear's head and fired just as it was about to plow Jerry over. The bear took a big swipe at Jerry and tore into Jerry's flesh, ripping open a portion of his left upper chest. He felt the bear's weight as it crashed into him and knocked him on his back with the force of three NFL linebackers. He heard his ribs crack and felt like his right shoulder had been knocked off away from the rest of his body and had the wind knocked out of him so that he could barely breathe. His only thought was to go down fighting and he hoped the end would be quick. He tried to grab the knife that hung on his belt but the bear had him pinned down and he could barely move. Jerry braced himself for the same fate as had befallen Puck. Instead, nothing happened. The bear didn't move. Trying to marshal his wits, Jerry slowly realized the bear was dead. The last shot must have got him; he didn't know how many of the others had hit their mark.

He began trying to extricate himself but couldn't use his arms because one was pinned and he couldn't feel the other. He was able to bend his knees just a little and dig his heels into the ground and push to get his body to inch out from underneath the bear. With each push his ribs and shoulder screamed at him but eventually he was able to get completely clear.

Jerry could only move with great pain but he made his way over to where Puck was lying on the ground with his side slashed open and his internal organs visible. There was blood everywhere. Puck was whimpering very softly, life seeping out of him, barely able to breath. Jerry bent over him and stroked his head softly. "Good boy, Puck," he said as tears began to erupt from his eyes. "You saved my life."

He knew Puck was in great pain. He knew there was but one thing to do. He emptied his .45 of the spent shells, took a bullet from one of the loops on his gun belt, and inserted it into the gun. "Goodbye, my friend," he sobbed and fired the bullet into Puck's head.

He sat on the ground for a long time, crying but with extremely mixed emotions. He was grieving over Puck's demise and yet he was happy to be alive and knew his trusted companion was the reason for that. He had no qualms about putting Puck down; he had been in terrible pain and it was the right thing to do. Most ranchers have to put animals down at one time or another and Jerry was always happy to relieve a being's suffering even if the only way to do so was by ending its life. "Damn!" he thought. "Why Puck? Why me?"

Walking, indeed every movement was very painful, but he nevertheless retrieved Rocket and, though it was chilly, he took off his coat, put Puck in the coat and carried him in front of the saddle. He knew the jacket would be ruined but he didn't care.

Puck had saved his life at the expense of his own. When Jerry finally made it back to the house, he was in a state of shock, bloody, battered and wheezing more than breathing.

Chapter 32

Jerry woke up and it took a while for him to figure out that he was in a hospital. He had no recollection as to how he had gotten there. It felt like he was tied up and he was groggy, like he had not been sleeping well. He saw monitors and lights and all sorts of equipment. He looked down at his right wrist and saw a needle and tube stuck in his wrist and vaguely remembered being given intravenous medication.

He slowly rolled his head and eyes over to his left and he saw Colin sleeping in a chair. "How the heck did he get here?" Jerry thought to himself. "What is he doing here?"

Jerry was trying to figure out what was going on when he sucked in a short but heavy breath as the bear attack jumped into his slowly-clearing consciousness. He remembered that Puck was dead but had saved his life. He thought about that for a moment and a tear formed in the corner of one eye and slowly rolled down his cheek. "What a great dog and friend!" Jerry thought.

Then, he remembered how he had felt when he thought he was about to die; he closed his eyes and pictured in his mind the bear closing on him and how he hadn't really been afraid to die, just sad because of "unfinished business." He remembered his thoughts about his children and his cry of help to God. Emotionally he experienced again what he had felt as the bear was closing in--the surreal sensation of complete calm before death and at least at that moment, how extremely insignificant were so many things he had thought were important. He remembered those thoughts but, presently, was too heavily medicated to know what he thought now that his life wasn't in danger. He tried to ponder whether he had reached out to God like the proverbial atheist in a foxhole or whether the apparent moment of death had brought hitherto unknown clarity on the subject of God's existence. For the time being, it took more effort than he was capable of to make any progress on that conundrum.

Jerry fell back asleep and slept for another two hours. This time when he awoke, he wasn't quite so heavily sedated and he felt some discomfort on his chest and shoulder; his chest felt like someone or something had cut into him while his shoulder gave off a general dull ache. He looked over to the chair where Colin had been sleeping but it was empty. He wondered if he had dreamed that Colin had been there.

Just then, the door to the room opened and a nurse came in and said, "Ah, you're awake, Mr. Johnston. How are you feeling?"

"I'm not rightly sure," Jerry answered slowly. "Earlier I felt OK but now I'm starting to feel like someone beat me up."

"Well," the nurse answered, "you were beat up but by a bear, not by a person."

Once again, a flood of memories of the incident cascaded over Jerry. He looked over to the empty chair again and asked, "Was my son here?"

"Yes," she answered. "He's still here. I think he went to the cafeteria to get something to eat. I am going to go get the doctor."

In a little while, the nurse came back with the doctor and also with Colin. Colin came over to the bedside and said, "Hi, Dad. How are you feeling?"

"Well," Jerry replied with a hint of a chuckle, "every minute that goes by I feel a little worse. Isn't it supposed to go the other way? Doctor, what's the story?"

The doctor gave Jerry a summary of his injuries—separated shoulder, broken clavicle, broken ribs, lacerated pectoral muscles, punctured lung and more—but Jerry was barely hearing it. He was looking at Colin and was so happy just because he was there. The doctor was talking about medications Jerry would be taking, next steps in his recuperation but sensed Jerry's inattention and said, "Colin, I hope you can remember what I've said. I'll write it all down but I hope you can help your dad and get him to do the things we're suggesting."

"Hmmpf," Colin laughed. "I'll remember it all but not sure whether I can accomplish the rest."

The doctor and the nurse left and so now it was just father and son. Colin said, "We called Ryan. He's on his way back from Chicago."

Jerry furrowed his brow and asked , "What's Ryan doing in Chicago?"

"You remember; he and Michelle went back to finish closing things up in Chicago. They will be here in a day or two." It was clear to Colin that Jerry did not recall this at all. "Anyway, Julie is at home with the baby but she'll come to visit when you're up to it. Emily got pretty choked up but said to let you know she's praying for you."

"That's fine, Son," Jerry answered. He looked intently at Colin and said "Thanks for being here."

Colin paused, trying to match his response to how he felt; trouble was he wasn't sure exactly how he did feel. All the old feelings, good and bad, were still with him and as usual it was hard which side of the ledger was predominant at any given moment. He finally settled for a simple, "No problem, Dad."

For a minute or so, no more words were spoken. They looked at one another but didn't speak as if words would only get in the way of communication. One thing that was clear to Jerry was that what he felt during the attack about his kids and, particularly, Colin was a legitimate true feeling. There was love in Jerry's eyes and Colin saw it. He wasn't sure what was going on but sensed it was good and so he didn't want to break the silence.

Finally, Jerry said, "Colin, I have to tell you something. When that bear was almost on me and I was sure that I was a goner, a few things ran through my head. One of them was how stupid I have been in regard to my relationship with you. I know there is a gulf between us; there's been one since the day your mama died and it's all my fault. I'm so sorry."

Colin had long hoped to hear those words but now that he had heard them he didn't really know what to say. After a few moments he said, "I know you blamed me for mom's death. I just never really understood why."

"No, Son. You've got it all wrong. I didn't blame you for her death, I blamed myself. I had pushed your mom to have a third child. You were just a constant reminder of my pushing her to get my way. You were a constant reminder of *my* responsibility for your mom's death. It was my fault, not yours."

Colin's eyes got a little teary and his voice trembled a little. This hardened, combat veteran couldn't help but go soft when the topic so long left unspoken was finally being addressed. When he spoke, there was a more than a touch of anger and a dash of sadness.

"Why couldn't you have told me this a long time ago? Do you know how long I have had to deal with this? Everybody else but you told me mom's death wasn't my fault. But you're the one I needed to hear it from!"

"I know; you're right. I'm so sorry."

Colin didn't say anything. He wondered if this was really from the heart. Was this a permanent change? When the trauma of everything was past and his dad was back on the ranch and in charge, would he feel the same way? Colin just didn't know what to say and so he stood there looking at his dad as if there was some further information he might discover. Finally, all Colin could muster was a nod of the head to say goodbye and he turned and went out.

Chapter 33

A day later, Jerry woke up and saw Fr. Jeff in his room. He knew Fr. Jeff well; they had had a friendly relationship in which the priest had tried to get Jerry to church and Jerry had consistently resisted. Jerry had never talked much to Fr. Jeff about why he wouldn't attend church. He didn't want to listen to what the priest might have to say.

Seeing that Jerry was awake, Fr. Jeff walked over to the bedside and said, "Jerry, I am glad that you are doing all right. How do you feel?"

"Terrible," answered Jerry. "I seem to either be in pain or so drugged up that I don't know what's going on. I'd like to get out of here but I know it's going to be a while." Jerry than looked at Fr. Jeff and was trying to decide if he wanted to talk about his appeal to God during the bear attack. It would open the whole can of worms he had avoided for so long. Nevertheless, he decided he had to.

"Father, I want to tell you something. When I was getting attacked by that bear, I cried out to God to help me." He looked at the priest as if he had said all that was necessary for him to respond.

Fr. Jeff said, "Do you find that unusual? It seems pretty normal to me."

"Well, not for me. For many years, I haven't had any use for God."

Fr. Jeff responded, "I don't know a lot but I've been told that it has something to do with your wife's death. Is that correct?"

"Yes."

"Tell me about it, Jerry."

Jerry told Fr. Jeff the whole story with Jackie and her dying and his praying and how he couldn't forgive or even believe in a

God that could do that. He ended with, "How could a just God do that to me?"

Fr. Jeff sat back and looked at Jerry straight in the eyes. He stroked his chin, having recognized Jerry's problem and now trying to figure the best way to explain it to him.

"Jerry, I've heard this kind of thing before. I recognize the symptoms. I think you have what I call Frank Sinatra Disorder." He let that sink in a moment.

Jerry said, "What the heck is that?"

"Obviously you know Frank Sinatra. One of his best known and popular songs was "My Way." The song was actually written by Paul Anka but Sinatra made it popular. Do you know it?"

"Yeah" answered Jerry, "I think so." Jerry then half sang some of the words from the song. "'For what is a man, la da de dah, blah blah blah, I did it my way.' Right?"

"Yep that's it. Does anything strike you about that song?" Fr. Jeff waited but Jerry slowly shook his head.

"It's a celebration of self. Every verse ends 'I did it my way.' My way, my way, my way. The whole thing is about how someone did everything in life *their* way. It's celebrated in this song even though, in my opinion, that's one of the biggest problems in the world today. Everyone wants to live and do things *their* way. They see the world through *their* eyes. But if everyone is doing that, there's bound to be a lot of conflict as all those egos clash.

Fr. Jeff leaned in and clasped his hands together on the table between them. "Jerry, you see your wife's death as practically a personal offense to you because you are looking at it as if you are the center of the universe. Is that what you feel?

"No," Jerry answered a little defensively, in part because Emily had used almost the exact same words. "I'm not an egotistical man. I don't think I'm particularly better than other men."

"And yet your whole description of your wife's death is filled with statements like, 'Why did God do this to me?' and 'Why wouldn't God do that for me?' I'm not trying to be cruel, Jerry, I am sure having your spouse die was a horrible experience. But I am saying that just because you don't understand it and just because you asked for something and didn't get it doesn't mean that there wasn't a reason for it."

"What reason could there be?"

"I can't tell you that; I don't know. But just because you and I don't know the answer doesn't mean that one doesn't exist. You don't believe in God but you do believe that if you can't understand why something, even a bad something, happened then it must be that there can't be any explanation. Don't you see how backward that is?"

"I don't know."

Let me put it another way. You were asking God to spare your wife, right?"

"Yes."

"Then you were mad at God for not doing so, right"

"Yes."

"Well, if you believe in a God that is so powerful that He has the power to spare someone from dying, perhaps that God has His reasons for what he does, even if He doesn't share them with you." After a brief pause, Fr. Jeff continued, "Let me take it a step further. You never questioned death before did you? I mean the fact that we all die? I presume that you always accepted death even for your wife but you just objected to the timing of her death because it didn't suit *you*. *You* were cheated of her companionship and her love. Do you see a common theme here?"

Jerry didn't make a sound but inwardly was groaning as the validity of Fr. Jeff's statements were starting to hit home.

"Before your wife died, did you believe in heaven and hell?"

"Yes."

"Assuming your wife is in heaven with God, is that bad?"

Jerry said, "No" in the upward rising tone one uses when there is a realization that one's position was incorrect.

"So, who is the only one who isn't happy about the timing?"

"Me?"

"Uh-huh."

Jerry sat quietly because there wasn't much to say. He couldn't outrun the facts. For years, he had been looking at Jackie's death as though it was a personal affront to him; as if his feelings were paramount. He hadn't been upset for her because he did think she was in a better place. How that belief jived with his rejection of God was something he hadn't even tried to work out in his mind. In any event, over the years, his question was basically "Why did this have to happen to me?" And then a wave of grief came over him as he thought about all the wasted years, the people who had been hurt and him being at fault for those things.

Fr. Jeff noticed the change in Jerry's expression and body language. "Feeling guilty? Feeling like you've done wrong?"

Jerry simply nodded.

"That's the beauty of Jesus Christ. He's always ready to forgive; always ready to take someone back."

"Fr. Jeff, I've got to be honest; just because I might see where I have been very self-centered and my rejection of or anger with God was a result of that self-centeredness, that doesn't mean that I am suddenly filled with faith and am ready to go out and preach the gospel. If nothing else, it's going to take some time for me to assess and adjust what I believe in and how strongly."

"That's entirely understandable. So let me ask you, do you believe in God?"

Jerry stopped to think. "You know, I used to say that I did without really thinking about it. But I guess I always had some doubts. I mean, some people I know would say that I was a fool to believe in God; that it was all just one more fairy tale. And sometimes just looking around at what was happening in the world, it would make you wonder. Sometimes I would think, "If He exists, why doesn't God just come down and show Himself and then we would all know for sure."

Fr. Jeff replied, "How sincere do you think people would be if God appeared in the sky like a giant Wizard of Oz or something and demanded their worship? You know, a big, threatening face taking up the entire sky and scaring everyone crazy. God wants a relationship with you but wants it from your heart and because you want it, not because you're scared of him or because you're just insincerely reacting to the obvious."

"So how do I go about getting faith in God?" Jerry inquired while leaning forward.

Let me start my answer by saying that just because I read the Bible and counsel people doesn't mean I know everything; far from it. It's like the old line the more I learn I realize the less I know. But I do think that the starting point is to spend time thinking about God to the point where it's like some kind of meditation. You could also, I suppose, call it prayer. But I think for most people when you say prayer they think of either set prayers they have memorized or just a bunch of thank-yous; you know like, "Thank you, Lord for this" and "Thank you, Lord for that." I mean there's nothing wrong with that kind of prayer but I'm talking about getting your mind off day-to-day things and just trying to mentally open a dialog with God. It's the step of moving away from your self-centeredness to where there is something else that becomes the most important thing in your life even if you don't spend the most time on it. It's just my personal belief, but I don't think God expects us to worship him all day long. He knows there are things we have to do while on this earth. But you should make some time for it every day.

Reading a little Scripture every day also helps, especially if you have a Bible that has lots of explanations of things. You'd be amazed at how many connections there are between things in the Old Testament and things in the New Testament. If you spend the time to read and learn, eventually you see there are some dots that can be connected. And when you connect the dots it becomes easier to see that it's not just another fairy tale.

There are lots and lots of books you can read that literally make the case for God and Jesus Christ. One of the best is called, "The Case for Christ" by Lee Strobel. He was a reporter who went about trying to prove or disprove that Christ was God by looking at physical and other evidence and by talking to experts in a number or pertinent areas. He concluded that Christ was, indeed, God and he believed it so strongly that he became a minister. You don't read the Bible at all, do you?" Fr. Jeff asked. Jerry shook his head.

"The bottom line I'm suggesting is that the starting point for many people in regards to faith, and certainly for you, is to turn their attention from themselves to God; or if you must in the beginning, to the existence of God. But you have to work at it. You're doing things that you wouldn't normally do. But that's why it's His way, and not my way or your way. You see, that's the core thing to understand. He is God, not us. Our life is to be built around Him. It's not something you just sprinkle on top of your own life. Some people just don't want to concede that there is a being greater than us."

Jerry already knew he was changing. He had already acknowledged God in his cry for help so he couldn't pretend that he was a total non-believer. What happened compelled him to admit his attitude had had more to do with anger with God than not believing in Him. And now, Fr. Jeff had shown quickly and clearly that Jerry's anger was more selfish and juvenile than anything else. He didn't know exactly how but knew things would be different going forward. After a long while, he said, "Fr. Jeff, I want to thank you for your time and all that we've discussed. You've given me a lot to think about."

Smiling, Fr. Jeff replied, "Jerry, this is what gives me pleasure now. Obviously, I don't know where all this will shake out but if there's even a chance that you will come back to God after our chat then it was worth this and a whole lot more."

Chapter 34

Jerry was laid up for two more weeks. Ryan and Julie and Emily all took turns visiting but not Colin. He had gone on a short motorcycle trip and would be back in a few days.

On the first Sunday after he got home from the hospital, Jerry went to 9:30 Mass to see if he might be able to see and talk to Jan; but she was not there. He thought about asking the priest or other people about Jan but he was too uncomfortable to do so. He was afraid whoever he might speak with would want to know his name and why he was asking about Jan and so on. Instead, he just made sure she wasn't there and she wasn't.

So, even though he was going to be a little late, he went over to Two Rivers where the boys were already there having their regular Sunday breakfast. They could guess that Jerry had been at 9:30 Mass to try and see Jan because he had done so before but had failed to see her. The fact that he made it to breakfast indicated that he was no more successful this time. They had all watched as Jerry had sunk down in the time after the failed proposal to Jan. He had told them enough about what had happened and her reasons that they pretty much knew everything that was going on.

"Howdy, Boys," said Jerry quite happily and with a big smile, "how is everyone?"

"We're all fine," answered Loren. "How are you? You seem pretty perky. Did you finally get to see Jan?"

"No," replied Jerry. "No such luck. But I'll keep working on it."

Tom said, "Well, you seem to be reasonably happy about something; or, at least, you don't seem to be in the same kind of funk as you were last time. Did something good happen?"

"You guys have been telling me for some time that I needed to have better relationships with my kids and to communicate more with them. Well, after my little encounter with the bear, I'm comfortable with the idea of having a good talk with all my kids and, well, trying to make things better than they have been."

"That's great!" exclaimed Gordon and everyone nodded in agreement.

Jerry grinned and said, "And, that's not all. Fr. Jeff from our church came to visit me in the hospital and we had a real nice talk. He might have changed my mind a little on certain things." Jerry was amused at the looks on the faces of his friends.

"You wanna' explain that a little?" said Tim.

"We talked about God and faith and that kind of stuff."

"Holy shit!" exclaimed Tom. "Pardon my French."

Loren said, "Don't tell me you're going to become a man of faith."

"Well, I'm going to give it a try," answered Jerry. "I will admit, though, that it's hard to turn on a dime in that regard. As you know, I was pretty negative on all that and now I have to do a one-eighty."

Tim asked," What was it that he said that made you want to change?"

Jerry told them about the Frank Sinatra Disorder. Tom said, "Hmm. I might be a little guilty of that myself." The others murmured a bunch of 'Me, toos.'

"So what do you plan to do? Do you think you have faith now like you once did?" queried Tim.

"Not really," answered Jerry, "at least not the way I think about it. I think a person of faith is pretty certain about the truth in what they believe. And from what this friend told me, it's something most people have to work at. I've been away from church or God for so long that I have some work ahead of me to get there. But that's what I'm going to start to do. Go to church, read the Bible, talk to people further along than I am. Mainly, though, it's about looking outward as opposed to inward all the time."

The group was just a little amazed at what their cynical-bordering-on-bitter friend had just said. It all sounded positive but it took a few moments to absorb the apparent change in Jerry.

So, Jerry," said Loren, "with all this change and all this work on faith and other things, why are you so happy?"

"I can't tell you precisely, Loren, but somehow it just feels right. For the first time in a long time, I feel like I'm on the right track. Now, I'm at the beginning of the right track with a long way to go but I think this is all going to be good. I feel like the anger that I had felt is subsiding, maybe even largely gone. I'm even trying to be more tolerant of people that have different political positions from me."

"Okay," said Tim, putting both hand up in the air. "This is getting scary now. Are you telling us that your political views are changing?"

"No, not at all," said Jerry. What I said was that I'm trying to be more tolerant of other people's views, even yours," he added with a smirk.

"Well, I'll be," said Tim with false gravity. "There's hope for the man, yet."

"So, what are you going to say to your kids?" asked Gordon.

"That's between me and them," responded Jerry. "But I'll tell you this: my goal is to have them all stay on the ranch permanently and be ranchers like me and my dad and my granddad."

Together with Barry, Tom and his brother were the three non-ranchers. Tom said, "You guys sincerely think ranchers are special. Why is that?"

The other three, all ranchers, looked at one another wondering who wanted to tackle that question.

Loren spoke up first. "To be honest, Tom, some of that feeling is probably just because we *are* ranchers. Maybe you feel the same way about bankers or a Barry might feel that way about lawyers. Also, I know it's risky to generalize but I have to say that almost all the ranchers I know are good people, people I trust. They work hard, they're willing to help others and do all the time and yet they are largely self-reliant."

Gordon said, "I think trust is the big issue. I know practically every rancher in this area and if I shook hands with any of them on something or some deal, I would have complete trust that the deal would be done and done fairly."

Jerry then added, "Most ranchers, and there's a fair number of women now, and their spouses have as priorities God, country and family. Making money, which seems to be a top priority for many these days, is not a priority for ranchers. Don't get me wrong; they want to make money. They just have other priorities. And I know, I'm an exception in the sense that I am lucky that I do make a lot of money and because God wasn't a priority. But I only make a lot of money because of what my dad and granddad left me. Most other ranchers aren't so lucky. As for God, well, He's now a priority in my life. So, I guess you could say we're teachable, too." Everyone laughed.

Loren said, "Lord knows, there's people like that in every profession and every walk of life. It just seems to us that the vast majority of ranchers are like that and I'm not sure you can say that about many other professions; maybe farming. There's something working the land and on the land that keeps people from getting twisted like city folk do."

"Most ranchers are pretty good stewards of the land," said Gordon. "We know we're just passing through, so to speak. But we were concerned with the land long before most so-called environmentalists were. Of course, we do use it for some things that they don't like and there is some merit to some of what they say but generally, we take good care of the land we use. And we really don't need some bureaucrat from Washington who knows nothing about ranching making up regulations that make our lives difficult."

"All true," said Jerry. "But go back to what I said earlier. Honor your God, serve your country and love your family. Again, ranchers aren't the only ones that do that but I bet our percentage is as high as or higher than any other profession. To me, that's why we feel ranchers are special."

"Yeah," said Loren, "even when we have cowshit on our boots." That brought another round of laughter.

Loren said, "Well, I'll tell you in that regard, it's getting harder and harder for ranchers to make it these days. A lot of them are just getting by and a lot of them are selling land that has increased in value in order to survive. It's not an easy living but people still want their cheeseburgers."

Jerry raised his coffee mug and proclaimed, "Here's to the ranchers. May they live long and prosper."

"Okay, Spock," joked Tim, realizing that none of the others might know what he was talking about.

Barry piped up and said, "And let's not forget their bankers and their lawyers."

"No," said Loren, half joking, "today I say we forget the lawyers and the bankers. Today is for the ranchers. To the ranchers!" And everyone clinked their mugs.

Jerry put the exclamation point on the discussion by saying, "Now that's what I'm talking about!"

Chapter 35

A few days later, Colin returned from his motorcycle trip in the late afternoon.

Jerry had just come in from one of the pastures and was getting a drink of water before doing a few chores close to home before dinner.

"Hello, Son," he said, "I'm glad you're back. I was hoping to talk with you a little more about what we discussed when I was in the hospital."

"Yeah, Dad, I'd like to talk to you, too. I've been doing a lot of thinking on my little trip."

Emily wasn't around at the moment so they sat down at the kitchen table.

Jerry spoke first. "Colin, I meant what I said the other day. I'm sorry that I let my guilt spill over into our relationship. It should never have been that way. But, I have to say, you can't understand how devastated I was when you mom died. It almost killed me. It was so unexpected and such a shock and I just wasn't ready for anything like that. I was devastated and from there I turned angry and bitter. The truth is, I blamed myself because I had badgered your mom to have another child."

"I know, Dad, I know. I've heard it all before. But I have to tell you that I can't just forget everything overnight. I've been dealing with this for as long as I can remember. It's been a big, festering wound that just can't be healed with one apology. I saw a lot of physical wounds in Iraq. They took months to heal if they even did heal. What I am dealing with isn't physical but that might make it even harder. I've been dealing with this for a very long time."

"I understand. I know it isn't easy but I don't know what more I can say."

"What do you want *me* to say? What do you want from me, Dad?"

Jerry thought for a moment and then said simply, "Forgiveness; forgiveness so that we can work toward having a real father-son relationship. You probably won't believe this but I had a talk with Fr. Jeff the other day and I think it's really changed me; that and the bear attack. I'm tryin' to regain my faith and ask for God's forgiveness. So that's what I would like from you."

Colin pondered that for several seconds. "Well, I won't lie to you; I don't think I'm ready for a normal relationship." Colin saw his father wince when he said that. He quickly followed with "Look, Dad, I am going to work at this, I am going to work at it every day and maybe, just maybe, things will get to where you want them to be. That's all I can promise you."

What Colin said reminded Jerry of his talk on faith with Fr. Jeff and that it had to be worked on every day. Jerry wondered if it was a coincidence.

"That's fair and all I can expect," said Jerry. They looked at one another for several moments as if trying to determine if that were the end of this topic.

Apparently it was for Jerry then said, "So, what are your plans?"

Colin laughed a wry laugh and said, "Funny you should ask. Even before our little talk, I was thinking about staying around here for a while, if that would be OK."

For the first time, Jerry saw Colin being a little uncomfortable, a little unsure.

Colin continued, "I came out of the service with some negativity, some darkness. Maybe it was what I saw; maybe not. But I felt unsettled and didn't know what I wanted to do. I hooked up with an old army buddy. He was struggling a little, too and we fell in with some not so nice people. I knew what I was doing was not me but for some reason I wasn't ready to be normal. So now, I think I need some time up in the mountains away from the rest of the world; clean, clear air and not many ways to get in trouble. I need to get my own house in order. Would that be OK?"

Jerry replied, "I would love it. I think it will be good for both of us." Then, being careful to not push right away to make it permanent, he said, "You stay as long as you want."

They stood up and shook hands. "Not a hug," Jerry thought, "but it's a start."

Chapter 36

So, the three kids were back, at least for now. Ryan and Michelle hadn't really committed to stay permanently on the ranch but they had no other options. Julie and Colin had returned home with the idea that it was for the short term and they didn't have any options either. So the three of them were back and assumed roles without being assigned. Ryan became Jerry's number two; Julie did marketing and advertising and Colin was out working with crews where his leadership experience learned in the military was quickly evident. Although he hadn't been around for some time and didn't know many of the crew members, his bearing, more than his status as the boss' son, commanded respect. He had learned the trick of making people respect and obey without ordering it. When he did give an order, it sounded like a request and the men responded.

Several months later, late in the afternoon, the three of them were discussing cattle markets and prices and when and how many head they should sell when Julie suddenly changed the topic and asked, "Colin, what's going on with you and Dad. I mean, of the three of us, you had the biggest problem with him but you seem pretty simpatico these days. How come?"

Colin looked at both of them, trying to decide how much to tell them.

"Well, Dad and I had a pretty good talk. He apologized for letting me feel guilty about Mom and asked me to forgive him. So, I'm working on that. But the whole thing has taken some of the edge off."

"Wow," exclaimed Ryan. "So that's it. We were wondering. What made him apologize?"

225

"He said it was the bear attack. That plus he had a talk with Fr. Jeff and I guess he's coming back to the Church, or at least to God."

"Wow again," said Ryan. He looked at the other two. "Maybe it's time that we all have a talk with Dad and try to sort a few things out."

"When?" asked Julie.

"No point in waiting," answered Ryan. "How about when he comes in?"

An hour later, Jerry did come in looking tired but content. He saw his three children and smiled. Although all were fully grown and then some, he still thought of them as his children. Julie said, "Daddy, we'd like to talk with you."

Jerry wasn't sure if he should be alarmed or concerned or pleased or what. A little tentatively, he said, "Okay."

Emily and Michelle were in the kitchen so they went into the great room and sat down.

Ryan started. "Dad, Colin's told us about the conversation you two had." Jerry looked over at Colin whose expression gave no clue as to what he had said or why or anything else for that matter. "I assume you'd agree that things between you and the three of us haven't been great for a long time. We all know why. But your talk with Colin has given us some hope that maybe things, actually, maybe you are changing."

Julie looked up and asked, "Daddy, what brought all this on?"

Jerry sighed and looked as though he had been asked to do something uncomfortable, which he had.

"Well, "he said, "as you may have guessed, a while back, in fact on New Year's Day, I had asked Jan to marry me and she turned me down. She basically said my poor relationship with you guys and my rejection of God over your mom's death were the reasons for turning me down. Of course, I wasn't happy about that and that's why for quite some time I wasn't myself, even the bad old self. Then, when I went through the bear attack and thought I was going to die, my main thought was how much I regretted my behavior with you and how I wished I had had a better relationship with you.

Then, Fr. Jeff visited me in the hospital and we had a conversation about my anger toward God and so on. In some ways, the problem I had with God was the result of the same thing that caused my behavior with you—I was looking at everything from my perspective and didn't try hard enough to look at things from the perspectives that other might have. Anyway, as a result, I'm working on my relationship with God while I am trying to rebuild my relationships with you guys."

"Wow!" said Ryan. "Who is this man?" They all laughed.

Jerry then spoke again. "Actually, I've been giving all this a lot of thought. We're all here but it seems like we're not together as one. There's this idea hanging over everything that this might all be temporary. I've been trying to think of how best to change that. One of the things I want to do as a way to start rebuilding relationships is to ask all of you to consider staying on the ranch permanently. I think that would make it feel better, more enduring.

So, I know that's asking you to make a commitment so I'm going to make one to you. You know I love this ranch and all it represents. I love owning this ranch; but if you'll agree to stay, I am going to give to each of you a 25% share of the ranch and I'll keep the remaining 25%. I want to ask Ryan to continue as the head of the ranch, he'll run things day-to-day. Julie, if you will agree to stay, you'll be in charge of all sales and marketing and communications and all that stuff that you know about. And Colin, if you'll agree to stay, you'll be Ryan's number two and right hand man. This is a big operation and he'll need all the help he can get. I plan on taking a step back and focusing on the long term. I have my eye on some ranches near ours that I think we can buy at a decent price and so we could expand some. But all major decisions, like whether to buy another ranch, will be made as a family." Jerry looked at each, trying to read their minds.

"How does that sound to you?"

Ryan glanced at his siblings and then said, "I think that's great, Dad, very generous; but I have to be honest with you. Things around here for the last few months have been pretty good and I do love it here; so does Michelle. But I can't give you a 100% guarantee that I'll stay. I'd like more time to see how it all works out. To be dead honest, a lot depends on you."

Julie and Colin nodded in agreement.

"Well, what are you expecting?"

Ryan thought for a moment and then looked over at his sister and brother. It was Colin who spoke up and said, "Dad, you say you'd like to have us her permanently. Well, I'd like to see that you have changed permanently; that you really are the changed man you claim to be. I'm sorry to be blunt, but for me, you're going to have to show me."

"Fair enough," said Jerry. "But like I said, I want to show you I am committed so I'll still give you each 25% and you don't have to commit until you're ready."

"Well, that's showing me something right there," said Julie.

Jerry looked at Colin who looked serious. "Colin?" he queried.

"I don't know, Dad. Do I get to keep my motorcycle?"

They all laughed and Jerry said, "Yes, but we all voted and you have to wear a helmet."

Then, in a serious tone, Jerry said, "Thank you." Then to lighten the mood he said, "I guess we're all ranchers now."

Somehow the kids all knew the meeting was over and they headed for the kitchen. Jerry hung back and when they turned around and saw that he was not coming, Jerry said, "You kids go help Emily with dinner. I'll be right there."

When they had left Jerry closed his eyes and said a prayer of thanks. "Dear God, he said softly," that couldn't have gone any better. Please, Lord, make me worthy of this gift you have given me. And give me the strength and wisdom to not blow it." Jerry continued to pray for a sometime longer and it felt good to him.

Chapter 37

When Jerry came out and into the kitchen, everyone was there including Emily and Michelle. It was evident that they had told Emily and Michelle the gist of what had transpired. Emily looked very happy even though she had watery eyes. She came over and gave Jerry a hug and then, keeping her hands on his shoulders, she just looked at him and gently shook her head but didn't say a word. Michelle was beaming especially because she knew what the new tack in Ryan's relationship with his father meant for Ryan. And Ryan's new and more defined role meant they were there permanently, well, at least semi-permanently, which pleased Michelle immensely.

Dinner that night was the best and most fun that anyone could remember. Jerry just marveled at how much progress had been made with his family. "What a jerk I've been," he thought.

The next morning, the happy mood was still evident at breakfast. It only got better when Michelle asked for everyone's attention and said, "Ryan and I set a wedding date last night. We're going to tie the knot on Saturday, September 13th so make sure you save the date."

Colin turned to Ryan and said, "Are you sure you want to get married on the 13th?

"Very funny," said Ryan.

Jerry thought, "Wow! Family banter; how much I have missed."

Michelle turned to Julie and asked, "Will you help me with the arrangements?"

"Well, "Julie answered with a roll of her eyes, "not that I know much about weddings but of course I'll help."

After breakfast, Ryan and Colin went out to start on the day's chores while Julie was preparing to go to the nearby ranch office building to work on some marketing plans. Jerry asked her, "Julie, can I ask about how things are with you and Christopher?

"What do you mean?" she asked.

"Well, how's the relationship going? Is it serious?"

"Yes, I think it is. I do love him and he loves me but so far we haven't gone much further than that." She laughed and then continued, "He's so shy that if we get to talking about marriage, I'll probably have to ask him."

"Would you say yes if he did ask?"

"I would."

"Well, Honey, I don't know him as well as I should if there's a serious possibility that he could marry you. Why don't you try to have him join us for dinner every Saturday?"

"Like you used to do with Jan?"

"Yes."

"Dad, is that over for good?"

"I hope not but time will tell."

"Okay; and I'll talk to Christopher about Saturday dinners."

Over the next couple of weeks everyone comfortably settled into their new roles. Ryan did, indeed, need Colin. He wondered how his dad did it alone and then remembered the kind of hours that his dad worked. Colin was a natural at working with the crews. They were mostly older than him but they all knew of his military service and that gave him standing that another man wouldn't get.

One morning at breakfast, Emily came into the dining room and said that there were two men at the front door asking for Colin.

Colin asked, "Did they say who they were or what they wanted?"

"No, said Emily, "but they said they knew you."

Colin looked puzzled but shrugged his shoulders and went to the front door. There he saw standing on the stoop his Army friend Little John and none other than Rolando Garcia. Colin opened the door so that he was out side with them and before he even said anything; his military instincts caused him to survey the landscape behind the two men to make sure no one else was around.

Little John laughed and said, "Don't worry; it's just us."

Colin continued his inspection but once satisfied said, "Howdy, boys. Rolando, I must say I'm surprised to see you. What's up?"

Rolando looked over to Little John to speak for them.

"Colin, Rolando and I have left our motorcycle clubs. Neither one of us is riding with the clubs anymore. I knew you had a ranch up here and I was hoping that we might find work. It's kind of hard for ex-bikers to find work if you know what I mean."

Colin looked over at Rolando as if to hear what he had to say.

"That's right, "said Rolando just a little nervously. "We're done with the gangs and we're looking for work."

Colin looked at them and then one more time scanned the horizon to make sure no one else was out there. "Is this okay with your clubs? What about Rocky?"

Little John replied, "Rocky's cool with it. I talked to him and because I was taking Rolando with me, it meant less competition for him. And he never thought much of me anyway so he was cool with the whole thing."

"Colin turned back to Rolando and said, "What about with you?"

Rolando answered, "I was a leader in the club. The guy who took over my spot was happy to see me go."

Colin looked at them and thought about how this might work.

"Guys, it's true that we're looking for a few more hands, but we're looking for guys who will be here long term not just for a month or two. What are your plans?"

"Well, Colin, we're both trying to start over. We came out of the service and made some bad choices. We admit that. I can't promise you we'll be here for twenty years but we're not going to collect one or two checks and move on. Like I said, we're trying to start over and we think this would be a good place to get established.

You know it's hard work; damn hard. Have either one of you ever done ranch work?"

They both shook their heads.

"Can either of you ride a horse?"

Rolando said, "Yes, I can. I grew up with horses in Mexico. I trained them and rode them all the time. I know how to shoe a horse, too."

"Well, we can always use someone who's good with horses."

Colin thought about the situation. On the one hand, it seemed risky to take to ex-bikers and outlaws into their ranks. He knew Little John but not so well that he was absolutely sure that there wouldn't be any trouble. But he had to give him credit for leaving that other world and also for apparently getting "clearance" from Rocky. And the same was true for Rolando. After all, it was Colin that told him to get out and go straight and get a job; that's what he was doing and since Colin had thought it was a slim proposition that he would, Colin now felt some obligation to see if it could work out.

Finally, Colin said, "Let me talk with my older brother. Can you guys come back around six tonight?"

They nodded and Colin said, "Okay, I'll see you tonight."

Colin went back inside and found Ryan before he went out to start on the day's work. He explained the situation to Ryan and asked what he thought. Ryan shrugged and said, "Hell, I don't know these guys, you do. I'm willing to go with your judgment but I'll admit it seems a little chancy."

Just then Jerry came into the kitchen and said with a big smile, "You know, I never knew I liked sleeping until seven so much. What's the big discussion about?"

Ryan and Colin explained to Jerry what they had been discussing. Jerry asked Colin, "What's your gut, Son?"

Colin said, "Honestly, my gut says these guys will be okay but I can't be too sure."

Jerry said, "Well, it's up to you boys; it's your show. But I will say that not too long ago I would have said why take a chance." Laughing just a little he continued, "But now I have a different perspective. As one who has benefited greatly from second chances, I'd say give'em a chance. But it's your call."

Ryan looked at Colin and said, "Sign'em up."

"Okay." Colin then turned to Jerry and said, "Dad, I have a date for this Saturday so I won't be at dinner."

Jerry replied in a kind of sing song voice that implied there were consequences, "You're going to miss seeing Christopher."

Colin laughed and said, "I'm sure I'll have many chances to see him in the future."

"Who's the young lady?" asked Jerry.

"Patty Neal," answered Colin.

"Again?" exclaimed Ryan. It seems like you've been seeing no one but her for the last couple of months."

"Well," said Colin with a very satisfied smile, "things have been going quite well."

Ryan commented, "Dad, you've got to see this girl. I mean she is hot."

"Where have you seen her?" queried Colin.

"That's for me to know and you to find out. But I will say, 'Congratulations, Little Brother.'"

Jerry said, "Well I guess this Saturday is out but maybe you should bring her over to one of our Saturday dinners. I'd like to meet her. Besides, I may be old but I'm not dead. I can still appreciate a good looking woman."

Ryan and Colin laughed. "Okay, Dad, I will."

As Jerry got into bed he realized that that night was one more night when he had special thanks to say. The last couple of weeks had been remarkable insofar as all the good things that had happened. Now, Jerry was thinking, I've got one son who's going to be married soon; a daughter that will hopefully be engaged soon; and a son who attracts women like bees to honey but maybe has settled on one. "Not bad," he thought, "not bad."

Chapter 38

So much good had occurred in Jerry's life over the past month or so that his life was now immeasurably better than just a few months earlier. But as good as he felt about most things now only highlighted to him all the wasted time and energy over the previous twenty-eight years. People always said don't look back but that wasn't Jerry's nature. Although he knew he couldn't, he just couldn't help wishing he could get some of those wasted years back. He'd curse himself for being so stupid and obstinate and then make promises to himself about how he would be for the rest of his life.

He felt good about most things but, of course, there was still one hole in his life. He knew that he loved Jan very much and wanted and needed her in his life. Almost worse than not having her was the real possibility that it might never happen. After all, she had been persistently successful in keeping him away.

One Saturday in early June when summer was a couple of weeks away on the calendar but already present in terms of warmer temperatures, Emily needed to go shopping for groceries for Saturday dinner. She had planned to go early in the morning and be back early but then the kids asked her to pick up various items for them. Since she was getting perishables at the grocery store, she got the other items first and got to the grocery store mid-morning, later than planned which turned out to be a happy coincidence; or possibly divine intervention. She spotted Jan in the produce section.

"Hello, Jan!"

Jan was momentarily startled but quickly recovered and said, "Well, Emily, how are you?" They hugged and held each other by their arms for a moment.

"I'm fine," answered Emily. "We've missed you. How have you been?"

Jan blushed a little at the reference to being missed because the reason was she had, in essence, been hiding. She knew that sooner or later someone in the family would probably "find" her but she had no other choice. She wasn't ready to just be friends with Jerry and would have found it too difficult to stay in touch with Emily or any of the kids given the situation with Jerry. She had considered moving away but she had come to like Livingston very much and was now well established in the school. She had concluded that she would just lay low and hope that she wouldn't be found for a long time when everything would then be less emotional. Now, Emily had found her which was sort of okay because she really liked Emily but she knew word would get back to Jerry.

"I've been fine. How are Jerry and the kids?" In spite of herself, she really wanted to know about Jerry but she thought she was being clever. By asking about Jerry *and* the kids it wouldn't seem like she was focused on Jerry.

Emily answered, "Oh, they're all fine." Then it occurred to Emily that maybe Jan was inquiring about Jerry's relationship with the kids so she added, "Jerry and the kids are doing great. I wasn't there but Jerry had some kind of talk with them and now everyone is as happy as can be. Ryan's now running the ranch and Julie and Colin are staying on and helping Ryan. I guess you could say that Jerry is now at least somewhat retired. He still is involved but not as much in the day-to-day. He's involved in some long-term things.

Emily paused and then said, "I know he misses you."

Jan gulped but didn't say anything but just looked at her shoes.

Emily then said, "I was in church a couple of weeks ago at 9:30am Mass and thought I might see you but didn't."

"Oh," Jan said, "a while back I started going to the 8:00am Mass. You know, I wake up pretty early and I was just sitting around so it seemed to make sense to go to the eight and then have more of the day available."

"Oh, I see," said Emily. "That makes sense." What Emily didn't say was that she hadn't been to the 9:30 Mass; she wasn't even Catholic but apparently Jan had either forgotten or never knew. It was Jerry that had been at the 9:30am Mass and more than once. Now that mystery was solved. Emily was mentally patting herself vigorously on her back.

Jan inquired, "And you say the kids are all doing well?"

"Very," replied Emily. Ryan and Michelle have set a wedding date in September. Julie is very serious with Christopher whom I think you've met. They might be engaged at any time. And Colin has been seeing a lot of a young woman that he went to high school with. They're all as happy as I've ever seen them."

"Well, that's wonderful," came the reply from Jan.

The two of them looked at one another realizing they were generally avoiding the elephant in the room—the relationship or non-relationship between Jan and Jerry.

Jan said, "Well, it was good seeing you. Say hello to everyone."

"I will," said Emily. "Good to see you, too."

Jan went home later and thought it very likely that she'd see Jerry the next day at church. To her relief, but also to her disappointment, he did not appear at Mass the next day. She thought that maybe Emily had not told Jerry of her new church-going schedule or, maybe, Jerry didn't care. Little did she know that Jerry considered the strategic campaign to get Jan back so important that he resisted his normal impulse to act impatiently and instead planned a more deliberate approach.

Therefore, it was two weeks later when Jerry went to the church, walking through the vestibule at 7:59am. He immediately spotted Jan who was sitting toward the front. He took a seat about halfway back. Jerry would be the first to admit that his attention was more on Jan than on the Mass but he felt this was one occasion when the Lord would forgive him.

When the Mass was over, Jerry went back to the vestibule and waited for Jan to make her way back. She was a bit startled when she saw him in part because she had become convinced that he wouldn't come since it had been a couple of weeks since her conversation with Emily so seeing him was a bit of a surprise.

"Hello, Jan," he said using a tone that he might with any friend. "It's good to see you."

"Hello, Jerry," she said with a suspicious smile. "I'm a bit surprised to see you here, but then again maybe not."

"You mean because of church? I've been going again for a while?"

"You're kidding! How did that come about?"

Jerry said, "How about I buy you a cup of coffee and I'll tell you the story."

She started to say, "I don't know…"

Jerry cut in and said dryly, "It's only a cup of coffee."

Jan laughed and said, "Well, okay then."

They went to a nearby coffee shop and Jerry told Jan the story of his encounter with the bear and of his discussion with Fr. Jeff. She listened intently and registered some surprise when he described how he had been humbled at various points in the conversation with Fr. Jeff. When he was done, he ended by saying, "I'm really a changed man." He put that out there and just let it hang in the air for a bit and let Jan chew on it. Moreover, Jerry carefully avoided saying anything about them or their past relationship or, particularly, anything about the future. Inside, Jerry was proud of himself because showing that kind of restraint was not normal for him.

And so it was he who announced, "Well, I have to get going. It was good to see you."

Jan said simply, "Likewise," and they went their separate ways. She was more than intrigued by the story of Jerry's fundamental changes; she thought they were remarkable given what she knew had been Jerry's feelings back in December and before. It got her thinking.

The next week Jerry purposefully did not go to eight o'clock Mass but did say a number of prayers and did some Bible reading before he went to Two Rivers church instead and had a fine breakfast with the boys. Jan had fully expected Jerry to be at her church for the 8:00am Mass and was surprised and once more even a little disappointed when he didn't show. Of course, this was exactly what Jerry had intended.

The week after, he did go to the eight o'clock Mass and did see Jan and this time he suggested breakfast, not just coffee, and she agreed. They discussed any number of topics but Jerry was careful to avoid any suggestion of any rekindling of their relationship or of their time before his proposal or anything that might suggest that he was thinking of them as a couple. He acted like they were just friends. Jan didn't know exactly what to make of it but she was certainly enjoying the attention and Jerry's company. She loved hearing about what Jerry's kids were doing and was very pleased that their relationships were all healthy. It made her think about how she would fit in.

This pattern of seeing each other Sunday morning at church and then having breakfast together continued for another few weeks. As before, Jerry didn't mention anything about them as a twosome. Then Jerry noticed an ad in the paper for a performance of Beethoven's sixth symphony which he remembered to be Jan's favorite. So, the Sunday before, at breakfast, he mentioned it to her and asked if she'd like to go. She looked at him with an accusatory half smile as if to say, "I know what you're doing" but she couldn't turn down the chance to hear her favorite.

At the intermission, Jerry said to her, "You know the kids would really like to see you. There's so much going on and they say they've really missed having you at Saturday dinner. How about you come over this Saturday?"

With the same half smile she asked rhetorically, "Just like old times?" Then she thought about it for a few moments even though she already knew what her answer would be.

"Okay," she said, "I'll look forward to seeing Ryan and Julie and Colin."

So the next Saturday Jan came over for dinner and it was like a birthday celebration. Everyone was so happy to see her and she had forgotten how close she had felt to all of them. Plus she got to meet Patty Neal who was now Colin's steady girlfriend. Jan couldn't get over the difference from the previous fall. Everyone was so happy. There was lots of good natured banter and Jerry was often the target but he just laughed along with everyone else. She noted how happy Michelle was about becoming a permanent part of the ranch. Julie was quietly gaga over Christopher who was rather quiet himself but he was also quite charming. And Colin, well, even to her old eyes, Colin was a hunk. Well-muscled, chiseled, flat stomach and a handsome face almost guaranteed that he could get nearly any single woman that he wanted. And the one he got, Patty, was quite a catch. But more than any of that, she was particularly struck at how much happier Colin seemed. The whole business of why his mom died and all that must have been put to bed somehow. He was beaming, and why not. He was young, handsome, had a beautiful girlfriend and had prospects for a wonderful life. And she was very proud of his military service and, as she had once before, told him so.

Jerry was seated at the opposite end of the table so Jan spent most of the evening talking with Emily and Michelle who were closest and then Colin and Patty. Previously, Jerry would have sat right next to her and might have even focused nearly exclusively on her to the exclusion of the kids. Now, it was almost the other way around. Jerry and Ryan and Julie were having a grand old time and even Christopher was laughing at some of the things being said which Jan was unable to hear. Every now and then she thought she saw Jerry sneak a glance at her direction but it was so quick and subtle she couldn't be sure.

At one point, Michelle and Emily and Jan were talking, and then Jan let the two of them carry the conversation while she surveyed the scene and tuned everything out except for her and Jerry. They each saw only the other clearly and everyone else was blurry. She was simultaneously thrilled and scared. Everything seemed so right, but she had been deeply, deeply hurt and disappointed on New Year's Day. She had been hoping that Jerry would propose; she had even laughed to herself that she might have to take matters into her own hands if he didn't. And she had been pretty confident that he would but then, of course, had the concerns about family and God. She had hoped those things might somehow improve before any proposal but it didn't work out that way. After she turned him down, she had made up her mind that she would never be married again. Getting involved with a man to that extent and then having to say no was just too much wear and tear on the soul.

Now, things had obviously improved and Jerry had changed for the better. Strangely, though, he was taking a much slower pace with Jan than before. She was more used to the old bull charging around and being so blunt and direct even when wooing her. Now he was measured and patient which made him all the more attractive to her. She knew she was falling but her defenses also kicked in and said, "Whoa, Girl."

The next thing that Jan was aware of was Michelle looking at Jan and saying, "So, what do you think, Jan?"

Jan looked back at Michelle and had no clue as to what Michelle was asking. She said, "I'm sorry, Michelle. I guess my mind wandered a bit. What was your question about?

Michelle and Emily both laughed. "Where were you?" asked Michelle, still laughing. "I was asking about what you thought about Ryan and I having baked Alaska at our wedding instead of wedding cake. Some friends of mine back in Chicago did that and I thought it was great. They didn't want to observe that silly custom of stuffing birthday cake into each other's mouths and I don't want to either. I think it's dumb. Ryan doesn't care. But I know this area is kind of traditional and I just wondered if you thought it would be a problem if we didn't go with birthday cake but had baked Alaska instead?"

"Jan looked at Michelle and said, "Michelle, it's your wedding. I say you do whatever pleases you and everyone else be damned."

"You go, Girl!" exclaimed Emily and all three clinked their water glasses and laughed.

After dinner, Jan helped Emily and Michelle do the dishes and then chatted a little with Ryan. Jerry kept a low profile. When it was time to go, he walked Jan to the front door and said, "Everyone sure enjoyed seeing you tonight. Same time next week?"

Jan said, "You sure have become an old smoothie in the last few months." She looked up and into his eyes and saw peacefulness and confidence. Down, Girl. "Okay, I'll come next week. Are you going to church tomorrow?"

"Wouldn't miss it," Jerry replied.

"Well, I guess I'll see you tomorrow, too."

"Good night, Jerry."

"Good night."

Jan and Jerry went to Mass the next day and then went to breakfast and talked about the previous night and any number of other topics but, again, nothing was said about them. Somewhat to her surprise, he talked freely and openly about his challenge of finding faith. He talked about how he worked at it every day and some days felt like there couldn't possibly be a question about believing in God and then other days little doubts would creep in. She was astonished when he said that he was going to start attending a Bible study group because he was convinced that by spending some time reading and studying the Bible with those that were smarter than him and had been at it longer would be beneficial.

It occurred to Jan that she was so comfortable being with Jerry now. One could even describe him as easy going now which would have been altogether wrong before. She decided she liked this version more, much more than the original charming but angry Jerry.

The next Saturday was, in many respects, a repeat of the previous Saturday. Everyone was so happy and seemed like one big happy family. One couldn't tell who were the Johnstons and who were those with different last names. They even discussed a little family business in front of the others. It was nothing huge or consequential but there wasn't a need to hide it from the non-family members.

Once again Jerry was sitting away from her, letting her interact with the others. By now, she realized he wasn't ignoring her; he was giving her space. He knew correctly that Jan would come to things in her own time. He really had changed.

After dinner, Jerry suggested that he pour a couple glasses of port and that they go out on the porch with the outdoor heater lit and enjoy the cool evening. The sun had set so Jerry had brought a couple of jackets.. They sat on the bench swing and looked out at a beautiful moonlit view that was so common in the Mountain West. "Someday Soon" by Suzy Bogguss was playing softly on the radio and Jerry was thinking about what a beautiful voice she had. Neither Jan nor Jerry spoke for some time.

Then, while Jerry was still studying the view, he heard Jan say, "You know, I really love you."

Jerry looked over at her. He was surprised but not totally shocked. Half of him had felt with absolute certainty that she was in love with him and would marry him. The other half remembered that New Year's Day and all the subsequent pain and heartache. He remembered that she had said that when she told a man that she loved him that that meant they were going to be married.

So, he laughed a little and asked her, "Does that mean we're going to get married?"

She stammered and started to say something but stopped, putting her hand over her mouth. Finally, she managed to say, "We'll see."

Jerry laughed very quietly. It was the laugh of a man who had good reason to hope he had won the battle. He had been smart enough to take his time and not make it a sprint. He had run the emotional marathon and the finish line was in sight.

He looked at her and said, "You know, I'm going to marry you."

"Jerry," she said, "you've clearly come a long way and I know I just blurted out that I love you. But before I commit to marriage I need to really be sure about everything. I need to be sure about you. It's all good today. Let's just see if it stays that way. Let's take it one day at a time."

One more daily challenge, he thought. One more thing to work on every day. But he read the expression in her eyes and the look on her face and he knew he had her. She might not want to say it out loud but he had her. Her look said she had just realized that she could no longer evade her destiny. She shivered a little, whether from the evening chill or her emotion she didn't know.

Jerry moved a little closer and put his arm around her and said, "And, just for the record, I really love you, too."

They sat together for quite a while. Nothing further was said. Really, nothing more needed to be said at that time. They were both enjoying the pace of their love unfolding and there didn't seem to be the need to mess with it.

Eventually, Jan leaned over and kissed Jerry and said, "I'd better be going."

Jerry replied, "I'll see you tomorrow at church."

Jan went home and surprised herself by thinking ahead about a wedding. Truly, she had fewer doubts than she had told him but at the same time she had been basically so scared of marriage since her first husband had died which was then compounded with the mess of the first go 'round with Jerry that there were some anxious feelings. She had more or less chosen to be a single woman and had enjoyed the perks of being single. Jerry had once nearly changed her mind but then, after she had turned him down, she had declared to herself, "That's it! Never again!" Now, she was going to go against that proposition again and it gave her a mild case of the jitters; a little because of Jerry but also just because.

But as she thought more about what she was stepping into, her anxiety eased. First of all, she loved Jerry and had seen enough of the "new" Jerry to be hopeful that living with him would not be a problem. But he still had to prove to her that he had really changed.

Second, she really loved his kids. They were all polite, well-educated and had proven themselves in various fields of endeavor. It was really the idea of joining and being part of a whole family that made her comfortable, actually eager. She wouldn't be their mom nor would she try to be; but all of the children had accepted her without reservation and she would think of them as her kids.

It occurred to her that she would technically be a rancher or, at least a rancher's wife. But she thought that she would find ways to help out with some of the chores and so at least as far as she was concerned, and she knew she was pushing the definition a little, she was going to be a rancher. It was a nice thought as she fell asleep.

Back at the ranch, Jerry was so pleased with how everything had gone that he decided to have a second glass of port out on the porch. It was pretty cool by now but he had a warm vest on and the port helped to ward off the chill as well. As he sat quietly, he really wasn't thinking; he was just there, his senses taking everything in, wallowing in his contentment. Eventually the port had its intended effect and Jerry got up to head to bed.

Coincidentally, he had the same thought about Jan being a rancher as she had had. His kids were all ranchers now and he knew how Jan would pitch in so, by golly, she would be a rancher. He thought again about his notion of a rancher and how ranchers honor God, serve country and respect family. It was surely true in the case of the Johnston clan.

As Jerry's head hit the pillow, the warm feeling of contentment together with the numbing effects of the port made for a delicious way to end a wonderful day. He wondered how many great days like this he had left; how much quality time was remaining. He had a friend with a ranch called QTR Ranch and the "QTR" stood for Quality Time Remaining. It made for a funny line and gave license to doing things one otherwise might not but it was also a reminder that nothing human lasts forever.

He remembered how things were just a year and a half go, and back beyond then, and wondered how he had possibly thought he was happy. He had been miserable and a miserable S.O.B if a fairly charming one. But now he was happy. Jan made him happy and he was sure that it would only get better with time. He was confident that he had changed enough to satisfy her and his kids over the long haul. That would be his daily challenge.

He knew that getting things right with his children was a key reason why he felt so good along with, of course, Jan. Was she a gift from God? For that matter, would he have been as happy if he had only fixed things with his kids but had not changed his thinking about God? He doubted it. He couldn't prove it but he thought changing his focus to God's way had changed him for the better, the much better. Have to take it on faith, he thought.

His eyes were getting heavy but he was feeling so good he resisted sleep as long as possible. One last time he thought about how wonderful life was now and how many good things had happened to him in the last few months.

As he thought those thoughts, he felt a wave of emotion. He felt the need to make aloud but quietly the exclamation, "God Almighty!"

As he finally drifted off, his final thought to himself was, "Yes He is, Jerry, yes He is!"

Note from the Author

I hope you enjoyed my book. If you did, I would be most grateful if you would go to www.amazon.com and rate it and review it.

I always appreciate any feedback. Email me at artmartinauthor@gmail.com.

Thank you very much!

CPSIA information can be obtained at www.ICGtesting.com
Printed in the USA
BVOW08s1805221115

428096BV00003B/40/P